"I've thought of you," Nikos said. "More often
than I'd like to admit."

"Save all your pretty little speeches for a woman
who's stupid enough to believe them." A tinge
of color blushed Ellen's cheeks. "I doubt you've
given me a thought over the years. After all, I was
nothing more to you than a two-week fling with a
silly little American virgin."

"Such anger. Why? Unless—"

"You're right. I'm overreacting. I apologize. I
haven't given *you* a thought in years."

*But her words were belied by the vulnerability
written on her beautiful face. Just what was
Ellen hiding?*

D0958167

BEVERLY
BARTON

on her guard

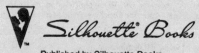
Silhouette Books

Published by Silhouette Books
America's Publisher of Contemporary Romance

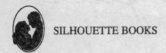 SILHOUETTE BOOKS

ON HER GUARD

ISBN 0-373-48471-2

Copyright © 2002 by Beverly Beaver

This edition published by arrangement with Harlequin Books S.A.

® and TM are trademarks of Harlequin Books S.A., used under license. Trademarks indicated with ® are registered in the United States Patent and Trademark Office, the Canadian Trade Marks Office and in other countries.

Visit Silhouette at www.eHarlequin.com

Printed in U.S.A.

To all my loyal "The Protectors" readers
who have asked for and patiently waited for
Ellen Denby's story. And for all the Ellens out
there, especially Ellen Micheletti, who was the
first reader to contact me about my Ellen after
she made her debut appearance in one of my
Silhouette Intimate Moments books.

Also...

A very special thanks to LH for the brainstorming
session that gave birth to Nikos Pandarus.

Prologue

The guard had only a millisecond warning before the intruder slit his throat with one swift, silent slash. As the man's body slumped to the ground, Wasim Ibn Fadil eased his knife back into its leather sheath, then motioned for the other three men in his entourage to move forward. At midnight, under cover of darkness and a cloudy night sky that masked the stars, the black-clad Wasim was all but invisible. Timing was important. His orders were to move in quickly, take the child and escape back to the sea.

Everything had been planned down to the minute, but Wasim was prepared for the inevitable twists that could not be foreseen. Preparation was the key to any successful operation. He had studied the layout of Theo Constantine's villa and the surrounding land, as well as the schedule and placement of the guards. Only recently had Constantine hired private guards for his home, having in the past relied upon loyal servants and his misguided belief that the Constantine family was always safe on Golnar.

This particular night had been chosen because Constantine and his wife were attending a party in Dareh, a thirty-minute drive from the villa, and were not expected home until one or two in the morning. No matter what might happen tonight, Wasim knew he must succeed. No other mission had ever been as important or as personal. This was his first time to lead a mission of great importance. His father trusted him not to fail.

One by one, Wasim and his men took out the other three villa guards—two more outside and another inside. Working together quite cohesively from years of fighting side by side on numerous missions, Wasim and his soldiers made their way upstairs without alerting the live-in servants of their presence. From studying the blueprints of the villa's interior, he had memorized the location of the child's room. Second floor, east wing, third door on the right. If necessary the nanny could be eliminated, but preferably she would be taken hostage, depending upon the circumstances. If Faith Sheridan posed too much of a problem, they would kill her; otherwise they would take her along with the child. The nanny might be able to keep the child quiet and soothe her fears.

Wasim motioned to Hamid, who opened the door to the nanny's quarters the moment Wasim entered the child's room. Aban and Bahir, both dressed all in black and carrying M-16 rifles, brought up the rear. Within seconds Wasim plastered his hand over the sleeping child's mouth. She whimpered and tried to pull away from him. He jerked her out of bed. In the process of squirming and wiggling, Phila Constantine knocked over a lamp on the beside table. While Wasim covered the little girl's face with a small rag doused in chloroform, Hamid dragged an uncooperative Faith Sheridan from the adjoining room.

Wasim handed the unconscious child to Aban, then

pulled a sealed envelope from inside his jacket and laid it on the girl's bed.

He walked over to the nanny, whom Hamid held captive in the doorway, and said softly in English, "Do as you are told or the child dies. Understand?"

With Hamid's hand over her mouth and his tenacious hold twisting her arms behind her back, Faith Sheridan nodded. Wasim saw the fear in the young woman's eyes. Taking great pleasure in her fright, he smiled at her. Her big blue eyes widened in alarm. She understood his threat.

Wasim hurried his men and their two hostages along the corridor, down the stairs and across the marble foyer. Just as they reached the front door, an overhead light came on. The huge, crystal chandelier shimmered, casting a brilliant glow over the grand entrance hall. An elderly man wearing a robe and house slippers stood in the doorway that led down the hall to the servants' quarters. The rifle in his trembling hands was aimed directly at Aban. Before the man could take action, Wasim fired his M-16. With one shot between the old man's eyes, Wasim eliminated the threat. But he had also alerted the rest of the staff.

The fifth member of their party, Riyad, brought a blue SUV out of hiding and skidded to a halt in front of the villa. The four men rushed outside, taking with them the unconscious child and her nanny. Only seconds after Riyad sped the SUV away from the house, three Constantine servants ran out into the driveway and opened fire with a rifle and two handguns.

Seven minutes later, Riyad parked the SUV he'd stolen last night, shortly after his arrival at the Dareh airport. On the beach below the villa, they boarded the two rubber rafts in which Wasim and his other soldiers had come ashore an hour ago. They carried their hostages with them out to sea. The cruiser waited for them two miles off shore. They would be back in Subria before daybreak. Wasim felt elated. His father would be very proud of him.

Nikos Pandarus hid in the hills outside Iaamar waiting for a signal from his contact. He had to get out of Tandu as soon as possible. His latest cover had been blow to hell and back. It had taken him fourteen months to infiltrate the weapons procurement program network and locate and disable a chemical weapons facility. He had been using the alias Jafari Naeem and passing himself off as an Egyptian during the assignment inside Tandu. While working undercover on this particular job, he had traveled in and out of the country, switching identities as easily as he changed shirts. Over the years, Nikos had become a master of disguise. He had built a reputation around a mysterious identity known to the world as *El-Hawah*— The Wind—a person no one could identify and that no two people would describe the same. When it suited his purposes, Nikos also became Mr. Khalid, one of his many aliases, and the one that had proved most useful time and again.

Fifteen minutes ago Nikos had used a burst transmitter to send a flash signal to MI6 via satellite. An agent used this type of transmitter only when he was in danger. And Nikos was in imminent danger. If he couldn't get out of the country by morning, the Tanduian soldiers were bound to find him. He'd left Iaamar less than twenty minutes ahead of them and only the cover of darkness had kept them from discovering his whereabouts before now.

If he could keep himself hidden, he'd be safe. Her Majesty's Secret Intelligence Service would do whatever it took to rescue him. In eighteen years of loyal service he had become their most useful operative. They would save him even if it meant deploying an SAS unit.

Nikos hunkered down behind a huge rock formation, placing his back to the flat surface as he braced his M-16 rifle between his legs. He'd wait it out. Help was on the way. But so was the enemy.

He was getting too old for this crap. He'd turn forty in a few months and it was past time for him to retire. If he made it out of Tandu alive, he'd talk to Gerald again and make it clear to the chief of MI6 that he was serious about leaving the agency, buying a house in the country and living a quiet, bucolic life. It wasn't too late, was it? He hadn't completely lost his soul.

Nikos's mind wandered back to the moment he had planted the bomb at the facility which had been prepared in advance to detonate just as a new shipment of machinery arrived. Everything had gone precisely as planned, except for one minor detail—Zara had betrayed him. She'd been his inside contact, a support agent of sorts. But as with so many of her kind, she'd sold him out for money. He'd known too many people like her—men and women—who would sell their own mothers for the right price. Usually his instincts cautioned him, telling him whom he could trust and whom he couldn't. But this time his gut instincts had failed him. Or maybe his male libido had temporarily blinded him. He and Zara had become lovers. No real emotional attachment; just hot sex. It was his own damn fault that he was in this predicament. It had been a long time since he'd allowed sex to alter his usually accurate perceptions. Another sign that he should retire.

Nikos didn't let women get under his skin. He neither loved nor wanted love in return. But sex was another matter altogether. He hadn't left a trail of broken hearts throughout the world, but he sure as hell hadn't lived a celibate life. Of course there had been someone special once…fifteen years ago…when he'd been young and foolish. A brief affair that could have become so much more if he hadn't been an undercover agent for the Firm.

Sounds echoed in the nighttime stillness. Nikos heard the

movement of troops on the road far below. Some of the soldiers would set up camp and at first light they'd search the hills. But if his luck held out—as it had for eighteen years—he'd be long gone before daybreak.

At 5:28 p.m. Eastern time, Ellen Denby took a call from Sir Matthew O'Brien, then told her secretary to leave for the day. It seemed to Ellen that she spent more and more time at the office; but why not? She really didn't have much of a personal life other than her volunteer work.

"Denby here," she said as she picked up the receiver. "What's up, Matt?"

"Hey former boss lady," he said. "I've got a major favor to ask of you."

"Which would be?"

"Fly to Golnar ASAP and bring along a team of Dundee's best."

Ellen's heart skipped a beat at the mention of Golnar. For the past fifteen years she had tried to put the past and its memories behind her, especially memories of the two weeks she'd spent on Golnar, the small Mediterranean island between Greece and Cyprus. But since Matt's last assignment for Dundee had included a sojourn on Golnar, Ellen had been forced to confront those long suppressed memories.

"Whatever's going on must be serious if you think a team of Dundee's best is needed."

"Remember Theo Constantine, the guy who's married to my wife's best friend? You told me that you'd met him once years ago."

She remembered Theo all right, although their acquaintance had been very brief. "What does Theo Constantine have to do with—"

"His daughter has been kidnapped," Matt replied.

Every muscle in Ellen's body tensed. Unbidden, tormenting memories flashed through her mind. *Take deep breaths,* she told herself. *Get control. Do it now!*

"Ellen?"

"Yes?"

"Are you all right?"

"Fine. Now what's this about Theo's daughter being kidnapped?"

"They came in late last night while Theo and his wife were at a party in Dareh. Our guess is they came in by boat, or at least they left the country that way. A stolen SUV was found on the beach. They killed four guards and the family's old butler. And they took seven-year-old Phila Constantine and her nanny, an American named Faith Sheridan."

"Why do you need Dundee's? This sounds like an international incident to me, something best handled by—"

"The kidnappers left a message warning Theo not to contact the local authorities or any government agencies. The letter said that Theo would be contacted with information concerning the abductors' demands. They said they'll deal only with Theo or his chosen representative."

"Does Theo know you've called me?"

"He contacted me and asked for my help," Matt replied. "I recommended he hire Dundee's and I told him that Dundee's CEO was the best hostage negotiator around, that she'd worked for years in that capacity for the Atlanta P.D."

"Did you tell him my name?"

"Yeah."

"And?"

"Nothing. But don't take it personally that he didn't seem to remember you. After all, the guy is probably in shock. His child has just been abducted by God only knows who."

Can I do this? Ellen asked herself. Can I actually return

to Golnar? Under usual circumstances—definitely not. But to help save a child—yes.

"Tell Mr. Constantine that I'll put together a team and we'll arrive in Dareh by Dundee jet as soon as possible. I'll contact you again and give you a more specific time after I've made some phone calls."

"Thanks, Ellen. I consider this a personal favor. Phila Constantine is Adele's godchild."

The minute she finished her conversation with Matt, a former Dundee agent now married to the princess of Orlantha, Ellen flipped open her personal phone directory that held all home and cell numbers for the Dundee employees. Which agents did she need? And who was available? Lucie Evans was a must. She held a degree in psychology and had trained as a profiler during her stint with the FBI. Sawyer McNamara was on assignment, but she'd see if the client would be willing to swap agents, something she didn't routinely do. But Sawyer's background with the Feds—handling numerous kidnapping cases—might give them the edge they'd need to save the Constantine child. The fact that Lucie and Sawyer mixed like oil and water made Ellen reconsider taking both of them along. She weighed the pluses against the minuses for a couple of minutes. To hell with it. She needed them both. They'd just have to put aside their personal hostilities for the duration.

Ellen tapped her fingers on the desktop as she contemplated the other agents she wanted for this particular job. Worth Cordell's expertise as a Green Berets Ranger just might be needed, as would Domingo Shea's particular talents that he'd honed to perfection as a member of SEAL Team Eight, that operated in Africa, the Caribbean and the Mediterranean.

Four hours later, all the Dundee agents she'd chosen—except Sawyer, whom they'd pick up by detouring to Florida—boarded the Dundee jet.

*   *   *

Half a world away Theo Constantine made a phone call to a private number in Istanbul and left a message for a Mr. Khalid. Though he knew Dundee's would supply him with a worthy team, there was only one man he trusted with the life of his child.

Chapter 1

Theo Constantine sent a limousine to the Dareh airport to pick up the Dundee agents the moment they arrived the following evening. Ellen and her crew were whisked through customs with great speed and efficiency. Before leaving Atlanta, Ellen had put together a file on Theo Constantine. It seemed the man she had met briefly fifteen years ago was a multibillionaire, having inherited a sizable fortune from his shipping tycoon father. The Constantines were natives of Golnar, an island nation whose citizens shared a mix of Greek and Turkish ancestry. Although the national language was Greek, most citizens spoke several languages, including English, due in part to the huge tourist trade. The Constantine family's influence was so great that they ruled the nation as if they were royalty. Dareh was the capital city and the center of culture and tourism.

With Ellen and the four agents settled in the limo and their luggage secured, the chauffeur, who had introduced himself as Peneus, maneuvered the limousine through the downtown area. Worth Cordell sat silently and paid little attention to the passing scenery visible at twilight. Ellen recognized a kindred soul in the big man—a wounded soul. He was even more of a loner than she and wasn't much of a conversationalist. On the other hand, the six-foot, red-headed Lucie Evans was an open book and a chatterbox. She devoured the sights and sounds of Dareh and commented on various items of interest.

Sawyer McNamara who'd been watching Ellen ever so subtly, turned suddenly to Lucie. "Will you shut up for five minutes? You haven't stopped talking since we got off the plane."

"Well, excuse me for taking an interest in my surroundings." Lucie glowered at Sawyer. "Some of us are more interested in what's outside the limo than what's inside." Lucie looked directly at Ellen.

Diplomatically changing the subject, Domingo Shea said, "What are the odds that the Constantine kid will come out of this alive?"

Ellen gave Dom an appreciative smile. She had personally interviewed and hired Dom without consulting Sam, the owner of Dundee's, or without asking for opinions from any of the other agents. Although most red-blooded women wouldn't look beyond Dom's incredible good looks—tall, dark and handsome in a way only a guy who was half-Irish and half-Cuban could be—Ellen had hired him for two reasons. One: His military record impressed the hell out of her. Two: She liked him, liked his forthright, what-you-see-is-what-you-get attitude.

By moving the conversation to the job at hand, Dom had defused a rather awkward situation for Ellen. She and several of her agents with whom she was friends knew that Sawyer McNamara "had it bad" for her. Lucie had been the one to point out the obvious to her three months ago. She'd told Ellen everyone else was aware that Sawyer was in love with her. Ellen and Sawyer had become friends over the years, working together on various cases in which the FBI had helped Dundee's. And when Sawyer left the Bureau and came to work for Dundee's eight months ago, Ellen and he had become friends and even dated occasionally. Their relationship hadn't progressed beyond a few heated kisses, but only because she was not ready to let it go any further. Sawyer was a great guy and she liked him a lot, but she was cautious when it came to romantic relationships, even if those relationships were casual. Ellen prided herself on being rational, unemotional and totally independent. On a strictly personal level, she made sure she never needed anyone and no one ever became too important to her. Ellen Denby took care of Ellen Denby.

"I'd say about fifty-fifty," Sawyer replied to Dom's question about Phila Constantine's chances of survival. "But we don't know what the kidnappers' demands are. If it's only money—"

"What else would it be?" Dom asked. "Constantine is a freaking billionaire."

Ellen sighed softly. "Logically, if the child of a billionaire is kidnapped, the ransom demand will be for money. A lot of money. But we can't be one hundred percent sure until Constantine hears from the people who abducted his daughter and her nanny."

"Why take the nanny?" Dom's gaze zeroed in on Lucie.

"It was either take her or kill her on the spot," Lucie replied. "More than likely they took the nanny so she could care for the child and to help keep the little girl soothed and quiet."

"I went over the file on Faith Sheridan," Sawyer said. "She seems to be squeaky clean."

Worth Cordell grunted. All eyes focused on the six-foot-four former Green Beret.

"You're a skeptical son of a bitch, Cordell," Dom said.

"What's your take on Ms. Sheridan? You think the nanny was part of the kidnapping scheme?"

"Maybe," Worth replied.

"Unfortunately it's happened before," Lucie said. "Sometimes the most trustworthy employees turn out to be disloyal, especially if huge sums of money are involved."

"Faith Sheridan doesn't fit the profile." Sawyer snapped open his briefcase, lifted out a file and tossed it to Lucie. The folder landed in her lap. She glared at Sawyer. "Take a look for yourself and see if you don't agree."

Lucie opened the file, scanned quickly through the pages, then said, "The woman's a saint. She was orphaned at twelve and grew up at a Girls' Ranch, worked her way through college and has a record anyone would envy. Everyone who knows her likes her. She's quiet, shy and sweet, and has worked as a nanny since she was twenty-two. Her first job, eight years ago, was for an American diplomat, taking care of his six-year-old son. She traveled abroad with the family and stayed with them for three years, until the boy was sent away to private school. Then she replaced the Constantines' first nanny, who retired due to poor health."

"So, what's your opinion, Madam Profiler?" Sawyer grinned.

Lucie frowned. "As much as it pains me, I agree with you. Faith Sheridan doesn't fit the profile of a woman who'd take part in a kidnapping scheme."

Ellen decided to allow Sawyer and Lucie to continue with their discussion, and perhaps defuse some of the tension between them. Those two seemed to always rub each other the wrong way; and no matter what the topic of conversation, they seldom agreed and usually wound up arguing. Their only common bond was the FBI. They were both former agents. Sawyer had been a by-the-book pro and

Lucie a fly-by-the-seat-of-her-pants rookie. Each had left the agency for personal reasons.

Searching for a distraction, Ellen focused her gaze on the scenes outside the limo window. Dareh combined the modern with the ancient. Once a seacoast village that grew and expanded over the centuries, the city spread out for miles across the shores and high above the Mediterranean. Endless miles of rock cliffs, interspersed with sandy beaches, spanned the coast and created a semicircle around Dareh and much of Golnar's northern and western shores. The city had changed quite a bit in fifteen years, had become more modernized; and yet it still possessed the same exotic charm that had captivated Ellen when she'd first visited the island.

During her stay here, she had to find a way to not let the memories from the distant past overwhelm her. Those two magical weeks on Golnar had happened to someone else, to another Ellen Denby. That girl—Mary Ellen—had been young and naive and much too trusting.

As the limousine passed through the northern edge of the city, Lucie peered through the window. "Look, isn't that an open-air market?" She pressed the button to lower the window. "Smell that delicious aroma. It must be from something that was cooked earlier today."

"What smell, the scent of goats?" Sawyer asked.

Lucie scowled at Sawyer.

Ellen knew that earlier in the day the singsong voices of buyers and sellers would have filled the autumn air and the aroma of fresh garlic and rich spices had floated on the cool October breeze. She remembered eating a bowl of broad bean stew purchased at this very market. She and Nikos had spent one morning browsing at the market. He'd bought her a red silk shawl that day and told her red was her color. She had burned the shawl a year later. After all this time, she could close her eyes and still see herself watching the crimson fabric wither and vanish, eaten by the hot flames.

Soon the limousine passed the marketplace and the faint aroma of food disappeared. Sunset cloaked the western horizon with a robe of vibrant colors. Nightfall would descend before they reached the Constantine villa.

After closing the bedroom door, Dr. Capaneus stepped out into the hall. Theo Constantine ceased his nervous pacing and looked his wife's physician square in the eyes.

"How is she?"

"Resting for the time being," the doctor replied. "I've had to sedate her. It's the only way to calm her."

"Will sedating her harm the baby?" Theo asked. After years of hoping for another child, their prayers had been answered. Only three weeks ago, Dr. Capaneus had confirmed that Dia was almost two months pregnant.

"It shouldn't cause any harm to the baby." The doctor grasped Theo's shoulder. "I'm going to leave Irina here to see after Dia. She'll contact me immediately if I'm needed."

"Thank you. I'll feel more at ease knowing Dia has a full-time nurse with her."

Dr. Capaneus patted Theo's shoulder. "Any word about our little Phila?"

Emotion lodged in Theo's throat making speech impossible. He shook his head. In his duties as personal physician to the Constantine family, Dr. Capaneus had delivered Phila seven years, four months and five days ago.

"If you'd like, go sit with Dia until she falls asleep," the doctor said. "I can find my way out."

Theo shook hands with Dr. Capaneus, then opened the bedroom door and moved silently toward the king-size bed he and Dia had shared for the past eight and a half years. Without saying a word, Dr. Capaneus's nurse, Irina, rose from the chair beside the bed and walked out of the room, leaving Theo alone with his Dia.

His beautiful wife, the woman he loved and adored, looked so pale and haggard, so terribly fragile. When he reached the side of the bed, he saw that her eyes were open, but the lids drooped sleepily. Carefully he eased down beside her. She lifted a slender arm, reached out and caressed his face. He clasped her hand to his mouth and buried his lips against the soft palm.

Tears gathered in his eyes. He shut them tight. *God, help me to be strong. I must be strong for Dia's sake.*

"Are they here, yet?" Dia's voice was weak, her words a mere whisper.

"Peneus phoned to tell me that they have arrived in Dareh and are en route at this very moment."

"Matt told you that they are the best, didn't he? They will be able to bring Phila home to us, won't they?"

"Yes, my love, they will bring her home. You must never doubt that Phila will be back in your arms very soon."

Tears trickled from Dia's eyes, cascaded down either side of her face and dampened her hair. "I—I must rest. Dr. Capaneus says that I must think of our unborn child." Dia's hand fluttered over her still flat belly, then spread out and settled atop her silk gown.

Theo kissed his wife's forehead and wiped away her tears with the tips of his fingers. "Yes, rest, my love, rest."

He sat with her while she drifted off into a drug-induced sleep. God knew she needed sleep. Neither of them had shut their eyes since Mrs. Panopoulas had telephoned him at Sophie and Zale's party to tell them what had happened at the villa. When they arrived home, they had found the local authorities swarming around the villa like maggots stirring about in filth. Wisely Mrs. Panopoulas had taken the note left by the kidnappers and put it in her pocket, then given it to Theo and told him where she'd found it. Even with his vast power and great influence, it had taken quite some time for Theo to persuade the police to handle the situation as a multiple-murder case and not to leak any information about the kidnapping.

"I will cooperate with you and help in any way you wish," Inspector Kaloyeropoulos had assured Theo. "I must admit that an incident such as this is beyond my realm of experience."

God, what a fool I was, Theo thought. For three generations the Constantine family had been safe in Golnar, protected by their power and prestige, and revered by the citizens. Only recently Matthew O'Brien had convinced Theo that times had changed, that he needed a squad of private bodyguards here at the villa to keep his loved ones safe. So he had hired locals for the job; and he had intended to do as Matt had suggested and send those men, two at a time, to the United States, to be trained by the Dundee agency, for whom Matt had once worked. If he hadn't been so old-fashioned in his thinking, if he'd hired professionally trained guards years ago, perhaps this horror could have been prevented.

Forgive me, Dia. Forgive your foolish, stubborn, old-fashioned husband. If any harm came to their precious little Phila, he would never forgive himself.

A soft rapping at the door drew Theo's attention and ended his mental self-flagellation. Easing quietly off the edge of the bed, he crossed the room and opened the door.

The housekeeper, her eyes swollen from crying, spoke softly in Greek. "You have a phone call from Mr. Khalid. He is waiting on your private line."

"Thank you, Mrs. Panopoulas. I will go to my office now." Theo motioned to Irina, who was standing several feet away. "Stay with Mrs. Constantine. If I'm needed, call Mrs. Panopoulas. She'll know, at all times, where I am."

Irina nodded, then went directly to her patient. Theo rushed downstairs and into his office. With his heart beating erratically, he lifted the telephone receiver.

"Nikos?"

"What's wrong?"

"Phila has been kidnapped."

"My God!"

"They took her from her own bed," Theo said. "They killed four guards and poor old Xerxes, who'd been hired by my father nearly fifty years ago. They left a note telling me they would not deal with the local authorities or any national agencies. They will deal only with me or my personal representative. The note said they would contact me soon with their demands."

"Do you have any idea who—"

"None. But I am a rich man. Perhaps all they want is money."

"Perhaps."

"I have enemies. I'm a businessman. My family didn't acquire an empire without making enemies. It could be an act of revenge, but I can't imagine anyone I know—" Theo's voice broke with emotion.

"Do not play a guessing game," Nikos said. "Not until we have more facts."

"Where are you? Is it possible for you to come to Golnar?"

"I'm in London. At Vauxhall Cross. I've only just yesterday completed an assignment. I'll let them know I need some time off for holiday. I'll get the ten-thirty flight out of Heathrow and be in Golnar before four in the morning, Golnar time."

"I'll send Peneus to meet your flight." Theo knew that if the Dundee agency could not help him, with their team of experts, including two former FBI agents, then Nikos would be his last hope. If he could not directly call upon any national agencies for assistance, then having a friend with direct ties to Britain's SIS could well prove to be Phila's salvation.

"How is Dia?" Nikos asked.

"How do you think she is? She is a mother whose little girl has been ruthlessly kidnapped by men capable of murder."

"I promise you that we will get Phila back."

"Yes." Theo swallowed hard. "We must."

The Dundee agents arrived after dark. The Constantine villa, just outside the small town of Coeus, presided over the area from its perch high atop the hillside. Jagged, weather-beaten bluffs behind the estate overlooked the sea. A series of terraces descended from the villa down to the narrow beach.

Theo met them at the door and welcomed them cordially into his home. Ellen realized the moment he shook her hand that he didn't remember her. His eyes held a blank stare that told her she was a complete stranger to him. But then why should he remember her? They'd met only once during the two weeks she'd spent on Golnar. And she had changed drastically since then. Gone was the clean-faced, starry-eyed kid, the carefree, little fool. Just because she would never forget anything or anyone associated with this island didn't mean someone she'd met back then would necessarily remember her. She doubted that even Nikos remembered her. After all, she'd been nothing more to him than a two-week vacation fling.

And he had meant everything to her.

"Please, come in, Ms. Denby." Theo looked behind her at the four agents. "All of you, please, follow me. You can use my office. It's fully equipped. Multiple phone lines, fax machine, Internet access and just about anything you will need."

"Thank you," Ellen said as she studied Theo's face. Dark circles under his eyes. A day's growth of dark beard stubble. And weariness etched into his features. This was a soul-weary father, Ellen thought. "I promise you, Mr. Constantine, that I will do everything within my power to bring your child home to you safe and sound."

Theo cleared his throat. "I…uh…would you and your agents care to freshen up and have some dinner first? My housekeeper has prepared several bedrooms for you and your team."

Ellen shook her head. "We ate on the plane, so we're good until breakfast. I'd like to see your office and take a look at the note the kidnappers left. Have the local authorities checked it for—"

"The local police aren't involved. The note specifically warns me to not let the police or any government agency handle this."

"All right. I understand." Ellen motioned to Sawyer. "First thing, contact your friends at the Bureau and see if we can get some unofficial help." She turned back to Theo. "Would you have our luggage taken to our rooms and then show us directly to your office."

Theo instructed the chauffeur in his native Greek language. Ellen assumed he was issuing orders to bring in the Dundee agents' luggage. "Follow me," Theo said. "My office is this way."

Ellen and her team followed him down the hall and into a two-story suite with a metal, spiral staircase that led from the main level to the second floor. The walls in the upstairs loft were lined with filled bookshelves. Downstairs the room contained a state-of-the-art office. A large fireplace graced one wall and heavy, dark wooden furniture dominated the room. Every piece of office equipment imaginable and a barrage of telephones comprised the work area.

Theo punched a button on the wall which activated a

switch that zapped an oil painting down behind a slender, antique commode. A well-stocked glass and chrome bar appeared. "I could use a drink. Would anyone care to join me?"

No one replied. Ellen shook her head. A telephone rang. Ellen glared at the assortment of phones. Theo's hands stilled over a bottle of Scotch.

"It's the regular household line." Theo pointed to the white telephone with the blinking red light.

Suddenly the phone stopped ringing. Ellen groaned. "From now on, one of my agents will screen all phone calls. Please instruct your servants to not answer the phone until further notice."

"All right," Theo replied, then lifted the bottle of aged Scotch from the bar and poured himself half a crystal tumbler. But before the glass reached his lips, a loud knock on the door interrupted him.

The door opened and a robust, black-eyed, middle-aged woman appeared.

"Yes, Mrs. Panopoulas?"

She replied to him in Greek.

Theo paled visibly. His hand holding the glass of whiskey shook. "She said there is a phone call for me and the man says it is about Phila."

"Is there a portable phone that connects to that line?" Ellen asked.

Theo nodded.

"Please get the portable phone for me," Ellen instructed the housekeeper, who looked to Theo for agreement. Had the woman understood her?

"Do it. Go. Now." Theo spoke to the housekeeper in English.

Mrs. Panopoulas scurried out of the room.

"She understands English?" Ellen asked.

"Yes, to a certain extent, and she can speak some English, also."

Ellen nodded, then told Theo, "As soon as I have the extension phone, then we'll pick up together. I want to listen to what our caller has to say, without him knowing I'm on the line."

"Do you think it's the kidnappers?" Theo's voice trembled.

"Possibly. So listen very carefully. It's important that you agree to nothing without checking with me first. Look at me, and if I can't reply with a nod or a shake of my head, I will write down a reply and hand it to you. Understand?"

"Yes, I suppose. I'm not sure."

Mrs. Panopoulas rushed into the room, the portable phone in her hand. She held it out to Ellen.

"Thank you," Ellen said.

The minute the housekeeper left, Ellen motioned for Theo to go to the lineup of telephones. When he was in place, she motioned again and simultaneously Ellen punched the on button as Theo lifted the receiver.

"This is Theo Constantine."

"How are you, Mr. Constantine?" The man's voice was deep, slightly accented and perfectly, deadly calm. "Are you worried about your daughter?"

"Do you have her? Is she all right?"

"She is quite well. Your little Phila and her nanny are our guests."

"What do you want?"

The deep chuckles Ellen heard over the phone line sent a cold, shivering wave through her body. She looked directly at Theo and their gazes locked.

"Do you want money?" Theo asked.

"Money is always good."

"How much?"

"A great deal to us, but not to a man as rich as you."

"Damn you, tell me—"

Ellen shook her head. Theo calmed.

"Five million dollars and..." The man deliberately let his words end midsentence.

Ellen picked up a pad and pen and wrote hurriedly, then walked across the room and handed the note to Theo.

"I've hired a hostage negotiator to handle the arrangements," Theo read from the note.

"An independent?" the man asked. "If you've brought in any—"

"An independent firm," Theo assured him.

"Tell your negotiator that we want five—"

"Tell me yourself," Ellen said, then motioned for Theo to hang up his phone. He hesitated for a moment, then did as she'd instructed.

"A woman negotiator?"

"Name your terms."

"Five million dollars and..."

He was playing with her as he had with Theo.

"And what?" she demanded.

"And the release of three members of the Al'alim who are being held as prisoners in Menkura."

Ellen sucked in a deep breath. God in heaven, this was no ordinary kidnapping where money was the sole objective. This had suddenly turned into a political matter and it was going to be damn difficult to keep this affair from becoming an international incident. And she knew better than anyone what the odds were of saving Phila Constantine, if she'd been abducted by the rebel army from Subria. These people were terrorists to whom murder was a glorious act, as long as it was done in the name of their cause. Every nerve in Ellen's body tensed. Don't think about it, she told herself. *Do not remember. Do not remember.*

Worth Cordell grabbed Ellen's shoulder and shook her

gently. She snapped out of her morbid thoughts, then nodded, indicating she was all right.

"How do you propose we arrange for the release of those prisoners?" Ellen asked.

"That will be your problem to solve, Ms. Negotiator."

"I'll need more information."

"And you will have it. In time." The phone line went dead.

The sorry son of a bitch had hung up on her. She turned off the phone, tossed it onto the nearby desk and exhaled a loud, mad-as-hell breath.

"We're in deep—" She stopped herself just in time, then glanced at Theo. "What do you personally have to do with the country of Subria and with the militant cult who call themselves Al'alim?"

"Al'alim? I have no ties to those monsters. None. I swear." Then suddenly, as if he remembered something he'd forgotten, Theo went chalk white. "Oh, God. Oh, God, no!"

Chapter 2

Countless stars sparkled in the predawn sky, and a cool autumn breeze blew in off the Mediterranean. The dark limousine stopped in front of the villa. Peneus emerged from inside, then quickly opened the back door. Domingo Shea, who'd drawn the early-morning watch, came out of the villa and walked over to meet Theo Constantine's guest. They'd been expecting the mysterious Mr. Khalid. Constantine had told the Dundee agents that this man was his friend and he had worldwide ties that might help them discover the identity of his daughter's kidnappers. Due to past experience on numerous other cases, Dom was skeptical about Khalid's usefulness. Dom was, by nature, skeptical about anyone who was as secretive as Khalid. Unknown elements in a person's background could as likely be evil as good. Which was Mr. Khalid? The savior Theo Constantine believed him to be—or the devil in disguise?

As Dom went to meet their newly arrived guest, he surveyed the man from head to toe. Khalid stood a good six-foot-four, and had a muscular yet lean build. He was as tall as Worth Cordell, but didn't have the body mass of the ex-Ranger. Khalid moved with the confidence of a well-trained warrior and the grace of a first-class athlete. Dom had figured he'd be wearing a *thobe,* the traditional flowing robe, or at the very least a *gutra* headdress. After all the guy was Arab, wasn't he? But Mr. Khalid wore black jeans and a black, long-sleeved shirt. His head was bare and his black shoulder-length hair was pulled into a loose ponytail. A neatly trimmed mustache and partial beard, as jet-black as his hair, shadowed the lower half of his face.

Mr. Khalid held out his hand to Dom and two dark gazes instantly collided. Whoever this guy was, he was cocksure, Dom thought.

"SabaaH ilkheer," Dom said good morning in Arabic. He knew about a dozen Arabic phrases, just enough to get by in a pinch.

Mr. Khalid's lips curved with a faint smile. *"SabaaH innuur."* Mr. Khalid ended the brief handshake. "I speak English quite fluently."

"So you do." Dom realized that Khalid spoke the language with an upper-class British accent, which meant he'd probably been educated in England.

"I am Khalid. And you are?"

"Domingo Shea, with the Dundee agency."

"Yes, Theo mentioned that Matthew O'Brien recommended his former agency to represent Theo in the hostage negotiations."

Dom motioned to the open front door. "Come inside. Mr. Constantine is expecting you. He's in his office."

Khalid nodded, then followed Dom. "Has he slept at all since Phila's kidnapping?"

"Not that I know of."

"Has he heard from the kidnappers?"

"One phone call. The boss took over the conversation

from Mr. Constantine. We're pretty sure the kidnappers are connected to the radical cult, Al'alim.''

Khalid said nothing, but Dom heard just the hint of an indrawn breath. As they headed down the hall, Dom asked, "You've heard of them, the Al'alim?''

"Yes, I have heard of them. Did they say what they want in exchange for Phila's safe return?''

"Five million bucks...and the release of three members of the Al'alim who are being held as prisoners in Menkura.''

Khalid's indrawn breath was louder that time, and he halted abruptly, a couple of feet from the entrance to Constantine's office. "I wish to speak to Theo alone, if you please, Mr. Shea.''

"Yeah, sure. Just as soon as Mr. Constantine says it's okay.''

Khalid nodded. Dom knocked on the closed door.

"Enter,'' Theo Constantine said.

Dom opened the door and Khalid followed him into the large library which doubled as an office. Constantine rose from where he'd been sitting on the leather sofa and rushed forward to grab both of Khalid's hands.

"Thank you for coming.''

"Mr. Shea has told me that the Al'alim are involved,'' Khalid said.

"Yes.''

"We should speak alone.'' Khalid glanced at Dom.

"Yes, we should.'' Constantine nodded to Dom. "Leave us, please.''

Dom left quickly and closed the door behind him. Once out in the hall, he paused. *Now, I wonder what that was all about? Those two know something about the Al'alim, maybe even know why the rebel group kidnapped Constantine's daughter.*

* * *

Nikos thought Theo looked rough, like a man who had suddenly been plunged into hell. He grasped Theo's shoulder.

"How could they have known about you?" Nikos asked, more to himself than to Theo. "No one has any idea that there is any connection between Theo Constantine and El-Hawah. Only the highest ranking officials at MI6 know that Mr. Khalid and El-Hawah are one and the same. Only those few are privy to my true identity. There's no way the Al'alim could know that you are friends with El-Hawah."

"Is it possible this is a coincidence, that the Al'alim took Phila for reasons that have nothing to do with you?" Theo pulled away from Nikos and paced the floor, his shoulders drooping from the heavy weight of worry. He paused, raked his fingers through his thick, ebony hair and looked pleadingly into Nikos's eyes. "Tell me that it is a coincidence? My God, you know what these people are capable of—" Theo's voice cracked with despair.

"Theo…" Nikos reached out to his friend.

"What if by some chance they do know we are somehow connected and they are using Phila as a means to smoke you out of hiding?"

"They asked for money and the release of prisoners," Nikos reminded Theo. "They did not mention El-Hawah. We can't jump to conclusions. I've already sent out feelers…before I left London. Someone out there knows something and it's only a matter of time before we find out what is being said in hushed tones throughout the world."

"Since the Dundee agency will handle the negotiations, I want you to tell their CEO about the possible connection between the Al'alim and you and I."

"The information we can give him will be limited." Nikos cursed his life as a spy, living a lie, never able to be totally honest with anyone. How would he live with himself if they found out that Phila had been kidnapped because of him? The only friendship he had maintained over the years was the one with Theo, whom he loved like a brother and trusted as he trusted no one else.

"The CEO of the agency is a she. And she was once a hostage negotiator for the police. Please, you must tell her what you can. It need go no further. I'm sure she will keep your secrets. But you should know that two of the Dundee agents were former FBI.'' Theo closed his eyes. Nikos had never seen such pain on his friend's face. "What if…what if the kidnappers want—''

Nikos grabbed Theo's shoulders and gave him a sound shake. "I will not let them harm Phila. I swear to you that I would give up my life to save your daughter.''

Theo grabbed Nikos and hugged him, then quickly released him and walked away; but not before Nikos saw the tears in Theo's eyes.

Ellen got lost in the crowd of revelers that lined the streets of Dareh. They pushed her along with them as they danced and sang and shared hugs. The music was happy and light. She didn't understand the language, but she understood the joy. Gaily clad girls in costume tapped their tambourines as they danced and sang.

The summertime warmth, combined with the crush of bodies, heated her flesh. Trickles of sweat dripped between her breasts, moistened her makeup-free face and dampened her strapless bra and bikini panties beneath her yellow sundress. She had come to Europe on this vacation trip for adventure and to reward herself for graduating from the University of Georgia magna cum laude. Coming to Golnar was turning out to be a wonderful decision. A Mediterranean island paradise with lots of gorgeous young men. She giggled at the thought of meeting someone and sharing a vacation romance. How lucky could a girl get—to arrive in the capital city on the very day of a Mardi Gras—like festival.

Ellen locked arms with two other women, friendly strangers. Caught in the rush of the crowd, they made their way merrily down the street. A group of ten or more revelers— including the two women flanking her—broke apart and headed straight into a café. After somehow managing to escape the rush, Ellen leaned against the outer café wall to catch her breath. She closed her eyes and sighed. Suddenly, without warning, lips touched hers. Briefly. Softly. Seductively. Her eyes flew open and she stared up into the face of the most devastatingly attractive man she'd ever seen. Not handsome by classical standards, but tall, dark and dangerous looking—and totally, undeniably male.

"What…why—"

He laid his index finger over her lips. "A kiss because it is festival time and we are celebrating."

A tingling awareness passed throughout her body as the man lifted his finger from her lips and trailed it across her chin and down her throat. Mesmerized by his incredible black eyes, Ellen couldn't look away. And she couldn't think straight, either.

"You are very beautiful," he said as his finger trailed lower and lower until it stopped at the top edge of her sundress.

"And you're very bold," she told him. "Do you try to seduce every woman you meet?"

"Only the beautiful American blondes."

When he smiled, Ellen went weak in the knees. Lord help her, this guy was lethal. She had wished for a tall, dark, handsome stranger to sweep her off her feet for a vacation romance. Now she realized the truth to the old adage, be careful what you wish for or you just might get it.

Ellen laughed and even to her own ears she sounded like a silly little girl. "How did you know I'm American?"

"Your accent. I'm very good at linguistics, picking up languages easily and identifying regional accents. You're from somewhere in the southern part of the United States."

"Amazing that you'd know. I'm from Georgia."

He laced her arm through his. *"You're not with your husband or boyfriend? Please, tell me you are alone."*

"I'm with some school friends. We're bouncing around Europe this summer. I lost the others in the crowd about half an hour ago."

"Then you must stay with me and let me show you Dareh."

"Are you by any chance a native?"

He shook his head. *"I am a British citizen."*

She stared at him, puzzled by his looks, which were decidedly not Anglo.

"My father was part Greek and part English," he explained, as if he understood her confusion concerning his physical appearance. *"And my mother was of Turkish descent."*

"How exotic, especially considering that I'm just plain old Scots-Irish." She kept staring at him, captivated by everything about this stranger. Stranger! *"Why should I trust you, Mr.—I don't even know your name?"*

"Call me Nikos."

"Just Nikos?"

He nodded.

"All right," she said. *"You may call me Mary Ellen."*

"Mary Ellen? Such a simple, ordinary name for such an extraordinary woman."

She bit down on her bottom lip to keep from giggling.

"Will you come with me, Mary Ellen, and share this day with me? If you don't come with me, you will always wonder. And so will I."

"I guess you know you're very persuasive."

Nikos led her down the street, away from the revelers. She looked up at him and smiled.

If you do not come with me, you will always wonder. She kept hearing Nikos's words repeating over and over again. Her head began to swim; the world went round and round. Everything went black. And when she opened her eyes, Nikos was gone. But a man held her arm tightly. A man as dark and mysterious as Nikos. But older. With a harsh face and a menacing expression.

She tried to speak, tried to ask him where Nikos had gone. But before she could say a word, the man slapped her forcefully across the face. She licked her lips and tasted her own blood.

"You will tell me what I want to know," the man said. "If you do not, both of you will die."

"No, please, I don't know what you want."

"Where is your lover? What is his real name?"

"Lover? I don't have a—" the second slap was harder and more brutal than the first. Ellen cried out in pain.

"Do not lie to me!"

"I'm not lying." She bowed her head, fear raging inside her like a forest fire, burning her from the inside out. "Please, please, believe me."

He grabbed her by the hair of her head and forced her to look directly into his cold, brutal face. "The man you met in Golnar. He was your lover. I want to know where he is."

"I don't know. I swear to you that I do not know where he is. It's been nearly a year since I saw him."

"You will pay a high price for your lies."

"I'm not lying. Why would I lie?"

"To protect him."

Suddenly she heard cries coming from the other room. Oh, God, the cries.

"Please, don't hurt him," she begged. *"I'll do anything you ask if only you won't hurt him."*

She could feel him in her arms, feel his small warm body lying against her own. Could smell his sweet scent.

Suddenly the crying stopped.

No!

The word screamed inside her head repeatedly. No... no...no!

Waking suddenly, Ellen shot straight up in bed. Sweat drenched, her heart thundering at breakneck speed, she flung back the covers.

She had believed herself invulnerable to the pain inflicted on her so long ago. The dreams came so seldom now that she had all but forgotten their power to weaken her physically and emotionally. But she should have suspected that this might happen, that returning to Golnar might trigger the nightmares she had fought so desperately to overcome.

Reaching out, she switched on the bedside table lamp. She picked up her wristwatch, noted it was a few minutes past six; then she got out of bed and walked to the windows overlooking the terrace. Morning light streaked the sky with various shades of pink and lavender. Despite every effort not to remember, her mind replayed a scene from her past. Another morning here in Golnar, when she'd looked at another dawn sky from the balcony of a little hotel. Nikos had come up behind her and wrapped his arms around her.

Ellen shuddered. Damn!

She rushed into the adjoining bathroom, stripped out of her oversize Georgia Bulldogs T-shirt and turned on the shower. While waiting for the water to warm, she glanced at herself in the mirror.

"Does Theo know where Nikos is?" she asked aloud. "I wonder if he's even still alive."

At six-thirty, Ellen answered the knock on her door. In jeans and a baggy olive-green sweater, Lucie Evans stood there, two mugs of coffee in her hands and a cheery smile on her face. With an Amazonian stature and long, curly, flame-red hair, Lucie would stand out in any crowd, but she did little to enhance her natural beauty.

"Dom just brought these up. Worth has taken over the watch and Dom's headed to bed for a few hours," Lucie said. "Dom wanted me to tell you that Mr. Constantine wants to see you downstairs. It seems Mr. Khalid arrived about an hour ago and the two have been holed up in the library."

"Put in a call to the office and see if they can get some information on this Mr. Khalid. I think it's a bit odd that Theo Constantine is so secretive about the man."

Lucie handed Ellen one of the mugs, then strolled into the bedroom. "Are you okay? You look tired."

"I didn't sleep well, but I'm fine."

Lucie sipped her coffee. "I hate these cases. When a child is kidnapped, it's pure torture for the parents. We haven't even seen Dia Constantine. Can you imagine what she's going through?"

A tiny shudder zinged along Ellen's nerve endings. "Yes, I can. And believe me, what Mrs. Constantine is going through is more horrible than you or anyone who has not gone through the experience could even begin to comprehend. And if that child is killed..." Ellen swallowed hard, then cleared her throat. "We're going to do everything in our power to see to it that that doesn't happen."

Ellen took several sips of coffee, then set the mug down on a tea table by a velvet upholstered chaise longue. "I need to go on downstairs."

"You should grab some breakfast after you talk to Mr. Constantine," Lucie said.

"Yes, Mother." Ellen smiled. "By the way, you and

Sawyer shouldn't wait for me. I don't know how long I'll be."

"Oh, great, something to look forward to. Breakfast alone with Sawyer," Lucie said sarcastically.

Another knock at the door stopped Ellen's departure. She opened the door and found Sawyer McNamara standing there holding a large tray. As always he was immaculately dressed, like a sleek, stylish model straight from the pages of *GQ*. Black slacks, gray-and-white pin-striped shirt, charcoal herringbone blazer and a dark red silk tie. If you didn't look beyond the fastidious facade, you might mistake Sawyer for nothing more than an attractive, mild-mannered gentleman. But you'd be wrong. Beneath the Beau Brummell camouflage, a fearless warrior lay dormant, needing only the right provocation to awaken.

"Breakfast is served," he said, then walked past Ellen and into the bedroom. He stopped dead still when he saw Lucie.

"Well, isn't this sweet of you," Lucie said. "But I had planned on going down to the kitchen for breakfast."

Sawyer glared at Lucie. "Please, go right ahead. Don't let me stop you."

"Thanks for this." Ellen eyed the tray. "But I've been summoned to the library. Let Lucie have it. Or better, yet, if there's enough, why don't you two share like a good little girl and boy? And try not to squabble once I'm gone."

Lucie reached out, grabbed the cloth covering the tray and exposed the breakfast-for-two. "Yeah, Sawyer, don't you want to have a nice, intimate breakfast with me, since Ellen isn't available?"

Sawyer set the tray down on the bed. "I don't want to share anything intimate with you."

"Children, children," Ellen scolded playfully. "Play nice while I'm gone."

"I'll see you later," Sawyer said to Ellen as he left hurriedly.

Lucie laughed. "Why don't you just tell the man that he doesn't have a snowball's chance in hell of ever scoring with you? Put him out of his misery. As it is, he's a bear to be around."

Ellen sighed. "I don't have time to deal with this now. Sawyer is always a consummate professional, except when he's around you. I swear, the two of you bring out the worst in each other."

"It might have something to do with the fact that he was a horse's ass to me when I worked under him—" When Ellen chuckled, Lucie said, "Let me rephrase that. When Sawyer was my boss while I was with the Bureau, we didn't see eye to eye on a lot of things. He's a by-the-book, unimaginative guy, with limited tolerance for opinions different than his own."

"You should hear all the nice things he has to say about you." Ellen winked at Lucie before leaving.

"Yeah, I'll bet," Lucie called as Ellen left the bedroom.

When Ellen reached the top of the stairs, a door on the far side of the hall opened and a stocky young woman with a thick mane of barely restrained dark curls waved at Ellen and came rushing toward her.

"Ms. Denby, please wait a moment."

Ellen paused. "Yes, what is it?"

"I'm Irina, Mrs. Constantine's nurse," the woman said. "Mrs. Constantine wishes to speak to you. She asks that, please, you come, now."

"I'm suppose to be meeting with…" Ellen sighed. "Oh, all right. I'll see Mrs. Constantine."

Ellen wasn't sure exactly what to expect, but she knew before she entered the bedroom suite that she would find a distraught woman.

What she found was even worse. Under normal circumstances, Dia Constantine would have been a strikingly lovely woman. But this morning, that beauty was masked by great suffering. The kind of suffering only a parent could know. *Only a mother could feel,* Ellen thought. Dark circles framed a set of bleary, gray eyes that stared from a pale face, as Mrs. Constantine struggled to rise from her bed.

Irina spoke frantically in Greek; then flew to her charge's side and tried to persuade her to lie down. But Mrs. Constantine would not cooperate.

"I wish to sit up for a while," she said in a weak, yet authoritative voice. She looked past her nurse to where Ellen stood in the open doorway. "Ms. Denby, please come in."

When Mrs. Constantine waved her nurse aside, she rose from the bed, eased her legs to the edge and placed her bare feet on the floor. Ellen approached the woman cautiously, realizing that anything she might say could do emotional harm to this fragile lady.

"Sit, please." Mrs. Constantine motioned to a chair beside the bed.

Ellen sat.

"I apologize for not greeting you yesterday evening when you arrived," Mrs. Constantine said, "but I'm afraid they are giving me medication to calm my nerves and… Are you married? Do you have children?"

"No."

"But you are a woman, so you must understand what a child means to a mother." Tears welled up in Dia Constantine's eyes.

Ellen clenched her teeth. *Take charge of your emotions,* she told herself. *Control. Total control.* Ellen prided herself on not showing her emotions in front of others. If she cried—which she seldom did—she cried alone, in private.

Ellen squared her shoulders. "I will…we will do everything in our power to help you and your husband bring your daughter home safely.''

"Money is no object. My husband is a very rich man. He…'' Mrs. Constantine fell apart before Ellen's eyes, unraveling like a tightly wound skein of yarn. Sobbing uncontrollably, she reached out to Ellen. "Tell them…'' She gulped several times. "Tell them we will pay them anything they ask. Oh, God, please, please, don't let them hurt Phila.''

When Dia Constantine grabbed Ellen's forearms, Ellen was shocked by the woman's strength.

"Please, say something to soothe her, Ms. Denby,'' Irina said in crisp, precise English. "I'll prepare a sedative to calm her.''

Ellen nodded, then spoke to Mrs. Constantine. "Tell me about Phila. How old is she? What's her favorite color? Does she have a pet?''

"She's seven. Her favorite color is blue. And she has a little cocker spaniel named Marmee, who just gave birth to a litter of four a few days ago. And she has a puppy, who is eight months old, named Lady. Mrs. Panopoulas is caring for Marmee and her babies, as well as Lady.''

Irina came forward, a hypodermic in her hand. Ellen held on to Mrs. Constantine's trembling hands while the nurse gave her an injection. Within moments, her speech slurred and she didn't put up a fuss when Irina eased her back down into bed.

Ellen rose from the chair, stood and took a deep, calming breath. Had she been a fool to take this assignment herself? She knew she was strong, that not much touched her because she guarded her emotions so fiercely, but this time, being back in Golnar and long suppressed memories bombarding her, could she maintain her iron control?

"Thank you for being so kind to her,'' Irina said.

Ellen nodded, then went out into the hall and down the

stairs. She tried to clear her mind of any thoughts that might interfere with her handling this job in a completely professional manner. As she approached the library, she heard the sound of two male voices that carried plainly through the open door. A very tall man in black clothes stood with his back to her as he spoke to Theo, who glanced past his guest and waved to Ellen.

"Ms. Denby, please come in. I'd like for you to meet my friend, Mr. Khalid."

Ellen took a couple of steps beyond the threshold. The man turned to greet her. Ellen stopped dead still. My God, it couldn't be! But it was. As if he had stepped out of her most recent nightmare, Nikos stood before her. His black eyes widened in shock.

"Mary Ellen?"

Chapter 3

Nikos stared at the woman. She was the same and yet vastly different from the girl he had known fifteen years ago. If possible she was even more beautiful now than she had been then. But there was no mistaking those stunning azure-blue eyes, that platinum-blond hair, though cut quite short now, and that incredible, luscious body. And yet this woman bore only a superficial resemblance to her former self. Gone was the exuberant smile, the tender young features and the twinkle of naive mischief in her eyes. But the woman standing before him, glaring at him with stunned disbelief, took his breath away, just as her younger counterpart had done.

"It is you, isn't it?" Nikos said, certain and yet unable to believe that this moment was possible. He had put any hopes of ever seeing her again out of his mind long ago. She had become a sweet memory, one he allowed himself, on rare occasions, to bring to the forefront of his thoughts and savor. She had been relegated to the part of his soul that existed in a fictional land called *"if only."*

She simply continued staring at him, neither speaking nor moving.

"What's going on here?" Theo glanced back and forth from Nikos to Ellen. "Do you two know each other?"

"Yes, we do, don't we, Mary Ellen?" Nikos took a tentative step toward her, but stopped instantly when he saw the expression on her face. She looked at him as if she were afraid of him. But why would she fear him?

"How do you know Ms. Denby?" Theo asked.

Nikos kept his gaze riveted to Mary Ellen. God, she was exquisite. Like something from a man's most erotic fantasy. A thick shock of white-blond hair, cut severely short, did nothing to diminish her ultrafemininity. Her face was classically beautiful, her fair, flawless skin lightly tanned. Not even the Spartan khaki slacks and crisp white blouse she wore could disguise the voluptuous figure hidden beneath.

"Is that your last name, Denby?" Nikos asked.

As if snapping out of a trance, Ellen sighed heavily, lifting and dropping her shoulders in the process. She huffed loudly, then closed the door and moved toward Nikos.

"We never exchanged last names, did we? And by the way, no one has called me Mary Ellen in a long time. I'm simply Ellen now." She halted several feet from him, but kept her gaze fixed on his face. "Nikos Khalid? Is that your real name?"

"It will do for now," he replied.

"Will one of you please explain to me how it is that you know each other?" Theo moved between them, glaring first at Ellen and then at Nikos. "If there's some reason why the two of you can't work together, I want to know now."

Nikos laid his hand on Theo's shoulder and gently shoved him aside as he moved closer to Ellen. "Don't you remember her? I introduced you to her at a party you held here at the villa. You told me what a lucky devil I was to have found such a rare jewel."

Theo jerked around and stared at Ellen. His gaze traveled over her from head to toe and then back up again. "When did we meet?"

"Fifteen years ago," Ellen said. "But only briefly. Obviously I didn't make much of an impression on you."

"Ah, but you did," Nikos corrected. "But I'm afraid Theo was slightly drunk that evening and when he drinks too much, he remembers very little the following day." Nikos squeezed Theo's shoulder. "I met Mary Ellen in Dareh during the Summer Festival."

"Fifteen years ago?" Theo absorbed the information. Suddenly his eyes widened. "This—this is the woman that you... My God!"

"Mr. Constantine, I see no reason why Mr. Khalid is needed here," Ellen said, her voice quite stern. "The Dundee agency is perfectly capable of handling the negotiations without any assistance."

"Perhaps you are," Theo said. "But Nikos is not here to assist you in negotiating. He's here because of his ties to…uh…to rebel factions worldwide. He has knowledge of and experience dealing with the Al'alim cult. I assure you that he will prove indispensable to us."

"I see." Ellen looked at Nikos, her eyes questioning him, doubting him. "And exactly what is it you do, Mr. Khalid, that has given you this vast experience with terrorists?"

"Theo, would you mind letting me speak to Ma…to Ellen alone?" Nikos eyed the door, then noted the direction with a nod of his head.

"Yes. Certainly." Theo walked to the door, opened it, then glanced back and said, "Ms. Denby, either work out your differences with Nikos here and now or bring in another agent to take your place. We have no time for old lovers to work through past mistakes. Not while my daughter's life is in imminent peril. Do I make myself clear?"

"Yes. You've made yourself quite clear," Ellen replied. Theo left and closed the door behind him.

Nikos crossed his arms over his chest and smiled. "You're still very beautiful, but you've changed dramatically. What happened to that sweet, wild, young thing who was filled with such *joie de vivre?*"

"She grew up, learned from her mistakes and moved on."

Not by word or action did Ellen show any emotion, but the coldness in her eyes spoke to him silently. She was angry with him. Angry and perhaps hurt. Was it possible that after all these years, she still resented the fact that he'd left her sleeping in their bed at the hotel, leaving her only a vague goodbye note? Surely she hadn't held on to that youthful rage for fifteen years.

"I've thought of you," he said. "More often than I'd like to admit."

"Save it, will you? Save all your pretty little speeches for a woman who's stupid enough to believe them." A tinge of color blushed her cheeks. "I doubt you've given me a thought over the years. After all, I was nothing more to you than a two week fling with a silly little American virgin."

"Such anger. Why? Unless—"

"You're right. I'm overreacting. I apologize. I haven't given you a thought in years, but I suppose seeing you again refreshed my memory and all that old anger resurfaced."

"Ah, I see. Of course, you had every right to be angry. I was your first lover and I left you with nothing more than a brief note. Very ungentlemanly of me." Nikos reached out and took her hand in his.

Ellen shivered. "My first lover, but certainly not my last." She jerked her hand from his. "I should thank you for being the first. You taught me more than you'll ever know.''

''Did I indeed?''

''Mr. Constantine is right. Unless you and I agree to forget we ever had a past association, we can't work together to save his daughter's life. And saving Phila Constantine and her nanny, Ms. Sheridan, is why I'm here in Golnar.''

''If you have no problem with our working together, I don't.''

''As long as you allow me and my agents to do our job, we will work with you, since that's what Mr. Constantine wants.''

Nikos eyed Ellen suspiciously. ''Do you hate me?''

She hesitated for a couple of seconds, then said, ''No. I have no feelings of any kind for you.''

''Setting me straight, are you, Ms. Denby?'' Nikos's lips twitched. ''You don't want me to have any misconceptions about our picking up where we left off fifteen years ago. Am I to assume you have a husband or a significant other in your life?''

''You can assume whatever the hell you want, Mr. Khalid.''

Ellen turned, opened the door and walked out into the hall. Nikos followed her as she made her way to where Theo stood halfway down the corridor. He was deep in conversation with another man, a big, burly guy, with the build of a professional wrestler.

Ellen walked up to Theo and said, ''Mr. Khalid and I are in agreement. We'll have no problems working together.''

Theo glanced beyond Ellen and looked straight at Nikos. ''Is that right?''

''I would never contradict a lady,'' Nikos said.

''Good. Good. Cooperation is the key to success.'' Theo

grasped Nikos's arm. "I'm going upstairs to see Dia. After you've had breakfast, we'll meet back in my office." He glanced at Ellen. "You and your people, too, Ms. Denby. We have much to discuss."

Ellen nodded. "We'll be there."

After Theo headed up the stairs, Nikos turned to the other man and said, "I'm Nikos Khalid."

"Worth Cordell." The guy's voice was deep and gravelly, with the power of a lion's roar. "I'm a Dundee agent, here with Ms. Denby."

Ms. Denby, not Ellen, Nikos thought. Professional relationship. Nothing more. Idiotic that he should be glad she wasn't involved with this man.

"I'm a businessman, with interests throughout the world," he told Worth, "but lately those interests are concentrated mainly in Asia and the Middle East. I've known Theo since we were in school together as boys in England."

"I'm sure he's glad you're here," Worth said.

"I'm here to help in any way I can." Nikos turned to Ellen and offered her his arm. "Shall we go to the dining room for breakfast?"

"Why don't you and Worth go ahead, Mr. Khalid," Ellen said. "I have something rather urgent that I need to attend to."

"Certainly. I look forward to seeing you later."

Without a backward glance, Ellen walked away. Nikos watched her until she disappeared down the hall.

"Ms. Denby is quite a woman," Nikos said.

"As a general rule, I'm a man who minds his own business," Worth said. "But in this case I'll make an exception. If you have any ideas about Ellen Denby, forget them."

"Are you warning me off, Mr. Cordell?"

"Not warning you off, Khalid. Just giving you a little

friendly advice. The lady never mixes business with pleasure. She's a true professional.''

''Is that right? Thanks. I'll remember that.''

''Be sure you do, because if you don't, she'll remind
you.''

The farther from the house she went, the faster she
walked, until she finally broke into a run. Memories attacked her like a swarm of angry bees buzzing all around
her, giving her no means of escape. Dancing with Nikos.
Laughing with Nikos. Kissing Nikos. Making love with Nikos. She could almost feel his body pressed intimately
against hers, could almost feel his warm breath and taste
his moist lips. A part of her hated him, but not for the
reasons he suspected. Yes, he'd broken her foolish young
heart when he'd deserted her without even saying goodbye,
but in time she had forgiven him.

When he'd gone away in the middle of the night, he had
left her nothing except a hastily written note lying on the
bedside table.

Mary Ellen, my love,
I will always remember you and the idyllic days we've
shared. If my life were my own, if I were a different
man, I would stay with you and beg you to be mine
forever. Forgive me for being selfish, for stealing your
innocence and enjoying the pleasure of loving you and
being loved by you for a brief time. Thank you for
giving me far more than I deserved.
    I wish you much happiness in the future. If you
think of me at all, please remember how truly special
you were to me.
N.

She had kept that letter for over a year, then she had
burned it the day she'd burned the red shawl. But the words

were etched on her heart as if they'd been seared there by a hot branding iron.

You can't do this, she told herself. You can't stay here and allow the past to destroy you.

But she had to stay. Phila Constantine's life might well depend upon her staying. An innocent child needed her.

Oh, God, please keep those memories at bay. I can deal with the memories of Nikos, but not...

The cries echoed inside her head. Soft whimpering at first. Then louder and louder, until they drowned out every other sound.

Ellen stopped running as nausea rose up inside her. She bent over and emptied her stomach, then wiped her mouth with her hand. After climbing the hill, she slumped down onto the grassy knoll overlooking the Mediterranean and tried to clear her mind while the soft sea breeze caressed her heated cheeks.

Although her eyes were open, she saw nothing except the color blue—blue sky mating with blue water. Fourteen years ago, the doctors at the clinic had tried everything to stop the nightmares, but nothing had worked. Not until one of the therapists suggested meditation. It had taken time to retrain herself, to teach her mind how to clear itself of unwanted thoughts, but now she was able to go into a mild trancelike state pretty much at will. Teaching herself how to wash away the painful thoughts had saved her sanity.

A silent, monotonous hum repeated over and over inside her head until she reached a state of deep meditation.

The other Dundee agents and Mr. Khalid waited with Mr. Constantine in his office, but Ellen was a no-show. Sawyer volunteered to go find her, but Lucie stepped in and raced out the door before Sawyer could stop her. Worth had said the last he'd seen of Ellen, she'd gone down the hall and out the side door. Lucie wondered what was up with Ellen. It wasn't like her to forget a meeting, and she must have forgotten it because the woman was never late.

As the cool breeze hit her the moment she stepped outside, Lucie shivered. The morning sunshine was bright and warm, but an autumn chill was in the air. After calling Ellen's name several times and receiving no reply, Lucie decided to follow the path that led from the villa and up a gradually inclined knoll that overlooked the sea. Perhaps Ellen had taken a morning stroll and for some reason lost track of time. As she approached the top of the hill, she saw Ellen sitting on the grass and staring at the sky.

"Ellen," Lucie called.

No reply. How odd, Lucie thought, then remembered having heard something through the Dundee grapevine about Ellen meditating on a regular basis. Was that how the CEO of Dundee's remained so cool, calm and in-control at all times? Lucie had tried meditation once, but hadn't been able to sit still long enough to get the hang of it. Her mother had always told her that she was like a worm in hot ashes. Always moving; never still.

As she drew closer to Ellen, she called her name again. Several times. When Lucie was almost upon her, Ellen turned her head and looked directly at Lucie.

"Did you forget about the meeting?" Lucie asked. "Everybody's in Mr. Constantine's office."

Ellen rose languidly from the ground, her movements slow and graceful. "I needed some time alone. I'll apologize to Mr. Constantine."

When Ellen walked toward Lucie, Lucie asked, "Are you all right? It's not like you to—"

"I'm fine…now."

"Anything you want to talk about? I'm a pretty good listener."

Ellen shook her head. "Thanks for the offer, but I really am all right."

"It's this case, isn't it?"

"What do you mean?"

"There's a child in danger."

"Yes, there is, but what has that to do with—?"

Lucie confronted her boss by making direct eye contact. "Hey, I'm not prying. It's just that the word at Dundee's is you're the Woman of Steel, you know, sort of a superwoman. And they say your only weakness is kids. A child whose life is in danger is your kryptonite, so to speak."

For a split second Lucie was afraid she'd overstepped the bounds and Ellen was going to give her hell. But instead, Ellen smiled faintly and reached up to grasp Lucie's shoulder. Lucie towered over her five-foot-four-inch boss by eight inches.

"I'm no superwoman, believe me. It's just that most of the male Dundee agents are a little bit afraid of me because they know I can kick their asses."

Lucie laughed. "I'll bet you could."

"Come on, let's get back to the villa before someone comes looking for both of us."

"Sure, but…" Lucie hesitated. "If while we're here in Golnar, you need someone to talk to…another woman… well, feel free to come to me."

"Thanks, Lucie. I'll keep that in mind."

Together the two women headed down the knoll and toward the villa.

Faith Sheridan had no idea where they were or what time of day or night it was. They could be anywhere, in any country. Their abductors had drugged her once they'd reached the boat that night. When she awoke—how many hours or days later?—she'd found herself in this small, dirty, dimly lit room. A room with no windows, and the only source of light came from a battery-powered lamp sitting on a wooden table in the corner. She wondered how long the battery would stay charged. Was it only a matter of hours before the light would go out and they'd be left in pitch-black darkness? When she'd come to—yesterday or the day before?—Phila had been sitting beside her on the cot and had been holding her hand. She'd grabbed Phila and hugged her fiercely, so very grateful the child was alive.

Since they'd been here, she had seen no one, talked to no one. An assortment of dried fruits and two loaves of bread, along with four canteens of water had been left on the table. The fruit was almost gone, but over half a loaf of bread remained. If necessary, she wouldn't eat or drink anything more, on the off chance that their abductors might not replenish their supply. Phila would need the food and water.

That first day after she awoke, Faith had beaten on the locked door and screamed for someone to help them. But no one came to their rescue. There was no heat in their little room, but thankfully their captors had left blankets. And there was no bathroom, but they made do with a metal pail, the equivalent of what was commonly called by folks where she grew up a slop jar.

Faith figured out that they were probably in the basement of a house or building. Two walls were some type of concrete and wood and the other two walls were hard packed earth. A strong musty smell and the stench of their own waste created an unpleasant odor. But Faith kept telling herself that things could be worse. They might be locked away in a dark, cold, damp, smelly cell, but they were alive, unharmed and had been given food and water. Their captors were keeping them alive. But for how long?

Poor Phila was terrified and clung to Faith during her waking hours. Faith tried to soothe the little girl's fears, telling her stories, singing songs and making promises she prayed to God someone would keep.

"Your papa will send someone to get us," Faith had said.

"But how will Papa know where we are?"

"He'll hire people who know how to search and find lost little girls." Faith had caressed Phila's round, soft cheek. She was such a pretty child and so very sweet. She had her mother's gentle disposition.

"Why did those bad men take us away?"

"I'm not sure, sweetheart, but however long they keep us here, we must be strong and brave."

"I'm not strong or brave. I'm scared. What if they hurt us? What if they—"

Faith had wrapped Phila in a motherly embrace, giving her comfort and reassurance. But there was no one here to comfort and reassure her, so she'd just have to mother herself. Wasn't that the way it had always been? For most of her life she'd been alone, with no family…no parents…no mother. A skinny, little orphan whom no one wanted.

After checking on a sleeping Phila, Faith hugged her arms around herself as she clutched the scratchy woolen blanket in which she was wrapped. Pacing the earthen floor, she shuddered as a feeling of helplessness overwhelmed her. That won't do! She might be trapped, but she wasn't defeated. Faith Sheridan had never been a quitter. There had to be something she could do. *You are doing something,* she reminded herself, *you're taking care of Phila as best you can. You're keeping hope alive for both of you.*

The Constantines were probably out of their minds with worry. Theo Constantine had no doubt called in an army of searchers to find his child. And if the monsters who had kidnapped them were asking for a ransom, she knew the Constantines would pay them whatever they asked, no matter how much. But what chance did Phila and she have to come out of this alive?

Tears gathered in Faith's eyes, but she swiped them away. She refused to give in to fear and despair.

Please, God, please, look over us, protect us and send us a rescuer as soon as possible.

Chapter 4

Ellen marched into Theo's office, her head held high, and her attitude one of confidence and professionalism. Lucie came in behind her, then closed the door. Ellen glanced around the room. Everyone was here, sitting at a conference table which Theo undoubtedly used for business meetings. Congregated together, the people in this room comprised a formidable alliance. If it were possible to save Phila Constantine and Faith Sheridan from the Al'alim, this group could. A former police hostage negotiator, two former Special Forces military men, two former FBI agents, a billionaire, and a... A what? An international criminal? An undercover agent? Exactly what was Nikos Khalid? Better, yet, who was he?

"I apologize for keeping you waiting, Mr. Constantine," Ellen said. "I took a morning walk and I'm afraid I allowed the beauty of your grounds to distract me."

"No need to apologize," Constantine said. "Please, come and join us, ladies. And since we will be working

together to save my daughter's life, I believe we should all
be on a first-name basis.''

"Certainly…Theo," Ellen replied.

There were two empty chairs—one between Sawyer and
Worth and another between Dom and Nikos. Lucie waited,
giving Ellen first choice. Which would be worse, Ellen
wondered, sitting beside Nikos or directly across from him?
She chose the latter and eased in between Sawyer and
Worth.

Sawyer leaned over and whispered, "Are you okay?"

Forcing a smile, she nodded. Thankfully, he let the matter drop. For now. She had made a mistake when she'd
begun a personal relationship with Sawyer after he'd joined
Dundee's. Although she had ended things between them
months ago when she realized how serious he was becoming, Sawyer seemed to still be having a problem letting go.

Ellen fixed her gaze on Theo. As a man accustomed to
being in charge, he sat at the head of the table. He took for
granted the privileges of his wealth and power. But in this
incidence, he was weak and vulnerable. His love for his
child put him at the mercy of that child's kidnappers. Now
it was part of her job to help him accept his limitations and
at the same time to convince him not to lose hope.

"Ellen, would you walk us through what we know at
this point," Theo said. "Help us see where we are and
what we can do."

"Yes. Certainly." She looked directly at Theo, avoiding
eye contact with Nikos; but she was acutely aware of his
presence. "We've received one call about the abduction. A
man, with a distinct accent, told me that they have Phila
and Faith Sheridan. We have no proof that this is true, but
it probably is. They have demanded five million dollars,
which Theo assures me he can get without any trouble. But
these people are also asking for the release of three prisoners—three members of the Al'alim."

"Why would they target Theo Constantine?" Sawyer asked.

Ellen assumed Sawyer's question was rhetorical, as did the others, who waited for him to answer his own question.

"The obvious reason is because he's a billionaire who can easily get his hands on five million dollars," Sawyer said. "But there are quite a few men just as wealthy, men with children, wives, family members who could have been abducted. So why Constantine?" Sawyer looked directly at Theo. "Why you? Why do you think this group would believe you could secure the release of their three Al'alim brothers?"

Ellen caught the quick sidelong glance Theo gave Nikos and the hard stare Nikos returned. She figured the other Dundee agents had picked up on the subtle exchange. Within seconds, Sawyer confirmed her assumption.

"Mr. Khalid, perhaps you can shed some specific light on this matter." Sawyer leaned forward and locked gazes with Nikos.

Nikos didn't bat an eyelash. "Theo is a man of wealth, power and influence. His family has been known and respected throughout the Mediterranean area, in Europe and the Middle East for three generations. The Al'alim might believe that if anyone could use his influence to persuade the government of Menkura to release three rebel prisoners, Theo could."

"And do you think the Menkuraian government can be persuaded to release these men?" Ellen directed her question to Theo, who remained silent.

Nikos replied, "I doubt seriously that anyone other than God could entice the Prime Minister of Menkura to release them."

"If the government won't agree to hand over these guys, then that leaves us with only one other choice," Dom Shea said.

All eyes focused on Dom.

"You're quite right," Nikos agreed. "The only other alternative is to send in a squad of highly trained mercenaries to break these rebels out of prison."

"Or a small, highly trained squad of Dundee agents," Worth said.

"And there you have another reason why Theo was chosen," Nikos explained. "He has the money to hire such a group. And if Matthew O'Brien had not arranged for Dundee's to spearhead this operation, then Theo could easily have paid the exorbitant price that mercenaries charge."

"As could any man as wealthy as he," Sawyer reminded the others.

"Perhaps my lack of a highly trained, professional group of bodyguards here at the villa made my family an easy target," Theo said. "Matthew had warned me that I was naive to believe my family was safe here in Golnar, simply because among our own people, we had been safe for generations."

"Possibly," Ellen agreed. "You had to be the ideal target for other reasons. These men were no doubt capable of masterminding a plan to get past even the most highly trained guards. No, I believe Mr. Khalid could be right. You were chosen because these people believed you would be able and willing to do whatever is necessary to free the Al'alim prisoners."

"We are overlooking one important factor," Lucie said. "Legalities aside, could we morally break three known terrorists out of prison?" She glanced from Sawyer to Worth to Dom.

"A valid question," Nikos said.

"As a father, my first reaction is to say that I'd go to hell and bring the devil back to earth and set him free here, if it meant saving Phila's life," Theo told them. "But how can we trust these rebels, these terrorists?"

''We can never forget we are dealing with ruthless, merciless killers,'' Nikos said. ''Can we trust them? Definitely not. Would they double-cross us? Most certainly. And if we were to free these prisoners, we could well be doing it for naught.'' Nikos glanced sympathetically at Theo.

Tears glazed Theo's eyes. He cleared his throat and swallowed hard. ''I refuse to believe that Phila has been killed.''

Ellen glared at Nikos. Why had he suggested to Theo that Phila might already be dead? Was he that much of a heartless bastard? Didn't he have any idea what emotional torment Theo and Dia were enduring? No, of course he didn't. He knew nothing about having a child's life threatened.

''I believe Phila and Faith Sheridan are still alive and that the kidnappers will call again very soon, probably today,'' Ellen said. ''And when they do contact us again, I'll ask for proof that Phila is alive. And I'll try to negotiate with them to change their terms.'' She turned to Theo. ''Do I have your permission to offer them more money?''

''Offer them ten million,'' Theo said. ''Offer them twenty.''

''They don't want more money,'' Nikos told Ellen. ''If money was their main objective, they'd have asked for a great deal more when they made the first call.''

''Perhaps ten million or more will be a greater bargaining tool than the release of their comrades. It's worth a try.'' Ellen sure as hell hoped it would be. The very thought of Dundee's taking part in freeing terrorists from prison sickened her. If anyone at this table knew what those sort of people were capable of, she did.

Push the thoughts from your mind, she warned herself. This is here and now. Not fourteen years ago. This is Theo and Dia Constantine's child in danger, not...

Unwittingly Ellen looked at Nikos and found him studying her. Was he trying to figure out what kind of woman she was and why she was so different from the fun-loving, carefree girl he'd once known?

"Is there something bothering you, Mr. Khalid?" Ellen asked.

Nikos's black eyes focused on her face, as if able to read her thoughts from her expression. "There is another alternative."

Ellen eyed him skeptically.

"I'm curious," Sawyer said. "What other alternative could there possibly be?"

"Find out where they're holding Phila and her nanny." Nikos's gaze connected once again with Theo's.

"Is that actually possible?" Theo asked.

Sawyer shook his head. "Not unless Mr. Khalid knows more about this kidnapping than the rest of us do."

"Do you know something that we don't?" Ellen asked.

"I know that Theo's money might be better spent paying informants," Nikos said. "Through my contacts, I can send out feelers, bait our hook with money and see what we catch."

"Put that in plain English, please." Lucie stared quizzically at Nikos.

"I have certain contacts throughout the Middle East," Nikos told them. "I've already made a phone call to set the wheels in motion. It might take time, but it is possible that we can find out where Phila and Ms. Sheridan are being held, and instead of taking a squad into Menkura to free three Al'alim bastards from prison, we could free Theo's daughter and her nanny."

"Wouldn't such actions be putting Phila and Ms. Sheridan at greater risk?" Lucie asked.

"Not necessarily," Dom said.

"Most definitely," Sawyer said simultaneously.

A sudden loud silence filled the room. Ellen sighed. A difference of opinion between two Dundee agents was not necessarily a bad thing. In order to make an informed decision, one needed to hear opposing sides in a matter. Her gut instincts told her Sawyer didn't like Nikos Khalid, but that didn't mean he would automatically disagree with the man. Sawyer's instincts were usually right on the money. He was smart, unsentimental and astute. If Sawyer didn't trust Nikos, then she'd bet money that Mr. Khalid wasn't trustworthy, at least on some level. But Ellen respected Domingo Shea's opinions and valued his insight into dangerous missions. Sawyer was the kidnapping expert, but Dom was the search and rescue specialist.

"Which is it?" Theo asked. "Is Nikos's plan more dangerous to my child or is it not?"

Neither Dom nor Sawyer replied; both looked to Ellen for affirmation. Being put in the middle wasn't pleasant, but it came with the territory of being the CEO of Dundee's.

"Actually, Theo, I'm sure we could give you pluses and minuses on both sides," Ellen said. "Anything we do that goes against the kidnappers' demands might put Phila and Faith in more danger. But on the other hand, we have no guarantees that if we do exactly as we've been told, they'll release Phila and her nanny unharmed."

"Then I say we give Nikos a chance to find out what he can," Theo said. "And if we learn where Phila and Ms. Sheridan are, then we'll go get them."

The tension in the room escalated. High testosterone levels saturated the atmosphere. There were five men involved, each with their own take on the situation, each believing their way was the best way. But Ellen didn't give a damn about male egos. Nobody was a hundred percent right or wrong. Given time to cool off, they'd accept that fact.

"You're the boss, Theo," Ellen said. "You make the final decisions. It's my job to advise you and carry out your wishes. My advice right now is for us to adjourn this meet-

ing and come back to the drawing board after we hear from
the kidnappers again.'' Ellen pushed back her chair and
rose to her feet.

Nikos stood, then one by one, the Dundee agents followed suit.

''Yes, you're right,'' Theo said. ''Ellen, you and your
people do whatever you need to do to get things ready for
that next call, but first, I'd like to speak to you…alone.''

The room cleared quickly, leaving Ellen still standing by
the conference table and Theo still sitting.

''Sit,'' Theo instructed. ''Please.''

Ellen did as he asked.

''Adele—Princess Adele of Orlantha—telephoned Dia
shortly before this meeting,'' Theo said. ''She and Matt
want to come to Golnar, to the villa. Adele is Dia's best
friend and I believe it would help Dia to have her here.''

''Yes, it probably would.''

''Then you see no reason why it would pose a problem
to have Adele and Matt here?''

''If having her best friend at her side throughout this
ordeal will help your wife, then by all means have the princess come to Golnar. But since she is a public figure, she
needs to issue a press release stating that she and her husband are coming to Golnar to visit friends, to take a holiday. You've been able to use your power locally to keep
the kidnapping a secret. We can't risk letting the international press get wind of this.''

''Yes, of course. I'll contact Adele and explain the situation.''

''Are you sure your phone lines are secure?''

''Reasonably sure.''

''I believe we need to be more than reasonably sure.''

''Is that something your people can handle?''

Ellen nodded. ''Yes, to a fair degree of accuracy.''

When Theo stood, Ellen did also. Theo came around the

table and grasped Ellen's hands. "I am putting my child's life in your hands." He gazed down at where he held her hands in his. "Yours and Nikos's."

"Do you trust Mr. Khalid with Phila's life?"

Theo released Ellen. "Yes, I trust him."

Theo's reply seemed to echo throughout the two-story room as well as inside Ellen's head. A definite yes. No hesitation. And apparently no doubts. How was it that Theo Constantine trusted Nikos so completely?

"I see the questions in your eyes," Theo said. "Forgive me, Ellen, but I cannot answer them. Only Nikos can tell you what you want to know. But suffice it to say that my friend Nikos would give his own life to save Phila."

The thumping beat of Ellen's heart rumbled in her ears. Tension tightened her muscles and jangled her nerves. She fought the sudden flashes of unbidden memories. Would Nikos truly sacrifice himself to save Theo and Dia's child? Was he that noble? If so, where had he been when she'd needed him? Why had he not been there to offer his life to save another's fourteen years ago?

"Are you all right?" Theo asked.

Brought back to the present by Theo's question, Ellen blinked several times, then replied, "I'm fine. Just thinking." She turned to go, then stopped and said, "Remind the servants that no one is to answer the telephone except me. And if for any reason I'm unavailable, then have one of my agents do it."

"Worth Cordell answered the phone when Adele called earlier today," Theo said. "Believe me, I and my household will follow your orders."

Ellen nodded, then left Theo's office. The moment she walked into the hall, she came face-to-face with Nikos. Apparently he'd been waiting for her.

"We should talk," Nikos said.

"We've already talked and said all that needs to be said," Ellen replied, then tried to walk away from him.

He grasped her wrist, but when she whirled around and took a physically defensive mode, he released her. "Who are you, Ms. Denby, and what did you do with my sweet Mary Ellen?"

"Your sweet Mary Ellen?" She laughed sarcastically. "The girl you knew died fourteen years ago and another woman—stronger, tougher, invulnerable—rose from her ashes and became the person I am today."

"Exactly what happened to you fourteen years ago to create such a drastic change?"

"You're asking a lot of questions and act as if you expect me to answer them. What about you, *Mr. Khalid,* are you willing to answer a few of my questions?"

"That depends."

A tight knot formed in her stomach; a sensual tingling radiated along her nerve endings. She had not reacted so strongly to a man's nearness in fifteen years. Not since... not since a handsome stranger had swept her off her feet during Dareh's Summer Festival. What was it about Nikos that affected her in a way no other man did?

"Who are you?" she asked. "What are you?"

"Today I am Nikos Khalid," he replied, his placid facial expression giving away nothing. "What am I? I am an entrepreneur, a world traveler, a man of influence and experience."

"Yeah? Well, if that's all you are, then I'm queen of the world."

Nikos chuckled. She remembered the sound of his laughter as if she'd heard it only yesterday. It was the same deep-throated rumble he emitted whenever he was amused by something. She had amused him during their two weeks together in Golnar years ago; and she had delighted in seeing him smile, in hearing him laugh, in sharing his exuberance for life.

"I believe I like this new Ellen, the strong, tough woman who believes herself to be invulnerable. She, like her young counterpart, has a sense of humor."

With his smile held in place, he looked at her with such intensity that she felt his gaze as if it had touched her physically. "I don't know why fate has thrown us together again after all these years...and it really doesn't matter why. I have a job to do, a child to save, so I'm warning you, Nikos Khalid—or whoever the hell you really are—if you do anything to interfere with my getting Phila safely home to her parents, I'll personally see to it that you pay with your life."

The smile vanished from Nikos's face. "Yes, I believe you would do just that. But believe me, the only reason I'm here, at Theo's request, is to do all within my power to help. Phila is as dear to me as any child could be."

"You don't have children of your own?" God in heaven, why had she asked him such a question? An inquiry that personal implied an interest that she preferred Nikos not suspect. "Forget that I—"

"I have no children. No wife. No family." He narrowed his gaze and tightened his jaw. "I lost my parents and my only sister when I was quite young, long before I met you in Dareh fifteen years ago."

How did he expect her to respond to this tidbit of personal information? Should she say she was sorry he had no one, that he'd lost his family long ago?

"What about you? Do you have a family?" he asked.

"My parents are both dead now. I was an only child," she told him. "And I've never been married."

"No husband? No children?"

"No. I'm quite alone."

"I, too, am quite alone," Nikos said.

"It's easier that way, isn't it? No personal entanglements, no sentimental ties to weaken us, to disappoint and hurt us."

"Nothing to make us vulnerable. Nothing that will endanger others."

She stared at him quizzically. What did he mean *nothing that will endanger others?* He didn't know what had happened to her. There was no way he could possibly know.

"In my line of business, if there was anyone I cared about, my enemies could use that person against me," he told her. "Do you understand?"

"Don't your enemies know that Theo is your friend?"

"I didn't think so. Now, I'm not so certain. I've been very careful to protect my acquaintance with Theo, always using the name Khalid in our association."

"But Khalid is not your real name, is it? Not the name by which you're known to your enemies." She held up her hand in a Stop gesture. "No, you don't have to answer." She harrumphed. "You were in this same business fifteen years ago when I met you, weren't you?"

"Yes. And I left you when I did—the way I did—in order to protect you."

Ellen stared at him for a couple of minutes, and then the reaction to his statement set in. She laughed. He stared at her, obviously puzzled. She laughed harder and louder. He grabbed her shoulders and shook her.

"What the hell's the matter with you?"

She sobered instantly and went rigid as a stone statue. Staring him right in the eyes, she said, "The pathway to hell is paved with good intentions."

Nikos loosened his hold. She shrugged off his hands from his shoulders, turned and walked away. Falling apart in front of Nikos was not an option. Hell, falling apart emotionally hadn't been an option for her in fourteen years.

But right this minute, if she didn't get away from him, she just might tell Mr. Nikos whatever-the-hell-his-real-name-was what an utter failure his attempt to protect her had been.

Chapter 5

Before Ellen got halfway to her room upstairs, Sawyer waylaid her in the corridor.

"Wait up, will you," he called.

She slowed her frantic pace, took a deep breath and turned to face him. "What is it?" Her voice held a shrewish edge she hadn't intended. "Sorry, I'm—"

"Not quite yourself," Sawyer finished her sentence for her.

"Yeah, something like that."

"I understand. I worked enough of these kidnapping cases when I was with the Bureau to know how they can affect a person. They have a way of getting to you, even when you think nothing else can rattle you."

Down the corridor, Lucie Evans opened her bedroom door and peered out at Ellen and Sawyer.

"The kidnapping of a child is especially difficult to handle," Ellen admitted. "Phila Constantine is only seven. Even with her nanny at her side, she must be terribly frightened. And she can't possibly understand what's happened and why.''

"It's a bad case." Sawyer grunted. "And it doesn't help that we have to deal with Constantine's friend, Mr. I've-got-connections. Who the hell is this guy anyway? He seems a little too slick, a little too sure of himself. And I don't like the way he looks at you. You'd better watch yourself around him.''

"Is that what this conversation is really about?" Ellen asked. She couldn't help wondering if Sawyer was simply acting proprietorial. If that was the case, she'd have to set him straight.

Lucie came out of her room and walked toward them. "Is this a private discussion or can anyone put in their two cents?"

"The conversation isn't private and it's over," Ellen replied, glad for the interruption. She really didn't want to get into anything personal with Sawyer right this minute.

"Too bad," Lucie said. "I have a suggestion for Sawyer."

"And that would be?" Sawyer glared at Lucie.

"If you want to know who Nikos Khalid is, why don't you call your old buddy Robbins at the Bureau and get him to run a check on the man," Lucie said. "But before you do, I'm willing to bet you a hundred bucks that there is no Nikos Khalid."

"For once we agree. I figure the guy is using an alias."

"That's exactly what I think." Lucie grinned.

"Run the check," Ellen said. "Call Robbins and see what he can find out about Khalid."

Both of her agents snapped their heads around and stared at her.

"You know Khalid is a fraud, don't you?" Sawyer smiled. "I didn't think you'd be taken in by his Arab sheik charm.''

"I don't think he's Arab," Lucie piped in. "Egyptian maybe. Or Turkish. Or perhaps he has a mixed heritage. But you're right about him projecting that Arab sheik machismo. Talk about overpowering masculinity."

"Be sure to send us an invitation to the wedding," Sawyer said.

Lucie made a face at him.

Ellen blew out an exasperated breath. "I should have known better than to have brought both of you on this assignment. Let's just call it a lapse in good judgment." She pointed her finger at Sawyer and then at Lucie. "I don't care that you don't like each other. I don't care that you can't get along. But I do care that two of my best agents are letting their personal animosity toward each other interfere with this assignment. Put aside your differences right now or one of you will be on a flight back to the States before dark. Do I make myself clear?"

"Sorry, Ellen." Sawyer shuffled his feet, then lifted his chin and stood at attention. "It won't happen again. Not while we're here in Golnar."

"Go put a call in to your contact at the Bureau and see if he can find out anything about Khalid," Ellen said, then turned and walked away.

After shooting a disapproving glare at Sawyer, Lucie quickly followed Ellen, catching up with her just as Ellen opened her bedroom door.

"Got a minute?" Lucie asked.

"Can it wait?" Ellen needed a few minutes alone, to collect her thoughts.

"Look, it's none of my business, but… Hell, I don't know how to ask you this."

"Just ask."

"Okay. Here goes—do you know Mr. Khalid? I mean, did you know him before you met him here at the villa."

"You're right—it's none of your business."

Ellen went into her bedroom, then leaned against the closed door and shut her eyes. Lucie was too damn perceptive. But the other Dundee agents weren't oblivious to the obvious. If Sawyer had noticed the way Nikos had studied her so intently, then Worth and Dom must have noticed, too. How long would it be before all her agents figured out what Lucie suspected—that Ellen and Nikos shared a past. *But if I don't let the past interfere with my ability to handle this job, then the affair I had with Nikos really isn't anybody's business.* The only problem was that she couldn't be sure the past wouldn't create problems for her in dealing professionally with this assignment. Maybe she was the agent who needed to take the next flight back to the States.

Wasim Ibn Fadil and his father shared the evening meal together, just the two of them, without his father's private guards. This house was a safe haven for them here in Zahur, one of several towns in Northern Subria with many rebel sympathizers. Although the town itself still remained in government hands, most of the local authorities looked the other way because they either believed in the Al'alim cause or because they feared Wasim's father, Omar Ibn Fadil. After Wasim's uncle—the great Hakeem Ibn Fadil—was killed eight years ago, his father had tried to fill the legendary leader's shoes. But Omar lacked the fire-in-the-belly zealousness his older brother had possessed. The cause had suffered a great setback when Hakeem died.

Wasim had been only twelve when his uncle was killed, and now he was a warrior of twenty. As much as he respected his father, a part of him wished that he had been born Hakeem's son. His father had many children, all younger than he. But his uncle had left only five daughters, no sons. Hakeem's only son had died a hero's death over fifteen years ago, when he'd been seventeen.

Wasim dreamed of becoming the next great Al'alim

leader. His people needed another charismatic warrior to inspire them in their quest to rid the world of infidels and reclaim Subria from the European dominated government that now ruled.

"We must talk, my son," Omar said. "What I say to you is a secret of great importance, to be shared with no one." Omar laid his hand on his son's shoulder. "I sent you on an important mission and you fulfilled your duties admirably. I am proud of you. But there is much that must be done. We cannot weaken in our resolve. Theo Constantine must do as we bid him to do. I cannot stress the importance of having our brothers freed from Nawar Prison."

"Nawar Prison? Is that where they are being held?" Wasim had heard of this horrible place, a hell here on earth.

His father nodded. "When you speak to Theo Constantine's negotiator, you will tell this American that a meeting will be set up to exchange the information they need for the first million dollars—good faith money. We will expect delivery of four million along with the freed prisoners in one week's time."

"I know that Shakir Abu Lufti and Jamsheed Abd Hamid were taken prisoners in the Battle of the Night six months ago, so they must be two of the three for whom we will demand freedom."

"Yes, Shakir and Jamsheed have earned their reward. If not for them, we would not have known about the third prisoner's existence."

Wasim puzzled over his father's reply, then said, "I know of no one else of importance being held in Menkura."

"The third prisoner was taken many years ago," Omar said, then lowered his voice to a whisper, as if he feared the walls could hear him speak. "We did not know of this man, not until Shakir and Jamsheed were taken. They discovered this man after they had been there for two months.

Because of the influence of the United Nations in Menkura, Shakir and Jamsheed were allowed to send one letter each to their families, three months ago, and we were given those letters, which were written in code. They told us of this man. He has been a prisoner in Nawar for eight years. He goes by the name Musa Ben Arif. When he was captured, years ago, he was thought to be a lowly servant of your uncle's, indeed, the man told the soldiers who captured him that he was proud to have served the great Hakeem Ibn Fadil.''

"Then his loyalty to my uncle will be rewarded," Wasim said.

Omar shook his head. "You do not understand. Musa Ben Arif hid his true identity to save his life. If they had known who he really was, they would have killed him. He has been waiting these many years, praying to Allah for deliverance, and his prayers were answered when Shakir and Jamsheed were imprisoned with him.''

"I am confused, Father.''

"Rejoice with me, Wasim," Omar said, a wide smile spreading his lips apart. "Musa Ben Arif is my brother, Hakeem.''

"Glory to Allah!'' Wasim could hardly believe their family and the great Al'alim brotherhood had been blessed with such good fortune.

Nikos sat alone on the terrace, the afternoon sun warm, the breeze from the sea cool. He had placed a call to "friends'' in London this morning, requesting a quick check of Ellen Denby, the CEO of Dundee's. He'd been curious about what might have happened to her fourteen years ago that could have changed her so dramatically. Whenever he'd thought of Ellen—and he'd thought of her more often than he wanted to admit—he had thought of her married, with children, a nice home, and fulfilling her dream of teaching. When they first met, she had been sweet, gentle and loving. People might say he swept her off her feet—and perhaps he did. But in many ways, he was the one who'd been swept away on a tide of passion unlike anything he'd known before or since.

Twenty minutes ago, he'd received a call that gave him a brief rundown of the lady in question. Fourteen years ago, Ellen had been found, nearly dead, in a park on the outskirts of a small Georgia town near Atlanta. When she came to in the hospital days later, she could tell the police nothing about what had happened. The doctors referred to her condition as selective amnesia. After leaving the hospital, she'd undergone extensive psychiatric treatment for the next six months. Those records were confidential. If he wanted to find out more, it would take time. Shortly following the conclusion of her treatment, she'd entered the police academy and upon graduation hired on as an Atlanta police officer. A year later, she'd trained to become a hostage negotiator and had worked in that capacity for six years.

Then something had happened. When she'd worked with the FBI on the abduction of a local star athlete's six-year-old son and the deal fell apart and the child was killed, Ellen left the APD and hired on with Dundee's. She'd taken over as the CEO when Dane Carmichael, the owner Sam Dundee's replacement, had retired from the agency three-and-a-half years ago.

Ellen Denby had a reputation as a tough, hard-edged female, with a kick-ass attitude. She was a martial arts expert, had a skilled soldier's knowledge of weapons and was considered a brilliant strategist and negotiator. She fraternized with her employees, but her personal life remained "off limits" to others. It seemed no one really knew her on a close personal level. Her most recent romantic relationship had been half a dozen dates with former FBI agent, Sawyer

McNamara. But their dating had come to an abrupt halt over two months ago.

"Did she have an affair with McNamara?" Nikos had asked his friend in London.

"Don't know. Want me to find out?"

He had almost said yes, find out. "No. It doesn't make any difference." Whether or not Ellen and Sawyer's relationship had been sexual, it was apparent that the man felt possessive where Ellen was concerned. But those feelings didn't seem to be reciprocated.

Damn his soul to hell, but he was glad. He wanted Ellen to be free of any emotional entanglements. If things worked out for him to retire soon, he thought he'd make a trip to the States. Maybe go to Atlanta. Even if Ellen denied it— and she probably would—there was still something between them. A smoldering ember that could easily burst into flames again. He'd felt it, in his gut. And so had she.

The call came in at three o'clock. Ellen picked up on the fourth ring.

"Constantine residence," Ellen said.

"I wish to speak to Mr. Constantine or his representative. I have been authorized to make arrangements for a preliminary meeting concerning his daughter's welfare."

A preliminary meeting? Ellen's heartbeat accelerated. "I'm Ms. Denby, Mr. Constantine's representative."

Ellen motioned to Lucie, who nodded and left immediately to go upstairs to Dia Constantine's room to inform Theo, and to gather the other agents for a post-phone call meeting.

"We will send our representative to meet with you in Dareh, on the first day of the Harvest Festival. Meet him at twelve noon at the Odyssea Café and bring one million in U.S. dollars."

"What will I get in return for that million dollars?"

Dom and Worth entered the office, but kept silent as they waited.

"The million is a good faith gesture and it will buy you the detailed information you need about the prisoners in Menkura."

"I have a counteroffer for you," Ellen said.

Sawyer and Lucie came into the office, followed by Theo and Nikos.

"I am not authorized to discuss a counteroffer," the man said. "You know our terms. We expect—"

"Take this counteroffer to whomever is in charge. Tell them that Theo Constantine is willing to pay more than five million dollars for the safe return of his child and her nanny."

"How much more?"

"Twenty million dollars."

Silence.

"Twenty million," Ellen repeated. "And no freed prisoners."

"No. I can tell you now that this offer will not be acceptable."

Ellen's heart sank. "Take the offer to your superiors."

"I will inform them, but… Be prepared to meet our representative. Only you. No one else. If our man is harmed or taken, the child dies."

"I understand."

"Bring the money in a black briefcase. Plain leather. Our man will have a similar one. He will be wearing a black *thobe* and a white *gutra*. He will answer to the name of Shabouh."

"If my counteroffer is acceptable—"

"I will not call you again before the first day of the Autumn Festival."

"I want proof that Phila Constantine and Faith Sheridan are alive and well. Otherwise, no deal."

Theo opened his mouth to speak and began to rise from his chair. Nikos grabbed Theo's arm and silently cautioned him to be quiet. Theo huffed out a shuddering sigh, then eased back down into his seat and closed his eyes, as if in prayer.

"Our representative will bring the proof," the caller said. "You bring the money."

"I expect you to report my counteroffer to your superiors," Ellen said. "Even if the response is negative, I am sure they would be unhappy to discover you had not informed them of Mr. Constantine's generous offer."

Silence. Ellen held her breath. Had she overplayed her hand?

"Yes, yes, I have told you that I will pass along the counteroffer. But do not expect an acceptance. Our prisoners are worth more to us than twenty million dollars."

Ellen's eyes widened. Oh, God! Who was worth more to the Al'alim than twenty million? Just who were these three prisoners and why were they so important to their rebel comrades?

The telephone dial-tone hummed in Ellen's ears. The conversation was over. The counteroffer had little chance of being accepted. That meant making some major decisions and making them today.

Ellen replaced the receiver in the base on the desk, then turned to the others in the room. All eyes focused on her.

"What did they say?" Theo asked. "Did they—?"

"They want a million dollars up front—good faith money," Ellen said.

"When? Where?" Nikos asked.

"Twelve noon, the first day of the Autumn Festival, at the Odyssea Café in Dareh."

"And in return they will give us what?" Sawyer asked.

"The detailed information we need about the prisoners

in Menkura," Ellen replied. "And the proof that Phila and Faith Sheridan are still alive."

Theo's grunt gained everyone's notice and refocused attention from Ellen to him. They all felt sympathy for the Constantines, but Ellen experienced an empathy that threatened to make her vulnerable. She cleared her throat and willed herself to banish everything from her mind except what must be done.

"I have refused to let myself think that Phila could be…dead." Theo crumbled before their very eyes. He shot out of the chair, rushed across the room to the windows and kept his back to them. His broad shoulders shook as he sobbed quietly.

Nikos followed Theo, stood beside him and spoke to him in a soft soothing voice. Ellen's gaze wandered to the two men. Friends. She could sense the depth of care and concern Nikos felt for Theo.

"What about the counteroffer?" Sawyer moved from the far side of the room and came closer to Ellen. "Did they out-and-out say no?"

"Pretty much." Ellen tore her gaze away from Nikos's wide shoulders. "I'm sure he'll pass it along to his superiors, but these prisoners in Menkura—they must be very special to the Al'alim."

"Why do you assume that?" Nikos turned sharply and directed his gaze on Ellen.

"He said that these men were more important than twenty million dollars. To a cause that is not funded by any government, twenty million is a great deal of money. Think how many weapons that could buy."

Nikos's features hardened. "There's something else going on here. Something we don't know about. The Menkuraian prisons are filled with Subrian rebel soldiers, but there are only two Al'alim followers in Subria worth anything to the organization. And I can't believe either would warrant them turning down twenty million dollars. Not when the Al'alim are in desperate need of capital.''

"And just how would you know all of this, Mr. Khalid?" Sawyer skewered Nikos with his suspicious glare. "What makes you an expert on the Al'alim and the prisons in Menkura?

"Yeah, I'd like to know the answer to that one," Dom said.

Theo whirled around and shouted, "Offer them thirty million! Hell, offer them forty million! Keep upping the amount until the money is worth more to them than anything or anyone."

Nikos grabbed Theo's shoulder, curling his fingers tightly over cloth-covered muscle. "The money is either a smoke screen or an after-thought. If twenty million won't buy them, a hundred million won't."

"Nik—Mr. Khalid is right," Ellen said. "I'd say there's a good chance that this whole kidnapping scheme was concocted to secure the freedom of whoever the third Al'alim prisoner is."

"There is no third Al'alim prisoner of any importance." Sawyer narrowed his gaze and glowered at Nikos. "Isn't that what you said, Mr. Khalid?"

"Yes, that's what I said," Nikos replied.

"And you got your information from…?" Dom asked.

"From privileged sources," Nikos replied.

Sawyer spoke directly to Theo. "This guy may be your friend, Mr. Constantine, but we can hardly take everything he says for gospel when we have no idea who the hell he is."

"I trust Nikos," Theo said.

"Do you trust him enough to put your daughter's life in his hands?" Sawyer asked.

Ellen saw the tension in Theo rising to the surface. The man was on the verge of exploding. And she sensed the harnessed anger inside Nikos. As much as she wanted these questions answered, she knew keeping peace among the central players in this rescue drama was essential to success. And success meant saving Phila and Faith.

Ellen watched Nikos eyeing Theo's trembling hands, his quivering lips, his pale face; and she knew the instant Nikos made his decision.

"If I explain certain things to Ms. Denby, in private, if I share certain information with her and ask her to keep it privileged and she in turn tells all of you—" one by one Nikos made direct eye contact with each agent "—that I am not the enemy, then will you accept me and accept my help? And believe my information is valid?"

"Nikos, there is no need," Theo said, then turned pleadingly to the Dundee agents. "Yes, I trust Nikos with Phila's life."

Sawyer shot Nikos an I-don't-trust-you-as-far-as-I-could-throw-you glare. "Explain yourself to Ellen and if she tells us you're okay, then we won't need to have this conversation again."

"All right," Nikos said to Sawyer, then leaned down and whispered something to Theo, who shook his head, but when Nikos said something else to him that the rest of them couldn't hear, Theo nodded.

"Will you, please, excuse me," Theo said. "If I'm needed, I will be upstairs with my wife."

The moment Theo exited the room, Ellen took charge and issued orders to her agents. "I want y'all to get busy making phone calls and see what you can find out about Al'alim prisoners in Menkura. Call in favors. Twist arms. Even make threats, if that's what it takes. If we're going to have a prayer of saving Phila and Ms. Sheridan, we need to know just what we're dealing with."

While the agents headed for the bank of phones in Theo's office, Ellen went straight to Nikos. ''Let's take a walk, Mr. Khalid. I believe you have something to tell me.''

Chapter 6

When Theo entered the bedroom, Irina rose from her chair and came to meet him. Glancing beyond the approaching nurse, he saw Dia sitting by the windows, staring outside, a glazed expression in her eyes.

"Take a break," Theo said. "I'll stay with Mrs. Constantine for a while."

"Yes, sir." Irina exited quickly.

Theo walked over to Dia, stood behind her chair and leaned down to kiss her temple. "Did you take a nap?"

Dia tilted back her head and looked up at Theo. "Yes. The injection Irina gave me helped me rest. But I don't want any more medication. It makes my brain fuzzy and I want to be alert. I need to be—" Her voice splintered with despair.

Theo rounded her chair, went down on his haunches in front of her and grasped her hands. "Ms. Denby spoke with the kidnappers and arrangements have been made to exchange a million dollars for the information about what we must do to free Phila and Ms. Sheridan. We'll have our little girl home with us very soon.''

''Phila is still alive.'' Dia clutched Theo's hands so tightly that her nails bit deeply into his flesh. ''I know in my heart that she isn't dead.''

Tears flooded Dia's eyes. Theo's heart broke in two just looking at her and knowing that at this precise moment he couldn't help her, that he was powerless to ease her suffering.

Reaching up, he wiped away her tears with his fingertips. ''Ms. Denby asked for proof that Phila is alive. She told them—no proof, no money.''

Dia gasped. ''Oh, God, Theo, what if—''

He kissed her, a quick, loving maneuver to stop the flow of her frightened words. ''Ms. Denby knows what she's doing. They agreed to provide proof.''

''When?'' Dia asked.

''Day after tomorrow. The first day of the Autumn Festival in Dareh. Ms. Denby is to meet their representative at the Odyssea Café.''

''However much money they want, you'll give it to them, won't you, Theo?'' She looked at him pleadingly.

He took her trembling body into his embrace and tenderly stroked her back. ''You must know that I would give them everything I have in exchange for our little Phila.''

While he held his wife, reassuring her with words and gestures, Theo's mind raced with thoughts about what the kidnappers wanted more than they wanted money. He could pay the ransom, but could he deliver the prisoners they demanded? Ms. Denby and her agents, all Americans, might not readily agree to anything more than diplomatic measures by which to free the Al'alim prisoners. And how would Nikos feel about returning three dangerous terrorists to their Subrian comrades? Nikos had dedicated his entire adult life to helping rid the world of men such as they.

Even if he could find a way to free the Al'alim prisoners, would he take part in the crime? And it would be a crime, one with international repercussions.

But to save my little Phila, Nikos would do it, Theo told himself. Wouldn't he?

Quietly, neither of them speaking, Nikos went with Ellen out onto the patio. Side by side but not touching, they walked to the edge of the balcony overlooking the sea below, then stopped and turned toward each other. Ellen searched his face for any clue to his true identity, to any hint of honesty in his eyes; but she saw nothing beyond what he presented to the world. Mr. Khalid was a handsome man, in his late thirties, probably of a mixed Middle Eastern and European decent. A man with no past and no future. A man of mystery, who could be either good or evil. Perhaps both.

Did Mr. Khalid have anything, other than obvious physical traits, in common with the man named Nikos who had once been her lover? Had time and life experiences changed him? Or had she truly never known him?

Odd as it seemed, she could sense that the Nikos she had fallen in love with that summer still existed in this man. She mentally shook herself. How unlike her to allow sentiment to affect her. She couldn't let her judgment be clouded by the affection she'd once felt for Nikos, any more than she dared to compare what was happening to Dia and Theo Constantine to what had happened to her.

"So?" Ellen stared at Nikos, putting on a mask of indifference that mimicked his own.

He shrugged. "So?"

"Don't play games with me. Either you tell me why we should trust you or—"

"Or what? Your power is limited by what Theo allows. He trusts me. Shouldn't that be enough?"

"Perhaps. But my agents and I would feel better about working with you if you can give me a reason why we should trust you."

"Is trusting me to do what's right for Phila Constantine the only reason you want this information about me?"

"What other reason could there be?" Was he implying that her interest in him was personal? Was his ego so huge that he believed she still cared about him in any way at all?

"Yes, that is what I'm asking you."

"All right, I'll tell you. Am I curious about you? Yes, I am. Is it personal curiosity or professional? Both. Is that honest enough for you?"

Nikos grasped her arm gently. "Let's walk farther away from the house."

"Why?" She resisted when he tugged on her arm, trying to urge her into motion.

"It's more private, down there—" he nodded the direction "—on the beach."

"Sure, why not? If you want total privacy, then by all means, let's go."

If he thought she would shy away from a walk on the beach with him, then he was wrong. Did he think she couldn't bear to remember the evening they had strolled along this very same beach and made love lying on their discarded clothes? Or was he hoping she would recall every moment of that evening and her woman's heart would soften? Did he believe she would trust him now simply because she had foolishly trusted him then?

Ellen jerked free from Nikos, then took the lead, going down the winding rock steps to the second terrace. Flowers, unharmed by early frost in their protected areas against the cliffs, filled the air with a faint, lingering scent. And the steady rhythm of the surf from far below throbbed like the echoes of a vibrant heartbeat.

Nikos followed her as she descended another set of rock

stairs, passed by the lower terrace and went down to the
narrow beach. Once her feet hit the sand, she paused and
waited for him to come to her side; then when he neared
her, she began walking along the beach.

"I ran a check on you," he said.

She stopped dead still, every nerve in her body screaming, every muscle tense. "What did you say?" She snapped
her head up and around.

Their gazes connected, an invisible current passing between them. "I wanted to know what happened to you
fourteen years ago," he told her. "I have contacts who can
get me almost any information I want or need, so I asked
for a background check as far back as fourteen years ago."

With her heartbeat drumming like mad inside her head,
she glared at him, fury boiling inside her. Oh, God, what
if he'd found out about... No! If he knew, he would already
have said something, would already have confronted her.
"You had no right to—"

"Did you ever remember what happened to you?" he
asked, genuine concern evident in his voice. "Do you know
who beat you, who almost killed you?"

"My past is none of your business. What I do or do not
remember is no one's concern other than my own."

"Were you raped?"

"What?"

"Whatever happened to you changed you, *agkelos,* so I
assume it was something truly terrible."

She glared at him, suddenly hating him beyond reason.
He was using their past history to sway her, to influence
her opinion of him. Did he honestly believe she was still
so vulnerable to his charm that by simply referring to her
by the pet name he'd used during their brief affair, she
would succumb to his wishes?

The very first day they met during the Summer Festival
in Dareh, he had said she was his *agkelos*—angel. *Because*

*not only do you look like an angel with your pale skin and
platinum-blond hair and wearing that yellow sundress, but
you are heavensent, a sweet, unexpected gift from the gods.*
He had called her *agkelos* in moments of play and whispered the endearment in moments of passion during their
two weeks together. The word alone conjured up feelings
within her that she had thought long dead.

Ellen forced a smile as she met his gaze head-on. "No
one would call me an angel these days. Bossy-butt, bitch,
she-devil—maybe. I'm nothing like the sweet, innocent girl
you once knew."

"Aren't you?" He reached out; his hand almost touched
her cheek before she jerked away from him. "You're skit-
tish, like a frightened colt."

"Once burned, twice shy. Isn't that what they say?"

"You didn't answer my question about what happened
to you fourteen years ago? I could have my people do a
more thorough check, dig a little deeper into your past."

No! She couldn't risk him finding out about her life before that night. If he discovered the truth, he would ask too
many questions. "There's no need to do that." When she
started walking again, he followed her. "I wasn't raped,
although the men who kidnapped me, threatened to rape
me."

"Then you do remember being kidnapped?"

"Yes."

"Why didn't you tell the police?"

"I had my reasons."

"Did you know your kidnappers? Were you afraid of
them, afraid they'd come after you again?"

"Yes, I was afraid," Ellen admitted. "I wanted them to
believe that I couldn't remember what had happened to me,
that I couldn't identify them."

"But by playing dumb you allowed these men to go free,
to prey on other women."

Ellen huffed. "By the time I awoke in the hospital, the men who'd kidnapped me and beat me were already out of the country. And as far as their preying on other women—they weren't sexual predators. I was chosen for a particular reason. They threatened me and beat me because they believed I had information they wanted."

"They mistook you for someone else?" Nikos asked.

Tell him, an inner voice urged. *Tell him what two weeks in paradise with him cost you.*

No, you mustn't, the more cautious part of her consciousness advised.

"They didn't mistake me for someone else," Ellen said, her voice deceptively calm. She had spent a lifetime trying to put the past behind her, desperately trying to forget what had happened and why. "They had tracked me from Golnar."

Nikos's dark eyes widened. "Why would... This was a year later, wasn't it? A year after we were together?"

"Yes, it was nearly a year later when they found me. You see they had been searching for you. *He* had been searching for you. A friend of a friend of a friend relayed the information that you—or someone they believed to be you—had spent two weeks on Golnar with a woman. All that relayed info took time to reach him and then he had to rely on his vast network of spies to find out my name, my nationality, and so on."

"You keep referring to this man as he. What was his name?"

"Don't you know? Over the years, have you made so many enemies who wanted to kill you that you can't—"

Nikos grabbed her by the shoulders and shook her. "What was his name?"

"He didn't introduce himself," Ellen replied calmly, totally in control of her emotions. She wouldn't fall apart.

She was strong. Stronger than the painful memories. "One of the men with him called him Hakeem."

For just a fraction of a second Nikos painfully tightened his hold on her, then released her and moved away. With a stricken look on his face, he gazed down at the sand at his feet and cursed furiously and loudly in Greek.

"Then you do remember him?" Her pulse raced at an alarming speed.

"Oh, yes, I remember Hakeem Ibn Fadil." Nikos raised his eyes until his gaze clashed with hers. "The man was a monster."

"Hakeem Ibn Fadil," Ellen repeated the name. "Are you saying this man who was searching for you was the infamous Al'alim leader whose terrorist acts made headline news around the world for so many years?"

"Yes, they are one and the same."

"But why was he—"

Nikos glanced away, as if he couldn't bear to look at her. "I was young and stupid, new to the business, and hadn't learned how to cover my tracks as well as I should have. God, Ellen, I had no idea that there was any way he could have found out about you."

She stared at him, uncertain what he was trying to explain.

"Don't you see—that's the reason I left you. I was trying to protect you. I knew I couldn't have a personal life, that if anyone became too important to me, they could use that person against me. If I had allowed you to…" Nikos raked his hand through his long hair. "Dammit, I believed we were safe here on Golnar. I honestly thought I'd covered my tracks, that no one would even suspect who I was."

"Tell me why Hakeem Ibn Fadil hated you so much, why he wanted to find you and kill you?"

"Ellen, I… It's more complicated than you can imagine."

"He came after me. He kidnapped me and my— He tortured me. Do you hear me, Nikos? He tortured me because he believed that I could tell him where you were. He thought we were still in contact because of… I lied to them over and over again, telling them anything I could think of, hoping to save…my life." Despite every effort to keep the memories at bay, they crept into her conscious mind. One-by-one. Fragments. Flashes. A sound. A touch. Moments too horrible to bear.

Regret and pain registered in Nikos's dark eyes as his gaze linked with hers. Ellen's gut instincts told her this man cared, that what had happened to her truly mattered to him.

"There were three of them," she said. "They had beaten me almost senseless and they had…" *No, don't go there; you can't deal with it and you know you can't.* "They received a phone call. I don't know from whom or about what. One of the men put a knife to my throat and said they should kill me then and there, but the other one told Hakeem that they should wait, that I might eventually tell them what they wanted to know. Hakeem hesitated, then agreed not to kill me. Not then.

"He and one of the men left, but one man remained behind. He talked to me, trying to get me to tell him where you were. He said…" She gulped several times. "He implied that he was better than you and that if I was being loyal to you because the sex had been so good, then he could show me—"

Nikos grabbed her face and cupped it with his hands.

"I don't know how I managed to force myself to respond to him, but I did," Ellen said, her voice quivering. "He was sexually aroused and therefore careless. I caught him off guard and grabbed his gun from where he'd stuck it under his belt. And I didn't give him a chance to say or do anything. I shot him and shot him and shot him." Ellen trembled from head to toe.

Nikos kissed her cheeks, her forehead and chin, all the while clasping her face tenderly. "I am so sorry, so very sorry. It was my fault. I am to blame. I foolishly believed that I could have you in my life for a brief period of time without it harming you in any way. How you must hate me."

Tears lodged in her throat. She refused to give in to emotion. But she could not control the shivers racking her body. Lifting her chin, she stared directly into Nikos's black eyes. "Why did Hakeem want so desperately to find you?"

"Because he believed I had killed his son. He wanted revenge."

The pain sliced through her in continuous agonized slashes. An eye for an eye, her tormented mind told her. "Did you—?"

Nikos took her by the shoulders again, met her questioning gaze and replied honestly, "Yes, I killed his son."

Ellen swallowed hard. The shivers increased until she was trembling forcefully.

Nikos wrapped his arms around her and pulled her close, then buried his face against her neck and whispered, "Forgive me. I never meant for you to become involved in my secret life."

Was it wrong to find comfort in this man's arms? If so, then it was a sin she could live with, because she needed Nikos. For just a few moments. She had needed him so desperately fourteen years ago, would have walked over hot coals to have reached him that night. She rested briefly, cocooned in his arms, greedily accepting his tender compassion.

"Tell me the truth," Ellen said. "Tell me about your secret life." She eased out of his arms. "Don't you think you owe me that much?"

Nikos looked away. "I owe you more than that, but I

cannot tell you everything. I would put not only my own life in danger, but other lives, too, if I reveal too much about myself.''

''Are you a criminal? Are you a spy? Are you some sort of secret agent? Tell me enough so that I can make sense of—''

''I've worked undercover for the past eighteen years,'' he told her. ''I've used dozens of different aliases and just as many disguises. Mr. Khalid is only one of my identities. I've worked with various governments and with numerous terrorist and rebel organizations, including the Al'alim. That's where I met Hakeem and his brother, Omar. I was passing myself off as an arms dealer. I can't tell you the particulars, but my cover got blown and I was forced to kill several of the Al'alim in order to escape. One of the men I killed was Hakeem's seventeen-year-old son.''

''You killed him in self-defense,'' Ellen said.

''Yes. I was fighting for my life. I was only twenty-three myself and new to the job. Hakeem swore revenge against me. He had known me only by my fake Arab name—Yusuf Ben Amir—but I had not disguised my appearance by doing anything more than dressing in the local costume. Hakeem put a bounty on my head—a million dollars to anyone who could lead him to me. I looked over my shoulder for years and always guarded my back, even between assignments.''

''Yusuf? That is the name he kept saying. He kept asking me to tell him where Yusuf was.''

''And you didn't know a Yusuf.''

''No, but I finally figured out that he was talking about you. He knew we'd been together on Golnar. I told him the man I'd been with was named Nikos, and he laughed in my face. He told me that you were a chameleon, a man of many names, many faces, and that because I was your woman I would know that, and shouldn't pretend that I didn't.''

"I thought he suspected the truth—that I was working undercover. After his son died, Hakeem tried to convince anyone who would listen to him that I was a danger not only to Al'alim, but to other terrorist groups. So, I simply changed my name again and was more careful about using disguises. I always stayed one step ahead of him.''

"Who do you work for? The CIA? Or is it another government, not the United States?"

"It's better for you if you don't know."

Ellen laughed. Nikos stared at her, obviously puzzled by her reaction. "Don't you realize that I'm not afraid," she told him. "Hakeem took everything from me fourteen years ago. I have nothing to lose anymore. Besides, Hakeem is dead, isn't he? Wasn't he killed in a battle between the Al'alim and the Menkuraian army nearly nine years ago?"

"Yes, Hakeem is dead, but his brother Omar has kept the Al'alim alive and thriving in the hills of Subria."

"What is the connection between Phila Constantine's kidnapping and your past association with the Al'alim? And don't try to tell me that there is no connection."

"I swear to you that I don't know. There is no way they can connect Theo's friend Mr. Khalid to Yusuf or to any of my other identities."

Ellen gasped.

"What is it?"

"I told him. I told him."

"You told who what?"

"Hakeem. I told Hakeem that you and I attended a party at Theo Constantine's villa."

"Why would you tell him—"

"I told him truths and half truths. I told him lies and made up stories and poured out my heart and soul to him.

I was scared out of my mind. I would have told him any-thing to save our...to save my life."

"Hakeem never contacted Theo, never went after him. If he'd believed he could use Theo against me, he would have. So why would the Al'alim come after Theo now? It doesn't make sense. Besides, Theo used to invite hundreds of people to his parties, especially beautiful women. There would be no real reason for Hakeem to have suspected that Theo and I were close friends. Unless you told him. Did you?"

Ellen shook her head. "I didn't know you and Theo were good friends. You never told me that. All you said was that you knew him."

"It's a coincidence that the Al'alim chose Theo," Nikos said. "It has to be."

"You want it to be. You don't want to believe that you could be responsible for Phila's kidnapping."

"The way I was responsible for what happened to you."

Ellen reached out and ran her fingertips over Nikos's cheek. "I was simply a casualty of whatever war you've been fighting for eighteen years."

"You suffered greatly, but you weren't a casualty," he told her. "You're still very much alive."

"Is that what you think? Then you're wrong. Mary Ellen Denby died fourteen years ago. She didn't survive. I live inside the shell that once was her body."

"You aren't telling me everything," he said. "There is more to what happened to you than you've—"

"Just as there are things you cannot tell me, there are things I cannot tell you."

"I see."

"No, you don't see, Nikos. You don't see at all, but it doesn't matter. What happened then is irrelevant to the present situation. All that matters now is that we work to-gether to save a child's life."

"What will you tell your agents about me?"

"I'll tell them that I believe we can trust you to do everything within your power to help us save Phila and her nanny."

"Thank you for trusting me."

"I didn't say I trusted you. I simply believe that you are honest about your willingness to do all you can for Theo's daughter." Ellen gave him a warning glare. "If you betray my trust, I will kill you."

Nikos looked at her and saw her for who she truly was today, not for the woman he had once known. "Yes, I believe you *would* kill me."

Chapter 7

Faith's stomach rumbled with hunger. She'd given Phila the last bites of bread and the last drops of water from the canteen yesterday. Or had it been earlier today? Unable to accurately judge the passing of time in their dark, dank prison, she could only guess. Poor little Phila had cried herself to sleep more than once since their capture; and to be totally honest with herself, Faith had to admit that she'd felt like succumbing to tears time and again. But she could not give in to panic and fear—if not for her own sake, then for Phila's. The child had been entrusted to her, and she took that duty seriously. One of the reasons she had chosen to become a nanny was because she believed no other job was more important than caring for and nurturing children.

"Faith?" Phila tossed back the wool blanket and rose from the small cot where she'd been sleeping. She still wore her pink silk gown, now wrinkled and filthy from wear, and her small feet were bare and dirty.

"I'm here, sweetie," Faith replied, then walked across

the earthen floor in her bare feet. They'd been taken so quickly from their beds the night of their abduction, that they had no robes or shoes.

"I thought it was a bad dream." Phila's large brown eyes filled with tears. "But it's real, isn't it? We're still in this awful place."

Faith sat down on the cot with Phila, then draped the edge of the scratchy woolen blanket she wore as a cape around Phila's shoulders, sharing the warmth of both her body and the blanket. "Yes, it's real. But once we're back in Coeus at the villa, this place will become nothing more than a bad memory."

"When will we go home? Will it be soon?"

"Yes, I hope so." Faith gave Phila a reassuring hug.

"You said my papa would send someone to get us. What's taking them so long? I want to go home now."

"Yes, I know you do, but…sometimes these things take a while. Your papa must find the right people to rescue us, and then they'll have to find out where we are. Remember, I told you to think of this as a game."

Phila's bottom lip trembled. "I don't like this game. I don't want to play it anymore."

"I'm afraid we have no choice. The bad men will not let us go. Not yet."

"I hate them!" Phila flung herself into Faith's arms and buried her face against Faith's bosom.

She stroked the child's back comfortingly. "It will be all right. We just have to be brave a little longer."

"It's awful in here," Phila mumbled. "It's cold and it stinks!"

Phila sobbed, her tears dampening the bodice of Faith's thin cotton gown. "They could hurt us, couldn't they? They might kill us!"

Faith closed her eyes and prayed for strength. "No, they won't kill us. I promise you that I won't let them hurt you."

Please, God, let me be able to keep that promise, Faith prayed. If necessary, she would die to protect Phila; but if they killed her, Phila would have no one standing between her and their captors.

What was that noise? Faith wondered. Had she imagined it? Suddenly the door—bolted from the outside—opened. Faith heard the hushed tones of a man speaking rapidly in a language she didn't understand.

"Someone's coming," she told Phila. "Be very quiet and still and don't say or do anything. Do you understand?"

"Yes." Phila's reply was little more than a squeak.

A tall man wearing camouflage fatigues and carrying a large, sinister-looking gun appeared first, then he stood aside to allow a woman to enter. She was wrapped in a long dingy robe and covered from head to toe, only the upper half of her face visible. A burlap sack hung over one of her shoulders. Scurrying into the room, her head bowed, she didn't even glance at Faith and Phila. Hurriedly she swung the sack around, opened it and removed the contents; then placed several packages of dried fruit, two loaves of bread and two canteens on the table. She retrieved the empty canteens, dumped them into her sack and started to leave.

Faith wrapped the blanket around Phila. "Stay here," she whispered, then rose from the bed and moved toward the woman, who kept her gaze glued to the floor. "Please, will you tell me where we are and why we're being kept here?"

The woman's sad black eyes lifted, and her gaze momentarily connected with Faith's before she bowed her head once again and raced from the room.

"She speaks no English," the young, clean-shaven soldier said. He was dark, his skin the shade of old leather.

"But you do."

"I speak good English." He grinned at her, showing a set of large, square, yellow teeth. Deep vertical lines appeared at either side of his large mouth.

"Yes, you do." Faith took a tentative step in his direction.

"Would you please thank our…our host for the food and water. Could you tell me where we are?"

The soldier laughed. "You are safely hidden away where no one can find you and the child." He glanced beyond Faith to the cot where Phila sat. "She is worth much to us. You are worth nothing."

When Faith noticed the way the man was looking at her, his narrowed gaze scanning her from head to toe and lingering on her breasts, she crossed her arms over her chest. A shiver of apprehension rippled through her body.

"Why were we abducted? Please, can't you tell me that much?"

"You ask too many questions."

He moved toward her. She retreated slowly. Holding the rifle in one hand, he reached out with the other and grabbed Faith by the back of her neck. She gasped. He leered at her.

"A woman should not talk so much," he told her. "A woman is here to please a man, to do his bidding. You wish to please me, American woman?"

Shivers racked Faith's body; fear clutched at her stomach. Before she could resist, he lowered his head and covered her mouth with his. His rancid breath stunned her; his brutal lips pressed feverishly. When she struck out at him, landing several blows to his chest, he ended the attack, but then grabbed her by her hair, yanking it until she cried out in pain.

Phila jumped up off the cot, ran across the room and kicked the solider repeatedly. He flung Faith onto the floor, then gave Phila a backhanded slap across her face. To show his contempt, he spat on the floor.

The moment he left, Faith tried to stand, but her weak legs gave way. She crawled across the damp earthen floor to Phila, drew the child close and hugged her. A large red whelt marred Phila's soft, pale cheek.

Whoever had kidnapped them and for whatever reason, Faith now understood that Phila was merely being kept alive for the ransom. Her worst fears had been confirmed. There was a good chance that they would both be killed.

Nikos Pandarus put in a phone call to SIS headquarters in London, gave his password and left the number where he could be reached. He sat alone in Theo's office that night and waited.

When he had pressed Ellen for the details of the event that had changed her life fourteen years ago, it had never entered his mind that she had been brutalized by Hakeem Ibn Fadil.

If he could change the past, he would. As much as those two weeks with beautiful, young Mary Ellen Denby from Cartersville, Georgia, had meant to him, he would have forgone the pleasure if he'd had any idea that by becoming her lover, he would be putting her life in danger. Yes, he had allowed their affair to go on too long. But he'd been so sure he was safe on Golnar. He had paid for everything in cash, used a phony ID and told only Mary Ellen that his name was Nikos. It had been his first real vacation in three years, since he'd joined the SIS when he was twenty-two and newly graduated from Cambridge. A contact group of lecturers at various universities were always on the lookout for ''firsts'' as MI6 prospects.

When he had agreed to go deep undercover and had asked for and received some of the most dangerous assignments, he'd been told that the price he'd have to pay for what he wanted was giving up any personal life. No wife and kiddies. No permanent girlfriend. No close chums. If his identity was ever discovered, the safety of those closest to him would be in jeopardy.

Nikos Pandarus ceased to exist. He'd gotten used to the solitary life, always alone. At first he had thrived on the excitement and danger, never considering the long-range consequences. But that summer when he'd come to Golnar for some much needed R&R, he had done the unthinkable—he'd fallen in love. He'd known from the very beginning that Mary Ellen and he had no future together, but he had wanted her more than he'd ever wanted anything. And when he'd walked away, leaving her nothing but a note of farewell, he had sworn to himself that it would never happen again. Leaving her had been the hardest thing he'd ever done.

Nikos swirled the brandy in the glass he held, then lifted it to his lips and took a sip. During the past eighteen years, he had been forced to stare into the ugly face of reality time and again. He'd told himself each time his actions had caused harm to others that he'd simply done what had to be done. No looking back. No regrets. Don't think. Don't feel. Just act. Somehow, he'd been able to put his love affair with Mary Ellen into a similar category. But that was when he'd believed she was off in America living the good life. Married. A mother. Teaching. Happy. Whenever he'd thought of her, she'd been that young, carefree girl whose laughter still echoed in his mind.

How did he live with himself now? How could he justify his actions? Had loving her been a good enough excuse for endangering her life? *But you didn't know,* he told himself. *You didn't know.*

What a cruel trick of fate. How many specific things would have had to fall perfectly into place for Hakeem to have discovered that the man who had killed his son, the man he'd known as Yusuf Ben Amir had spent two weeks on Golnar with an American woman named Mary Ellen Denby? How could Hakeem have known that Mary Ellen had meant anything more to him than a woman to warm his bed? What had made him believe that she knew Nikos's real identity and knew where he could be found?

The phone rang. Nikos had told the Dundee agent on duty tonight—Worth Cordell—that he would man the phones. Undoubtedly Ellen had spoken to her people and informed them that Nikos could be trusted, because Cordell hadn't given him any flack.

Nikos lifted the receiver. "Yes?"

"Black Wind, this is Red Velvet, please hold."

Nikos's true identity was known only by SIS Chief Townsend and two of the Firm's top-ranking officials. To others he was known simply as Black Wind. His reputation as an MI6 operative had grown to legendary proportions over the years. Within the ranks, he was considered a mysterious superhero. Few of his missions had failed. He'd never been captured, even when he'd been caught in the act. Although he knew better than anyone that he had not single-handedly thwarted numerous terrorist actions over the years, he'd been given credit for jobs well-done in Europe and Southeast Asia, but his real area of expertise was the Middle East and Africa. He had infiltrated rebel organizations which could by their very existence pose a threat to world peace. Gathering information had been his major goal, but on various occasions he'd been forced to take action without any backup, although usually the Special Air Service chaps did most of the hands-on dirty work.

"Black Wind?" a familiar voice spoke.

"This line is secure," Nikos said.

"How are you, my boy?"

Gerald Townsend still referred to Nikos as a boy, despite the fact that Nikos was now thirty-nine. A Cambridge contact had first approached Nikos about joining the "FCO Co-ordinating Staff," as MI6 was known. After a lengthy chat with that contact at the Carlton House overlooking St. James's Park, Nikos had been recruited officially by Gerald Townsend, then a Grade 5 officer.

"I'm greatly concerned," Nikos said. "If you aren't able to find the whereabouts of Phila Constantine and her nanny, we may be forced to do the unthinkable."

"I understand your predicament. Naturally I cannot officially request any diplomatic negotiations to discuss the release of three Al'alim prisoners from Menkura, nor can I sanction any action involving the unlawful release of those prisoners."

"What have you been able to do…unofficially?"

"I've made some inquiries. There seems to be no room for negotiations. Menkura is not inclined to release any Al'alim prisoners, not even to save Theo Constantine's daughter and her nanny, an American citizen. And the U.S.'s stand on hostage negotiations is the same as ours— we don't deal with terrorists."

"I feared as much." Nikos set his brandy glass on the desk. "That leaves us only two options."

"How much time do we have?" Gerald asked.

"Ms. Denby meets with their representative in Dareh day after tomorrow. My guess is that we'll be given no more than a week, ten days at most to produce the three Al'alim prisoners."

"You are assuming that the man in charge is thinking in a reasonable manner."

"If the one giving the orders is Omar Ibn Fadil, then we can count on a modicum of reason. The man isn't a hothead the way his brother was. But if someone else is behind Phila's kidnapping, then we may have more problems than we'd first anticipated."

"I'll do everything within my power to find out where the hostages are being held. Unofficially, of course."

"Theo will gladly pick up the tab for the cost of that information."

"Yes, of course. And if we're able to find them, I can arrange—unofficially—for a few former SAS chaps to handle the rescue. You remember Geoff Monday, don't you? He can round up some friends for you."

"Theo has put Ms. Denby in charge, and something tells me that she's not going to willingly allow anyone other than her own people to handle the rescue. She's got a former Ranger and a former SEAL on her team who will know what they're doing. Unfortunately the Dundee agents don't quite trust me. So how would I explain Geoff Monday and his men being involved?"

"Tell Ms. Denby they're your associates. Or pass them off as nothing more than mercenaries. You can think of something."

"Yes, I'll think of something. But first you have to find the location. If you don't—"

"I understand what the consequences are if you're not able to rescue the child and her nanny. Freeing three terrorists won't be easy for you, but the alternative is not something that is acceptable to you, is it?"

Nikos swallowed hard. No, the alternative was not acceptable. He could never live with himself unless he did everything possible to save Phila.

"There's something you should know," Nikos said. "Theo authorized Ms. Denby to offer the kidnappers twenty million dollars. They turned her down."

"My God! Why would they— The money isn't their main objective, is it? Those three prisoners being held in Menkura are very important to them. We're quite certain about the identity of two they will undoubtedly want released, but have no idea who the third man might be."

"That's what we have to find out."

"Someone's been in hiding, covering up his identity. That's what you think, isn't it?"

"Something like that. See if you can find out who, if any, of the Al'alim's major players, seems to have dropped out of sight lately, say in the past year or so."

"You do realize that we can't allow three Al'alim leaders to be returned to Subria and handed over to Omar Ibn Fadil."

"I'll need them only long enough to exchange them for the two hostages. After that…"

"Yes, quite right." Gerald paused, no doubt contemplating the steps that would have to be taken to recapture the freed prisoners. "Contact me tomorrow after Ms. Denby is given more details. In the meantime, we'll keep doing all we can to find out where they're holding the Constantine child and her nanny."

The dial tone buzzed in Nikos's ear. He returned the receiver to the cradle, then picked up his unfinished drink and downed the remainder of the brandy in one long swig. The liquor burned a path straight to his stomach. He blew out a hot breath, then set the empty snifter on the desk and walked out of the room. He needed a few hours of sleep in order to be alert tomorrow. Although Ellen would have to go in alone for the meeting, Nikos had every intention of being close by…closer than her backup team of Dundee agents.

Ellen had slept fitfully for hours, tossing and turning, fading in and out of happy dreams that metamorphosed into nightmares. One moment she was in Nikos's arms, feeling loved and protected. Then suddenly his face was replaced by Hakeem's evil visage. Another dream about her holding an infant, whose sweet smell lingered long after she awoke, changed to visions of weeping children crying for their mothers. Lost babies. Lost children. Lost forever in darkness.

She woke, damp with perspiration, her heartbeat racing and her mind slightly confused. For years now she'd been able to keep the nightmares at bay, except when she worked on a child abduction case. Then the dreams returned, as inevitable as the sun rising in the east. But this time, with this particular case, old memories intermingled with the nightmares, making them far more devastating than usual.

Ellen got out of bed, slid her feet into her white, terry cloth house slippers and made her way into the bathroom. Leaving off the light, she turned on the faucet, gathered cold water in her cupped hands and splashed herself in the face.

You are not going to give in to those painful memories, she told herself. *You know what will happen if you do. You'll be consumed and destroyed. You climbed out of that dark hole once, inch by slow agonizing inch. But could you do it again?*

Returning to the bedroom, she picked up her lightweight white, terry cloth robe from the foot of her bed, put on the robe and walked out onto the balcony that ran along the back side of the house. The predawn breeze chilled her with its cool breath. She crisscrossed her arms and hugged herself. In the distance the surf hummed rhythmically as it rolled ashore and then returned to the sea far below the villa.

Ellen wondered if Dia Constantine was sleeping, perhaps fighting demons in her drug-induced dreams. Or was Phila's mother awake and aware of each passing moment? If so, then she was thinking of nothing except her child, wondering if Phila was alive or dead. Praying that no one was hurting her baby. Afraid to allow herself to imagine the worst possible scenarios. Ellen moaned. A quiet, tormented sound, ripped from her heart. She was unable to ease Dia's suffering. She couldn't even promise the woman that her child would be returned to her unharmed.

But she was not powerless. Not as long as options existed.

Why were the kidnappers making them wait? Was someone enjoying the thought of prolonging Dia's and Theo's agony? If so, then someone truly hated them. Someone wanted them to suffer the torment of the damned. Another whole day before the Autumn Festival began in Dareh. Another thirty hours before she would exchange a million dollars for information. And each moment was sheer torture for Phila's parents.

But they were feeling only a fraction of the pain they would feel if anything happened to their child.

No, Ellen, don't go there. Come back to the present. Leave the past dead and buried, an inner voice demanded her obedience. The inner voice of sanity and reason.

Ellen felt his presence before she actually heard him or saw him standing in the shadows. Go back inside and lock the door. Lock him out of your life. If you let him in, he'll keep probing, keep asking questions, and sooner or later he'll wear you down. Is that what you want? she asked herself. Do you want him to know everything?

"I couldn't sleep," Nikos said as he came toward her.

With the Mediterranean moon casting soft, subdued light over him, Ellen noted that he wore black silk pajama bottoms and an open black silk robe. His long, flowing hair hung loosely about his shoulders. His muscular bronze chest glistened like polished metal. Her heart skipped a beat and for a split second, she felt twenty-one again and totally hypnotized by a tall, dark stranger.

"I didn't realize you were in the room next to mine," she said.

"I did not request it, if that is what you're thinking."

"It wasn't an accusation, just a comment." She turned to go back inside.

"Wait." She paused. "Please, stay," he said, his deep voice seductively mellow.

"Why?" she asked, and all the while she knew. Whatever had been between them fifteen years ago had not died, not completely. He felt it just as she did, the alluring attraction that drew them together.

"I think you know why." He moved closer.

With her back to him and her head slightly tilted so that she could see him, she watched as he came to her. She could have walked away. It would have been so easy. A few steps to the door, a few more into the bedroom and to safety.

Nikos came up behind her, gently grasped her shoulders and turned her around to face him. She looked up, fixing her gaze on his face. She didn't flinch; didn't blink. "I'm not Mary Ellen. If you're looking for her, you won't find her."

He lifted one hand, placing his index finger over her lips, as his other hand glided down her arm to grasp her wrist. "I understand. I am not the same Nikos that you once knew." His finger skimmed over her lips, across her chin and down her throat, stopping at the rounded curve of her oversized T-shirt's modest neckline.

"Our minds are playing tricks on us, trying to make us believe things that aren't real," she told him.

"Ah, but that is where you are wrong, *agkelos*. It is true that neither you nor I are the same as we were in the past, but this feeling between us is very real. Passion does not know how much time has passed. It is not aware of our maturity, does not care about the life lessons we have learned."

"Is that what you call it—passion?" She forced herself to not break eye contact, to not allow him to see how profoundly he affected her. "I call it insanity, and insanity in the young can be excused, but not in people our ages."

He brought his hand up to her face and cupped her chin. "Just how old are you? You still look so young."

"I'm thirty-six."

"Ah, a woman in her prime."

She shook her head; he removed his caressing fingertips.

"How old are you?" she asked. "Or is that also top secret information?"

"I will be forty very soon," he replied. "And I often wonder where the years have gone. It seems as if only yesterday I was twenty-five and in love for the first time in my life." He lifted her hand and laid it on his naked chest. "In love with Mary Ellen Denby."

She sucked in her breath. "I believed you when you told me you loved me. But then after you left the way you did, I doubted you. I doubted myself. You have no idea what—" *See, I warned you,* her inner voice cautioned. *He's seducing you with every word, every look, with the very nearness of his hard, lean body.*

"I truly believed that by leaving you, I was doing what was best for you." He pulled her body up against his. "I thought I was protecting you. I had no idea that Hakeem would ever find out about us."

Ellen could not deny the chemistry that existed between Nikos and her, as powerful this very moment as it had been fifteen years ago. Loving him had cost her dearly, but only with him had she known true passion. If she knew what was good for her she would resist the temptation to once again experience Nikos's possession. She had trained herself not to think about him, but how was that possible now that she must see him on a daily basis? Perhaps fighting the burning desire was the wrong way to squelch it. She didn't love Nikos now. He could no longer hurt her. Giving in to her needs could well be the surest way to defuse the passion.

"I don't want to talk about Hakeem or about what happened." Ellen lifted her arms up and around his neck and pressed herself against him intimately. "I don't want to relive those two weeks we shared. I have no love to give you, Nikos. There is none in me. But I'm not the idealistic young fool I was when we first met. I don't believe love is necessary for a good physical relationship."

"The passion will be enough for you?" His gaze questioned her more profoundly than his words.

"Passion is all we have. Perhaps it is all we ever had," she lied. As deeply as it hurt her to remember the depth of her feelings for Nikos, she knew that she had loved him with a mindless, all-consuming hunger unlike anything she'd ever known before or since. She had lain in other men's arms, experienced the heat of physical desire and walked away without a backward glance. She had known satisfaction with others, but never true passion.

For her, love was impossible; passion was not. With Nikos she could know passion again.

But at what price?

"Perhaps you are right," he whispered against her lips. "But it was a passion I would die to know once again."

She wanted his kiss more than she'd wanted anything in a very long time. The desire inside her burned white-hot. When Nikos's lips covered hers, she responded feverishly, giving herself over to the moment.

Suddenly a series of blood-curdling screams rent the predawn solitude. Ellen pulled out of Nikos's embrace and gasped for air.

"My God, who's screaming?"

Nikos grabbed Ellen's arm, then rushed her into and through her bedroom and out into the hall. Sawyer, Lucie and Dom, all three in their sleep attire and holding their weapons, dashed out into the corridor. And Worth, who was on night duty, flew up the stairs, taking the steps two at a time.

The screaming continued for several seconds. Then utter quiet. Ellen's heart caught in her throat. She recognized the cries of terror. Once, years ago, those tormented cries had belonged to her.

Chapter 8

"The screaming was coming from the Constantines' bedroom," Lucie Evans said. "I'm right next door and heard it immediately. I'm pretty sure it was Mrs. Constantine."

"Probably a nightmare," Ellen said, relief calming her.

Sawyer McNamara scowled at Ellen and Nikos, but he said nothing, for which Ellen was thankful. Obviously all of her agents had seen Nikos and her coming out of her bedroom. At four-thirty in the morning. They were all probably thinking the same thing; in their place she'd be thinking it, too. A man and woman, in their robes, who emerge from the same bedroom at the crack of dawn had probably been sleeping together. Of course, what she did or didn't do was no one's business. Her private life had always been just that—private.

Theo Constantine opened his bedroom door, stepped out into the hall and looked directly at Nikos. "Dia had a terrible dream. She woke believing that Phila was in grave danger, more than ever before. I couldn't convince her that nothing had changed. Dia is afraid that Phila is dead. Nothing I said to her calmed her. She's terribly confused. She kept saying something about the baby being dead. But our unborn child is very much alive." Theo glanced at Ellen. "I held her down while Irina gave her an injection. But she's still weeping. Ms. Denby, would you—" Theo clenched his teeth tightly in an effort to control his emotions. "Dia is asking to speak to you."

"I'll go in and see her," Ellen said, then turned to the other Dundee agents. "Y'all go back to bed." She looked at Worth. "Were the servants disturbed by the screaming?"

"Yeah, they're all awake and waiting to hear what happened," Worth said.

"Go tell them Mrs. Constantine had a nightmare, but she's all right now."

Worth nodded, then headed downstairs. Domingo Shea went back to his room, and after giving Ellen a questioning glare, Sawyer followed him into the room they shared.

Lucie came up to Ellen and whispered, "I'm going to head down to the kitchen and see if Mrs. Panopoulas minds if I fix us some coffee. You look like you could use a jolt of caffeine."

"I won't be long," Ellen said. "Why don't you fix the coffee and I'll come down to the kitchen in a few minutes."

Offering Ellen a halfhearted smile, Lucie nodded in agreement.

Nikos put his hand on Theo's shoulder. "Is there anything I can do?"

"Yes. You can bring Phila home to her mother and me," Theo said. "I don't know how much more Dia can take before she breaks."

"Come with me to my room and we'll talk," Nikos said. "You're in pretty bad shape yourself."

Theo shook his head. "I shouldn't leave Dia. She might

need me. I can't do anything to help Phila. I have to leave that to you and Ellen. But maybe I can help my wife.''

"Let Ellen go in and speak with Dia,'' Nikos said. "If you want to stay right here, outside the bedroom door, I'll stay with you.''

"Yes, I prefer to stay close by. In case…''

Ellen glanced from Theo to Nikos, then turned and walked into the semidark bedroom. Nurse Irina stood to the left side of Dia Constantine's bed. As Ellen came near, Dia lifted her hand and reached out for Ellen.

Poor, pitiful woman, Ellen thought. The most frustrating part of handling a child's kidnapping was keeping the parents' emotional agony from bleeding over into your own emotions. Hardening her heart was never easy for Ellen, despite what others thought. She put up such a good front; no one ever realized how deeply this type of case affected her. Of course, on some level, she did remove herself emotionally, but she did it because she knew that otherwise she'd be unable to do her job effectively.

Ellen sat on the edge of the bed and took Dia Constantine's trembling hand into her own steady hand. "Your husband told me that you wanted to speak to me.''

"I feel as if I'm losing my mind,'' Dia said, her words already slightly slurred from the effects of the sedative.

Theo had explained to Ellen that the medication Dr. Capaneus had ordered for Dia was strong enough to sedate her, yet mild enough not to harm the fetus. The doctor feared that Dia's emotional agitation would be more detrimental to her pregnancy than the drugs to give her a few hours of emotional peace.

"The dream was so real. Phila was crying for me. She kept calling me. Mama. Mama. But I couldn't find her. I searched everywhere.'' Dia lifted her head off the pillow and stared straight ahead as if she saw something on the far side of the room. "She was in a cage. Locked in a cage.

And she was all alone. Faith wasn't there. Where was Faith?''

"Mrs. Constantine, please, don't do this to yourself." Ellen gently grasped Dia's chin and nudged her head back onto the pillow. "You aren't helping Phila and you're hurting yourself and your unborn child."

"The baby's dead."

"No, your baby is all right. It's not dead."

Dia laid her hand over her belly. "Yes, my little one is well. But the other baby is dead. I saw him. Tiny little baby."

Every muscle in Ellen's body tensed. "You had a nightmare. It wasn't real. Rest now. I promise you that we'll do everything we can to bring Phila home to you. You mustn't give up hope."

Dia squeezed Ellen's hand. "If my little Phila dies, I will die, too. Don't you understand?"

"Yes, I understand." Ellen released Dia's hand and grasped her shoulder. "Look at me."

As fresh tears flooded her eyes, Dia tried to focus her gaze on Ellen.

"No matter what happens, you will not die," Ellen said. "You feel as if you're dying now, as if you're already half dead. But you will not give in to the demons trying to destroy your mind. You have a husband and an unborn child. They both need you." When Dia's eyes widened, Ellen knew she'd heard her and understood what she was telling her. "We will save Phila. You must believe that. You must hold on to that hope."

"Poor Theo." Several huge tears trickled down Dia's cheek. "He is suffering even more than I am because he suffers for me, too."

"Rest now, Mrs. Constantine. And when you wake, see if you can find the strength to offer your husband comfort."

"Yes, I'll do that." Dia closed her eyes. "Theo... My dear Theo."

As Ellen rose from the side of the bed, she saw Theo and Nikos standing together just inside the open doorway. When she passed them, she paused.

"After your wife has rested and she wakes, tell her how much you need her," Ellen said. "Tell her you don't have the strength to go through this ordeal without her at your side."

"But I don't want to burden her more than—"

"What your wife needs right now is for you to share your feelings with her." Ellen forced her gaze to remain fixed on Theo because she didn't dare look at Nikos. "She needs to share your weakness as well as your strength. Don't shut her out."

Theo nodded, then moved slowly toward the bed. When Ellen went out into the hall, Nikos followed her and caught up with her before she reached the top of the stairs.

"I heard what you said to Dia. It was amazing. I could have sworn you understood exactly what she's going through, that you could feel her pain."

"I'm an experienced hostage negotiator, which means dealing with the hostage's family, too," Ellen told him. "And as a Dundee agent, I've dealt with several child kidnapping cases."

"And you can draw from your own experience, having been kidnapped yourself."

"Yes, that fact can work to my advantage."

"Or to your disadvantage."

Ellen glared at Nikos. "Only if I allow my emotions to get in the way of logic."

"But you don't allow that to happen, do you?"

"No. I keep my emotions in check."

A tentative smiled played at the corners of Nikos's mouth. "Passion is an emotion, *agkelos.*"

"Yes, you're right, it is. And in a moment of weakness, I almost gave in to it…out there on the balcony with you."

"Almost?"

"Let's make a deal." Ellen steeled herself with resolve, determined to regain control, to rein in her desire for Nikos. "We will work together to find a way to free Phila and Faith. Then, when this is all over, we'll rent ourselves a hotel room and we'll get out of our system whatever is left over from the past, then go our separate ways."

Nikos stared at her, a stunned expression on his face. "Are you really as cold and unfeeling as you want people to believe you are?"

"What's the matter, Nikos? Isn't that what you usually do? Sex for the sake of sex, then hail and farewell."

Ellen knew that Nikos wanted her and would not end his pursuit simply because she asked him to. A man like Nikos did not take no for an answer, not when he believed that she desired him as much as he did her. For a few moments earlier this evening she had considered having sex with him to defuse that almost uncontrollable desire, but showing him even a glimpse of weakness on her part had given him an edge. She had to take that advantage away from him. By offering him the sex he wanted once this assignment ended, she had accomplished the desired effect. She realized now that Nikos wanted more than sex from her. He wanted what she could not give him.

"Yes, of course. No emotional entanglement to worry with later." He studied her face, as if seeking something he'd suddenly realized was lost. "Isn't there anything of Mary Ellen left inside you?"

More than I want to admit. Mary Ellen was weak, powerless, naive and even stupid. And afraid. But Ellen was strong and powerful. Smart and worldly-wise. And fearless. Ellen could not be hurt the way Mary Ellen had been.

"I'm going down to the kitchen," Ellen said, deliberately not responding to his question. "I need some coffee."

Nikos offered her a gentlemanly bow. "Then I will see you later...Ellen."

"Nine o'clock. Theo's office. We'll go over the last-minute details for tomorrow's rendezvous in Dareh."

Wearing their robes and house slippers, Ellen and Lucie sat in a secluded corner of the huge kitchen, sipping coffee. Mrs. Panopoulas worked busily preparing breakfast for the household. Several other servants wandered in and out of the area, each performing a specific job, no one paying much attention to the two American women.

"So, do you want to tell me or do I guess?" Lucie nailed Ellen with her sharp stare. "What's up with you and Nikos Khalid?"

"It wasn't what it looked like," Ellen said.

"Then what was it? And don't try to tell me it was nothing. We all saw you and Mr. Khalid come out of your bedroom together. I thought Sawyer was going to blow a gasket."

"My personal life is none of Sawyer's business."

"It's none of my business either...unless it affects our assignment."

Ellen's mouth tightened. "I never let anything interfere with doing my job when I'm on an assignment."

"Before you go getting all defensive, think about it this way—what if you'd seen Mr. Khalid and me coming out of my bedroom, wearing our nighties, at four-thirty in the morning."

Ellen blew out an exasperated breath. "Okay, you've got me there. Sure, I would have assumed you'd had sex with him."

Smiling, Lucie widened her eyes as if to say "see what I mean?" "You've got to know that if you're involved with

Mr. Khalid, it's bound to complicate things. And I'm not talking only about Sawyer's jealousy. That you could deal with. But Ellen, honey child,'' Lucie enunciated the last two words, stressing her South Alabama accent, ''we're all well aware of the fact that this Mr. Khalid is a dangerous character. And you know what they say about lying down with dogs.''

Ellen grinned, then chuckled. Lucie stared at her inquisitively.

''I don't think Nikos is infested with fleas,'' Ellen said. ''Bugs maybe, but not fleas.''

''Okay, how about filling me in on the joke.''

''Strictly between us girls?''

''Uh-oh. When you refer to us as girls, you scare me.'' Lucie scrutinized Ellen's expression. ''Oh, all right. Strictly between us girls.''

Ellen glanced around the kitchen, then lowered her voice when she noted that they were alone except for Mrs. Panopoulas who was too far across the room to overhear their conversation. ''I knew Nikos years ago. Fifteen years ago to be exact.''

Lucie let out a long, slow whistle. ''Old lovers?''

''Yeah, something like that.''

''So who is he really? An international criminal or a—''

''I'm not sure who he's working for, which government, but my guess is he's either CIA or SIS.''

''Was he an agent fifteen years ago?''

''Yes, but I didn't know it at the time.''

''Long affair?''

''You're getting awfully nosy,'' Ellen said.

''Brief affair?''

''Two weeks.''

''Must've been some two weeks. Mr. Tall, Dark and Deadly looks like he'd be hot in the sack.''

"That comment was a bit too personal." Ellen rose from the table, picked up her and Lucie's empty cups, then walked across the room, lifted the glass pot and poured them more coffee.

Lucie waited for Ellen's return, then reached up to take the cup of hot coffee from her boss. "So, are you going to tell the others?"

"I'll tell them I knew Nikos years ago and that's all I'll tell them. And I'll reassure everyone that as far as helping us rescue Phila, he's totally trustworthy…or at least I think he is."

"Then you don't really trust him, do you?"

"Not one hundred percent," Ellen admitted. "But to be honest, I'm not sure how much of that distrust comes from my personal feelings about Nikos and how much comes from logic."

Nikos thought the morning meeting with the Dundee agents went well. Deliberately he had arrived fifteen minutes late, and just as he suspected, Ellen had taken that time to inform her agents she and Nikos had known each other in the past. And she had also stressed that she believed he could be trusted to help them rescue Phila Constantine. During the meeting, all the Dundee agents—except Sawyer McNamara—seemed somewhat more comfortable around him.

Theo had not sat in on the meeting, preferring to remain upstairs with Dia. Nikos wondered what it must be like for the couple to live each moment scared out of their minds, afraid that they would lose their daughter. He'd heard people say that you didn't know what love was until you'd loved a child of your own. A selfless love unlike any other. Good parents always put the needs of their child before their own needs.

During the meeting, Nikos and the Dundee agents had

gone over the plans for the exchange of a million dollars in cash for information. Because the banks were closed tomorrow for the Autumn Festival, Theo's local banker would meet Ellen and Nikos at eleven o'clock in the lobby of the Larnaka Hotel in downtown Dareh, only a couple of blocks from the Odyssea Café. Lucie and Sawyer would pose as customers eating lunch at the café and arrive at precisely eleven-forty-five. Worth and Dom would be strategically placed in adjoining buildings to the right and left of the café, each armed and ready to strike if anything went wrong. Nikos would take an active part in the scenario, passing himself off as a waiter. It would be his job to get photographs of the man meeting with Ellen. But what no one else knew—not yet—was the fact that two former SAS soldiers, who'd be flying in from London today, would be across the street with the telescopic lenses of their M-16 assault rifles trained on the table where Ellen would be sitting with the Al'alim's representative. And a couple of SIS agents would be making a thorough check—unofficially—of all incoming boats and planes, on the lookout for the Al'alim contact as he arrived and departed. It just might be possible to follow this man straight back to his superiors. Possible, but not probable.

Nikos could count on Gerald Townsend to arrange whatever assistance he needed. More than once, Gerald's willingness to bend the rules had saved not only Nikos's life, but salvaged a gone-bad assignment.

After the strategy meeting, the Dundee agents had scattered, including Ellen, who acted as if nothing had happened between Nikos and her, as if they hadn't been on the verge of making love that morning. Maybe she'd come to her senses faster than he had. Rekindling an old romantic fire was usually a mistake, but in this case it could prove foolhardy—perhaps even deadly.

Sawyer McNamara hung around after the others left, apparently waiting to speak to Nikos alone. Nikos had picked up rather quickly on Sawyer's possessive attitude concerning Ellen. Were they still romantically involved? If so, Ellen certainly didn't appear to return the man's affections.

"Is there something else we need to go over?" Nikos looked point-blank at the other man.

Sawyer scowled, baring his teeth like an animal preparing to attack. "What's your game, Khalid? Who the hell are you?"

"I am Theo Constantine's friend."

"Are you also Ellen Denby's friend?"

"No, Ellen and I were not and are not friends. We were lovers."

Sawyer's jaw tightened; a vein in the side of his neck bulged and throbbed. "Stay the hell away from her. Do you hear me?"

"If she were your woman, you would have every right to warn me off," Nikos said. "But she isn't, is she? You would like for her to be yours, but Ellen belongs to no man."

"Damn you, Khalid!" Sawyer balled his hands into fists.

"I understand the attraction. She is a beautiful, desirable woman." Nikos sensed that Sawyer was on the verge of taking a punch at him. "But there is no need for us to fight over her, is there? Not when we both know she has already rejected you."

For a split second Nikos wasn't sure whether his words had incited Sawyer to violence or had defused a volatile situation.

With tension vibrating between them like electrical currents, Sawyer took a deep breath, released it and said, "If you hurt her…"

I've already hurt her. Damaged her beyond repair. Knowing me, loving me, destroyed Mary Ellen Denby. "I won't hurt her. I can't. The lady's heart is untouchable. But then you already knew that, didn't you?''

"Yeah," Sawyer said. "And now I'm wondering what part you played in making her the woman she is today." With that said, Sawyer walked away, leaving Nikos alone in the office.

Nikos took full responsibility for the transformation in Ellen. He could blame fate, blame Hakeem, blame the damn SIS, but in the end, the guilt lay at his feet. He had inadvertently put her life in danger by prolonging what should have been a weekend affair. But he'd been young and cocky and filled with the lust for danger and adventure. Playacting had been fun then; now it was second nature to him. He'd been so sure no one would even suspect his true identity those two weeks he'd spent with Mary Ellen in Dareh.

If he could change the past, he would. He'd return Ellen's sweet, untarnished soul to her. But he could do nothing to erase his grievous mistakes. All he could do was make sure she never again suffered at his hands.

Princess Adele of Orlantha and her husband, Sir Matthew O'Brien, arrived at the villa in the early afternoon, shortly after lunch. Nikos and the Dundee agents greeted the royal couple in the huge foyer, while two servants brought in their luggage and carried it upstairs. Ellen had known Matt for several years, but she'd never seen this side of the former Air Force "cowboy." The new-bridegroom-madly-in-love-with-his-wife part of him. The way the couple looked at, spoke to, and touched each other was the kind of romantic hogwash that sold millions of dollars worth of candy, cards, flowers and lingerie on Valentine's Day. It was enough to turn your stomach—or to make you sick with envy. Love was new and exciting for them, filled with the promise of a real happily forever after future. Maybe some people were lucky enough to grab the brass ring and hold on to it. Some people. But not Ellen. And apparently, not Nikos, either.

While Matt introduced his wife to his former Dundee buddies, Ellen felt Nikos watching her. Was he thinking what she was? If fate had been kinder... If Nikos had chosen a different profession... If life was fair...

"It is good to see you again, Matt," Nikos said. "And you, too, Your Highness."

"Mr. Khalid." Princess Adele took Nikos's hand and held it for a few moments. "You look different. Something is—where's your scar?"

"Mysteriously gone." Nikos smiled.

"Oh, I...well...I am so pleased that you are here," the princess said. "I'm sure your presence is a comfort to Theo. He knows you will move mountains to save our precious little Phila."

"I'll do everything within my power."

"As you requested in the message Theo gave me, I instructed our ambassador to Menkura to make inquiries about the government's policy on releasing Al'alim prisoners," the princess said.

Ellen glared at Nikos. He'd sent her royal highness a request via Theo without consulting her first? Dammit, didn't he know she was supposed to be in charge of this mission?

"And what did your ambassador find out?" Ellen asked.

Princess Adele frowned forlornly as she turned to Ellen. "I am afraid that the news is much as we expected. Menkura's policy is to show no weakness by releasing prisoners. Not even if their own prime minister was taken hostage would they release prisoners to save his life."

Ellen huffed, releasing a loud, disappointed sigh. "May I ask, Your Highness, how many people you brought into your confidence concerning Phila Constantine's abduction?''

"Hey, Ellen, you're way off base," Matt said. "Adele didn't—"

"I can defend myself," the princess told her husband, then said to Ellen, "Phila is my goddaughter. I would do nothing to endanger her. Matt and I shared this information with no one. I spoke to our Menkuraian ambassador in strictest confidence and used a hypothetical scenario of what might happen were I or any member of the royal household kidnapped and the ransom asked was that Menkura free members of the Al'alim they hold as prisoners.''

"I apologize," Ellen said. "I—"

"Ms. Denby is upset with me," Nikos said. "You see, she's accustomed to being in charge and I'm afraid I didn't ask for her permission before I sent you the request through Theo.''

Adele's brows lifted as her eyes widened and her mouth formed a perfect oval. Matt glanced from Ellen to Nikos.

"Well, now that we have that cleared up," Matt said, "we'd like to see Theo and Dia.''

"Yes, of course you would." With a warm smile and a friendly manner, Lucie stepped in and took charge. "Why don't I go upstairs and let them know that y'all are here.''

"Yes, please, Ms. Evans," the princess said. "I'm quite anxious to see Dia.''

"And I'm eager to see you, my friend," Dia Constantine said.

All eyes turned to the staircase where, halfway down the stairs, Theo stood with his arm around his wife's waist. Dia still looked pale and weak, but she appeared to have recently showered—her damp hair was neatly combed—and she was dressed in gray slacks and a white sweater instead of her gown.

"Dia!" the princess cried and rushed across the foyer while, aided by her husband, Dia hurried down the stairs.

The two old and dear friends came together in a weeping, clinging, hugging moment that brought tears to Lucie's eyes. All the men shifted their feet and looked away, pretending to be unaffected by the poignant scene.

Ellen walked away, heading for Theo's office. She needed to keep busy, to find something to occupy her mind. Despite her outward show of utter calm and control, she was always a bit nervous, a bit antsy, before a mission. Even though tomorrow was only a preliminary event to what would come later, Ellen was well aware of how many things could go wrong. Especially if Nikos and she weren't on the same page with the exchange operation. If Nikos had neglected to tell her about sending Princess Adele a message, what else hadn't he told her? Did he have some sort of contingency plan for tomorrow, something to which she wasn't privy?

Before she made it halfway down the corridor leading to Theo's office, she heard footsteps behind her. Instead of turning and confronting her shadow, she marched forward and straight into the office. Just as she started to slam the door, a big, dark hand reached out and grabbed the door's edge.

"We need to talk," Nikos said.

"Nothing personal," she told him.

"Strictly business."

She nodded. He entered the office directly behind her, then closed the door.

Ellen spun around and glared at him. "You don't play well with others, do you?"

"I'm sorry I didn't tell you about sending the princess a message through Theo. But I saw no need to—"

"This isn't one of your espionage missions. It's not some cloak-and-dagger undercover operation." Ellen reached out and tapped him in the center of his chest. "You aren't the one in charge. You aren't the one making the final decisions. This is a group effort. You're on a team. My team. What one knows, we all know. That's the way a team effort works."

"I apologized, didn't I?"

"What else don't I know?" Ellen threw up her arms in an angry, frustrated gesture. "Other than, of course, who you really are and what government you're working for and if we can trust you out of our sight."

"My mother was Turkish," Nikos said. "Born in Cyprus and educated in England. My father was the product of a marriage between a Greek father and an English mother. He, too, was educated in England. My parents were wealthy, cultured world travelers. And they were deeply in love. I was the eldest child and my sister was born three years later."

Ellen stared at Nikos, stunned by his sudden personal revelations. "What has this to do with—"

"When I was nineteen and a student at Cambridge, I left school on holiday and was en route to meet my parents and my sister, Chloe, in Cyprus. It was to be a special visit home for my mother. My father had booked a suite at the best hotel in Pafos. But before I arrived, my parents, my sister and a small group of tourists were killed by a bomb explosion. The following day a militant terrorist organization took credit for the bombing."

"Oh, Nikos."

Ellen laid her hand on his chest. She felt the tension in his body as he stood stiffly, his face tight, his expression one of barely contained rage.

"When I graduated from university, I was approached by a contact for Her Majesty's Secret Intelligence Service." As if he had willed himself under control, the pressure inside Nikos subsided. "It didn't take much persuasion for them to recruit me. I was more than eager to do my part to rid the world of its villains.''

"You're an MI6 agent," Ellen said.

He nodded. "I've worked undercover for the past eighteen years." He laid his hand over hers where hers rested on his chest. "My real name is Nikos Pandarus...and only three other people besides myself and Theo—and now you—know my true identity. SIS chief, Gerald Townsend, and two of the Firm's top officials."

"Why are you telling me all of this now?"

Nikos squeezed her hand. "Because I want you to trust me. Because I need for you to believe me when I tell you that I'm one of the good guys. And because you're right— if we're going to save Phila, we have to work together."

"I think I've always known—deep down inside—that you really were one of the good guys."

He lifted her hand from his chest and brought it to his lips. "I'm sorry, *agkelos*. I'm so very sorry about what happened to you."

An oddly warm yet disturbing feeling fluttered inside Ellen. Caring? Compassion? Or love? She believed the sincerity of Nikos's words. He was racked with guilt, placing the total blame for what had happened to her squarely on his own shoulders.

Oh, dear God, Nikos, you only know the half of it.

Within the walls of Nawar Prison, located in the coastal region of Menkura, a good ten miles from the nearest town, the inmates were allowed thirty minutes of outdoor exercise before the evening meal. Musa Ben Arif imagined the sound of the surf; and in his mind's eye, he pictured the beautiful waters of the Black Sea. For eight long years he had dreamed of walking out of this living hell and boarding a ship that would take him home. Home to the mountains of Subria. Home to his people.

Soon. Very soon. He must hold fast and continue his prayers. He would trust Allah. And trust his brother, Omar, to find a way to free him. Had he not proven himself worthy by years of suffering? Surely having Shakir Abu Lufti and Jamsheed Abd Hamid brought to Nawar three months ago had been a sign from Allah. In all the time he had lived within these walls, trapped and punished for being a true believer and leading the Al'alim to greatness, he had waited. And planned. And schemed.

Eight years, five months and twenty-four days ago in the *Bohaira* Battle, when he realized it was inevitable that he would be captured, he had swapped clothes and identities with one of his loyal followers—Ben Arif. The alias he had assumed then had kept him alive all these years, but soon he would become Hakeem Ibn Fadil again. And revenge would be his. One of the strongest forces alive and thriving within him had helped him survive—the hatred he felt for El-Hawah. Killing the man of many faces, many names, many incarnations, would be his first act of retribution.

He would do whatever it took to kill the man who had murdered his son. Even if it meant destroying half the world.

Chapter 9

One call from Theo Constantine to the Odyssea Café's owner secured Nikos a very temporary job. Attired in the white twill pants and red-and-white-striped cotton shirt that was de rigueur attire for the wait staff at the restaurant, Nikos handed menus to the couple sitting at the table near the street. Sawyer and Lucie appeared to be nothing more than tourists on holiday here at Dareh's most famous sidewalk café. The only other early lunchtime customer—an elderly lady—sat several tables away, leisurely sipping from a cup of tea. While the Dundee agents discussed the variety of choices on the menu, Nikos glanced toward the building on the right, a delicatessen. Standing just inside the door, a newspaper in one hand and a mug of coffee in the other, Worth Cordell kept watch.

Lucie ordered quickly, but Sawyer couldn't make up his mind. A delaying tactic to keep Nikos close by until Ellen showed up. Nikos appeared slightly agitated, then casually glanced at the building to his left, an antique shop where

Dom had been stationed. But Dom wasn't inside the shop. Instead he was heading directly toward Nikos.

"Waiter!" Dom called as he sat down at the table next to Sawyer and Lucie's.

"What's up with him?" Lucie whispered.

Nikos smiled at Lucie. "Please, excuse me. I'll see to the other gentleman while your husband decides what he would like to order."

Reminding himself to act naturally, Nikos approached the table where Dom waited, then handed him a menu and asked, "May I help you, sir."

Dom flipped open the menu, pointed to an item and said, "What's this, some kind of chicken dish?"

Nikos bent down a little closer and peered at the menu.

"There's a marksman across the street," Dom said quietly. "In a second-story window of the florist shop."

"There are two marksmen," Nikos replied.

"Two, huh? I spotted only one. Where's the other?"

"Second floor of the Dionyssos souvenir shop."

"I'll get Worth and we'll—"

"Yes, sir, that dish is made with chicken." Nikos grinned, then in a lower voice added, "They're my men. Ellen knows about them."

Dom scowled at Nikos. "When did you tell her?"

"Right after we met Mr. Mehran to pick up the money."

Dom narrowed his gaze, a hint of skepticism in his expression. "A backup team for the backup team, huh?"

"Something like that." Nikos shook his head. "I'm sorry, sir, but we don't have bacon and eggs. Perhaps you'd like to try something else."

"No, thanks." Dom rose from his chair. "I'm not very hungry after all." As nonchalantly as possible, Dom went back to the antique shop and took up his watch directly inside the door.

The Al'alim contact was supposed to show up at noon.

That gave them practically no time before the festivities for the Autumn Festival officially began. Right now the celebrators were in various churches, their minds being properly prepared to appreciate the festival as a time to give thanks to a generous God who had provided a bountiful harvest. Old traditions died hard. For some unknown reason, people felt more comfortable drinking to excess, eating to the point of gluttony and indulging in every carnal act imaginable if they did a little praying beforehand.

Just as Nikos returned to take Sawyer's lunch order, he caught a glimpse of Ellen in his peripheral vision. Dressed in tan dress slacks, a white button-down shirt and a black blazer, she marched across Lidinis Street. Looking every inch the modern businesswoman, either a young executive or an up-and-coming assistant, she carried a plain black leather briefcase. An inconspicuous attaché case—stuffed with a thousand one thousand dollar bills. U.S. currency. Good anywhere in the world. Just looking at her, no one would suspect that she was in possession of a million dollars or that the fate of two hostages could well depend upon how she conducted herself in the upcoming fateful meeting.

Sawyer ordered quickly, leaving Nikos free to go to Ellen. He approached her, a smile plastered on his face.

"May I help you?" He handed her a menu.

She returned the menu to him. "Just coffee for now. I'm meeting someone and I'd rather wait for him before I order."

Nikos hurried off into the restaurant's interior and straight to the kitchen, where he gave the cook an order for Lucie's and Sawyer's meals. Then he went to the huge stainless steel coffee machine, picked up a white ceramic mug from the stack to the left and filled the cup to the brim with steaming hot coffee. He checked his watch. Precisely twelve noon. The Al'alim's representative should be here soon.

This morning around seven-thirty, he had received a call from one of his SIS colleagues with news that four possible suspects had arrived in Dareh. One by boat last night. Three by airplane this morning. All were of Middle Eastern descent. Passports were varied. None from Subria. But then passports could be forged. The Al'alim contact wouldn't be using his real name.

One man had gone straight from the airport to a breakfast meeting with an import/export dealer. The man who'd come in by boat last night had gone directly to the hospital where he'd stayed at the bedside of a dying relative. The other two men had checked into two different hotels. Those were the ones being kept under surveillance.

Nikos placed the coffee mug in front of Ellen. "Do you require cream or sugar?"

"No, thank you."

While Ellen made an effort to sip on the black coffee, Nikos made a show of inspecting all the umbrella-covered tables. He rearranged two umbrellas, wiped off three perfectly clean tabletops and straightened already straight chairs. As inconspicuously as possible, he checked his watch again. Ten after twelve. The man was late. Had he already come by and figured something wasn't quite right? Had he spotted Dom? Or Worth? Or worse—had he spotted one or both of the snipers across the street?

Nikos returned to the kitchen, picked up Sawyer's and Lucie's orders and hurried back outside with their lunch. While he was setting Lucie's plate of *Makaronia tou Fournou*—a macaroni casserole made with ground meat—in front of her, he noticed her gaze wander across the sidewalk to Ellen's table.

Nikos tensed momentarily when he saw a man in a black *thobe* and a white *gutra* walk up to Ellen. While continuing his duties, giving a stellar performance as an attentive waiter, Nikos approached Ellen's table.

"Saba'a AlKair," the man in the black *thobe* said to Ellen.

Nikos held his breath, waiting for Ellen to respond to the man's good morning greeting. He had rehearsed with her the one thing she was to say to the man in Arabic.

"Ma Ismok?" Ellen asked.

Nikos could see now that the man was quite young—a boy really, not much out of his teens, if that. The youth's black eyes widened, apparently surprised that Ellen would speak to him in Arabic.

"My name is Shabouh," the youth replied.

Ellen's heartbeat pounded an erratic drumroll inside her head. Stay calm, she cautioned herself. This meeting has to come off without a hitch. You're surrounded by seven well-trained operatives, capable of taking this man out at a moment's notice. You're safe. The only thing you have to worry about is doing whatever you can to keep Phila and Faith alive.

"Won't you join me?" Ellen motioned to the chair across from her.

The man nodded, then placed the black briefcase he carried down on top of the table beside Ellen's case. That's when she noticed he wore thin dark gloves. No fingerprints!

Nikos breezed up to the table and held out a menu to Ellen's lunch guest. "May I help you, sir?"

Ignoring the proffered menu, Shabouh glanced up at Nikos. "Water, please. Bottled water."

"Certainly, sir."

The moment Nikos was out of earshot, Shabouh said, "The information you need about the prisoners and the proof of the child's well-being that you requested are in my briefcase." He reached out and patted the case.

"The money is in mine."

"Once we know the prisoners have been freed, you will be given instructions concerning the exchange."

"Did you tell your superiors about my counteroffer of twenty million dollars?" Ellen directed her gaze to the man's dark, pensive eyes. It was often possible for her to detect a person's truthfulness by studying the expression in their eyes.

"Five million and three prisoners in exchange for the child and her nanny. That is the only acceptable deal."

"I can offer more," Ellen told him. "Would thirty million be a more enticing offer?"

The man glared disconcertingly at her. "No."

With a white linen cloth draped over his arm, Nikos returned with the bottled water and set it in front of Shabouh. "Will there be anything else?"

Shabouh shook his head. "Leave us."

Ellen stole a quick glance at Nikos, who smiled at Shabouh and then at her. "Whenever you're ready to order lunch, please let me know."

The moment Nikos left them, Ellen said softly, "How does forty million sound?" She could tell instantly that the young man hesitated as he considered the offer.

"No more bargaining," he told her. "The three prisoners in exchange for the child and her nanny." Shabouh rose from the chair, picked up Ellen's briefcase and then said, "There will be no more contact between us until the prisoners are released from their Menkuraian captivity."

Ellen held her breath until Shabouh walked away from the sidewalk café and down the street. He glanced from side to side and then over his shoulder, obviously checking to make sure he wasn't being followed. Ellen hoped the SIS agent Nikos had assigned to tail this man was able to work under a cloak of invisibility. Just a hint of a double-cross might be enough to end Phila's life. After releasing her pent-up breath, Ellen stood, dropped some money on the table to cover the two drinks, lifted Shabouh's case and walked in the opposite direction.

She strolled briskly along the sidewalk until she reached the corner of Episkopi and Nicosia Streets. Off in the distance, she heard music and laughter. The first festival parade wasn't far away. Without a backward glance, she marched directly toward the Greek Orthodox church on the corner, a three-story, whitewashed stone building. She went inside and sat down in one of the back pews, then bowed her head and waited.

Just as they had planned, Nikos, disguised in a priest's robes, met Ellen twenty minutes after she entered the church. He came up the aisle, sat beside her, and called her *agkelos* in a hushed tone. She stood as he did and walked with him toward the altar. They turned to the right and Nikos guided her through several rooms, then straight to a back entrance and out into the alleyway behind the church. She immediately noticed the brown van parked about ten feet away, and made no objections when Nikos took the briefcase from her and knocked on the van's double back doors. One door opened and a dark-sleeved arm reached out and took the case.

Nikos herded her quickly back inside the church. They stood together in a small, dimly lit storage room.

"How long will it take?" she asked.

"Not long. They're set up to dust for fingerprints, check for possible DNA samples and make sure there are no bugs or bombs anywhere in the briefcase."

"I have to admit that it didn't occur to me that Theo might be the real target and this entire scheme simply a smoke screen." Ellen offered Nikos a weak smile.

"It's an unlikely scenario," Nikos admitted. "But better to play it safe than sorry. I doubt there's a bomb inside, but I wouldn't rule out a bug of some sort."

"Were you able to get a picture of Shabouh?" Ellen asked.

"Yeah, I should have gotten at least one good shot with my handy little camera."

"I didn't see a thing. You must have had the camera hidden quite well."

He lifted his arm, pulled back the robe's sleeve and exposed the silver wristwatch. "What we have here, my dear Ms. Denby, is a smashing little invention straight from MI6. It tells the time and takes photos at the same time."

"Something straight out of a James Bond movie." Ellen laughed.

Nikos adjusted the face of his wristwatch. "This little gadget could be something in a 007 movie, but believe me, other than useful gadgets, I don't have much in common with Ian Flemming's glamorous super spy."

"A lot more real danger and a lot less glamour, huh?"

"Definitely." Nikos smiled, but there was a quiet sadness in his eyes. "I'm wondering if our man will be able to track Shabouh once he leaves Golnar. He probably knows he's being followed, so it won't be easy to keep tabs on him. And it would be fairly easy to get lost in the festival crowd."

"Did you by any chance recognize Shabouh? Was he anyone you knew?"

Nikos shook his head. "Afraid not. But I'll give these SIS chaps the watch, and when they develop the film they can run our young rebel's picture through the Firm's data bank."

"Theo and Dia must be half out of their minds waiting for us to return to the villa."

"No doubt. But Matt assured me that he and his wife would do their best to help keep up Theo's and Dia's spirits."

"Their spirits will be lifted once they see proof that their child is still alive,'' Ellen said. ''The only thing worse than having your child kidnapped is not knowing if he…or she is alive or dead. Until you have proof one way or another, you would wonder forever.''

Nikos's gaze raked over her face, as if searching for some hidden meaning to her words. She'd said too much, made him curious.

''I've dealt with enough child kidnapping cases to be able to put myself in a mother's place,'' Ellen explained. ''If there is no proof the child is dead, especially if a body isn't found, a mother's heart or a father's heart would never accept the truth. Deep down inside, a kernel of hope would exist. But once you see the proof…'' A memory flashed through Ellen's mind. She shivered uncontrollably. Another flash, more vivid than the first. *No, God, no! Not now…not here with Nikos.*

''Ellen, what's wrong?'' He grasped her upper arms.

''Nothing. I just had a sudden chill.'' She jerked away from him.

''You went white and started trembling. You acted as if you'd seen a ghost, so don't tell me it was nothing.''

How could she tell him the truth? She had seen a ghost…a ghost that lived inside her mind, inside her heart…a ghost that never left her.

A loud knock on the door saved Ellen from further explanations. Nikos opened the door. A tall redheaded guy wearing typical vacationer's street clothes came in carrying the black briefcase.

''It's clean,'' he said. ''No bomb, no bugs and not a sign of a print or anything identifiable.''

Nikos removed his wristwatch and handed it to the SIS agent. ''These photos are top priority. I want a report ASAP.''

''Yes, sir. You'll be notified in the usual manner.'' He handed Nikos the briefcase. ''There are only two items in the case—a letter with instructions concerning the prisoners in Menkura and a videotape showing the Constantine child is alive, as of yesterday.''

''A tape, huh? Is it something the parents should see?'' Nikos asked.

The redheaded agent shook his head. ''God, no!''

Wasim Ibn Fadil returned to his hotel room, placed the black leather briefcase on the bed and then discarded the *thobe* and the *gutra* he'd worn in his Shabouh guise, along with his gloves. As instructed, he opened the briefcase, then smiled broadly when he saw the stacks of thousand dollar bills. A million dollars in U.S. currency! And to think Theo Constantine had been willing to give him forty times that in exchange for the child. That much money could have done a great deal for the Al'alim. But even twice that was not worth as much as the return of Hakeem Ibn Fadil. His uncle's name alone brought smiles to the lips of his followers and hope to the hearts of the downtrodden. Upon the great Hakeem's return, there would be cheering in the streets and prayers of thanks offered continuously.

After removing the stacked bills from the briefcase, Wasim counted the money, then patiently placed the cash into the empty suitcase he had brought with him when he checked into the hotel earlier today. Glancing at the clock in his room, he saw that he had over two hours before his plane left Dareh.

As he waited, he went over the precise plans he would follow upon leaving Dareh. Knowing he would no doubt be followed by someone, he would do nothing to disguise himself before leaving Golnar. Wasim's father had told him that despite the warnings to Theo Constantine, the man was no fool—he had hired a renowned agency to handle the negotiations. And that agency had ties to various U.S. government agencies, and perhaps British agencies as well.

Wasim would take a plane directly to Athens, check into Room 24 at the small Aegon Hotel on Leoforos. He would stay overnight and leave the following morning, carrying an empty suitcase. The money would be left behind in a pillow slip and picked up by a maid and given to Wasim's friend Aban, who was already in Athens. Wasim's journey home would take several days; he would travel from Athens to Rome and from Rome to Hungary and from there to Turkey, where he would lose whoever was tracking him. If all went as planned, by the time he reached Subria, his uncle Hakeem would be a free man.

After viewing the videotape of Phila Constantine on a VCR in the back of the SIS van behind the church, Ellen disagreed with the agent's stern warning that the parents shouldn't see the tape. Nikos sided with the agent.

"Haven't Theo and Dia been through enough?" Nikos turned off the VCR and popped the tape out of the machine. "If they see this, it will rip them up inside. Phila sitting on that dirty cot, holding a faxed copy of the front page of yesterday's Dareh newspaper, tears streaming down her little battered face—"

Ellen held out her hand. "Give me the tape, please."

Glaring at the tape he held, Nikos hesitated. "You can't honestly think they'd want to see their child in such a pitiful condition. Isn't it best if they—"

"You may be the superspy, but I'm the expert in this situation, not you." Ellen wiggled the fingers on her outstretched hand. "Give me the tape."

Reluctantly Nikos handed over the tape, all the while scowling at her. "If you're determined to do this, then show it to only Theo."

Ellen returned the tape to the black leather case, placing it carefully beside the documents that held the instructions about the three prisoners to be rescued from Menkura.

"Theo's limousine is waiting for us," Nikos told her. "We'll discuss this further on the ride back to the villa."

Ellen waited outside the van while Nikos spoke to the agent for several minutes. When he joined her, sans his priestly robe, they reentered the church and walked out together, straight to the waiting limo.

Crowds of Golnarians lined the streets, dancing, singing and drinking Ouzo. The Autumn Festival had begun and already the city had taken on a carnival atmosphere. Ellen's mind rushed back fifteen years to the day she met Nikos during the Summer Festival. Parades and parties and masked balls. Food and wine and flowers. And such gaiety. Now as in the past, laughter wafted up and down the streets, mixing and mingling with the light, rhythmical music. *Tsif-teteli* and *rembetiko* songs.

Just as Nikos opened the limousine door for Ellen, they heard a loud shout. When they looked up, they saw a group of brightly clad young women, tambourines in their hands, dancing down the street. Ellen tried to stop remembering, willed herself not to recall that first instant when she'd seen Nikos. Her heart had stopped at that very moment and when she'd breathed again, her life had never been the same. She'd been swept away by his masculine charisma and the exotic spell of festival time.

Ellen shook off the veil of memories, then slid into the back seat of the limo. Nikos joined her. The minute the chauffeur started the engine, Nikos turned to Ellen.

"I remember a day similar to this. A summer festival and a beautiful young American girl."

Ellen crossed her arms over her chest and avoided looking directly at Nikos. Ignoring his comment, she said, "It'll take us forever to get through Dareh. The streets are clogged with celebrators."

"I'm sure Peneus knows a way out of town taking some back streets that won't be as crowded."

"The sooner we return to the villa the better. Dia and Theo need to see the proof that their daughter is still alive."

"I realize that Theo put you in charge of the negotiations process, and therefore the proof that Phila is still alive falls under your jurisdiction, but—"

"No ifs, ands or buts. The subject is closed. Theo and Dia will see this tape." Ellen patted the briefcase she held in her lap.

"It's not necessary. We've both seen the tape. We can verify that it proves Phila and Ms. Sheridan are alive. There's no need to do more than assure Theo and Dia of that fact."

"You really don't understand, do you?"

"What is there to understand? You're willing to torture them with the sight of Phila dirty, ragged, trembling, in tears and badly bruised, where I would spare them that horrible sight."

"Is that what you think you'd be doing—sparing them? Ha!"

"Can you honestly tell me that if it was your child, you could bear to see her in such pitiful shape?"

"God, yes!" An adrenaline rush surged through Ellen, flushing her face, flaring her nostrils and putting fire in her eyes. "If it were my child, I'd weep with joy to see her alive. I'd need to see her alive, no matter what her condition. Alive means hope. Alive means a chance for survival."

Nikos stared at her in disbelief. "But once they see that tape, they won't be able to erase Phila's pathetic little image from their minds."

"Don't you get it? Dammit, Nikos, what they'll see on this tape isn't half as horrible as what they've already imagined. The images they have in their minds now are so horrific that this—" she slapped her hand down on the briefcase "—will actually give them some relief."

"You know this for a fact? You've dealt with something like this before?"

"I know it for a fact," she told him, amazed at her own ability to control the anguish threatening to overpower her. "If this were a tape showing Phila Constantine's bloody, lifeless body, proving that she was dead, I'd show it to her parents."

"I don't know you at all, do I? What kind of person would—"

"Don't you dare chastise me. Don't you dare judge me."

"I've spent a lifetime fraternizing with some of the most vile, inhuman creatures on earth and there have been times when I've feared that I'd lost my own soul." Nikos reached out to touch her face, but suddenly dropped his hand to his side. "What is it that I don't know about you? How did you lose your soul?"

She closed her eyes for a brief moment, shutting out the sight of Nikos's accusatory stare. *Why don't you tell him?* a taunting inner voice dared. *Tell him and then see if he's so quick to judge.*

"If my child had been kidnapped and held for ransom— whatever that ransom might be—and I was told he or she was alive...or dead, I'd want to see the proof with my own eyes. If he were dead, I'd have to see his body. The heart plays dirty tricks on us, giving us hope when there is none, or taking away all hope when we should keep hoping."

"Ellen?"

"I haven't lost my soul," she told him. "I'm simply on guard twenty-four seven, protecting myself." Always on her guard, never letting down her defenses, knowing the staggering price one paid for caring too much, loving too deeply, and being defenseless against evil.

"I'm sorry," Nikos said. "I have no right to judge you."

She turned from him and faced the other side of the

limousine, determined to not allow his apology to affect her in any way.

"Ellen?" He touched her shoulder.

She tensed and shrugged off his hand. "Please, leave me alone."

Thankfully he did as she requested.

Lucie Evans watched Phila Constantine's bruised, dirty, tearstained, five-foot-high face on the big screen TV in the media room on the first floor of the villa. The child's huge brown eyes stared pleadingly at the people assembled to view the videotape. Dia and Theo. Sir Matthew and Princess Adele. Nikos. And the five Dundee agents. Phila's tiny, quivering voice, punctuated with panicky sobs, echoed through the surround sound system. Ellen stood directly behind the sofa, her hand resting on Dia Constantine's shoulder, as if channeling strength and bravery to Phila's mother through her touch. Theo and the princess sat on either side of Dia.

Lucie couldn't bear to watch. Twice during the first showing of the five minute tape, she'd closed her eyes. The second time, she moved farther and farther back in the room until she stood near the door. She feared the third viewing would be her undoing. No matter how many kidnapping cases she'd worked on for the FBI, she'd never learned to distance herself from the parents' emotions when a child was the victim.

Using the remote control she held in her hand, Ellen rewound the tape. Lucie breathed a sigh of relief. Standing in the back of the media room, Nikos Khalid continued staring at the now blank screen.

"Theo, there's no need for you and Dia to watch this again," Nikos said. "We need to study the tape, but—"

"No!" Dia called, her voice strong and steady. "No, I want to watch it again. Please." With tears trickling down her cheeks and a fragile smile on her lips, she turned to her husband. "You understand, don't you?"

Theo, his own face damp with tears, nodded. "Yes, I understand."

"Well, I don't," Nikos said.

Dia glanced over her shoulder and fixed her watery gaze on Nikos. "Phila is alive. This tape proves that as of yesterday, she was alive. I know she's frightened and—" Dia gasped for air "—I know from seeing that ugly bruise on her face that someone hit her. But she isn't dead. Don't you see, my worst fear has been eliminated."

"It's all right." Theo wrapped his arm around Dia's shoulders and hugged her close. "Nikos doesn't understand because he has no children of his own. He's thinking of us, of how difficult it is for us to see Phila frightened and crying...and hurt."

"In the days since she was taken, I have imagined far worse," Dia admitted. "In my nightmares... Oh, God, in my nightmares, she..." Dia burst into fresh tears.

"Why don't we take a break?" Ellen suggested. "Theo, you and Dia should take a walk, get a bite to eat, talk things over. Let us study the tape, then you and Dia can return and watch it as many times as you'd like."

"That's a good idea." Theo rose to his feet and held out his hands to his wife.

Princess Adele stood up beside Theo. "Let's put on our wraps and you and Theo and Matt and I go out on the terrace and watch the sunset."

Dia accepted Theo's outstretched hands and allowed him to help her to her feet. As her husband and best friend led her from the media room, she paused momentarily and glanced back at Ellen.

"Ms. Denby, I want to thank you," Dia said.

Ellen nodded.

"We're going to get Phila back, aren't we?" Dia's gaze

fastened on Ellen's solemn face. "We have hope now, don't we?"

"Yes," Ellen replied. "We have hope."

Lucie turned and rushed out of the room. If she had stayed another minute, she would have made a fool of herself. On the verge of tears, she couldn't hurry down the hall fast enough. She didn't know how Ellen did it—how she remained so untouched by the contents of the videotape and by the Constantines' suffering. Talk about a steel magnolia!

Lucie shoved open the office door and sighed with relief when she saw the room was empty. No servants cleaning up. No Dundee agents making a beeline there before her. She bent over, touched her toes, repeated the process a dozen times, then stood up straight and took a deep breath. Everyone had their own way of calming themselves, of regaining their composure. Some people counted to ten. Some people, like Ellen, meditated. Lucie exercised. A trick she'd learned as a teenager.

"That's one of the reasons you weren't cut out to be a federal agent," Sawyer McNamara said as he entered the office.

Gasping, Lucie whirled around and gaped at Sawyer. Damn irritating man. Mr. Go-by-the-book McNamara. The guy thought he was perfect and expected everyone else to be perfect, too. Her experiences with him when they'd both worked for the Bureau had not endeared him to her. He never made allowances for human foibles.

"Jump up my—"

"Now, now, Ms. Evans, is that any way for a lady to speak?"

"We've covered this ground before—I'm not a lady and you're not my boss. So, get off my back. Don't take it out on me because Ellen prefers tall, dark and dangerous Nikos to got-a-cob-up-my-ass you.'' Lucie punctuated her statement by pointing her index finger directly at Sawyer.

Sawyer frowned. ''You can stop beating me over the head with that particular club. I get the picture. And despite what you may think, I'm not the kind of guy who falls apart just because a woman rejects me.''

''Okay, I accept that that might be true in your case, if you'll accept the fact that, in my case, showing normal human emotion doesn't make me an inferior agent.''

''Despite your thirst to right the wrongs of the world, you don't have the type of personality it takes to be a top-notch agent, either for the FBI or for Dundee's. You should have chosen a profession more suited to your personality.''

Lucie gritted her teeth and groaned. ''Who died and made you the king of the world? You have such a narrow view of life that—''

''You two at it again?'' Domingo Shea stopped in the open doorway. ''Don't let Ellen hear you squabbling or one of you will be on the next plane back to the States.''

''We aren't squabbling,'' Lucie said. ''Just swapping opinions.''

''You were swapping opinions loud enough so I could hear y'all from halfway down the hall. When this assignment is over, I'm going to recommend to Ellen that she put a memo in both of your personal files that y'all are not to work together ever again.''

''Suits me fine,'' Lucie said.

''Where is Ellen?'' Sawyer asked.

''She and Nikos are still in the media room.''

''What's your take on this guy?'' Sawyer glared at Lucie, giving her a silent warning not to respond to the question he'd asked Dom.

Dom shrugged. ''Ellen says he's okay. That's good enough for me.''

''What was that all about this morning right before the

exchange in Dareh…when you left your post and came over to the café? I got the impression something was up."

"Yeah, something was. Our Mr. Khalid forgot to tell me or Worth that he had a backup team of his own stationed across the street in the upstairs of two buildings. Until he clarified the situation, I thought maybe our kidnappers had brought along their own snipers and I couldn't figure out why."

"Snipers? Professional snipers?"

"Look, Sawyer, my guess is that Nikos Khalid—or whatever his real name might be—is an operative for either our CIA or the Brits' SIS. Ellen's not giving away any of his secrets, but she's put her trust in him on this assignment. That should tell us something."

"Yeah, you're right. Ellen's too smart to fall for a line of bull—even from an old lover—so that means he's on the up and up."

"But knowing that, you still don't trust him, do you?" Dom grinned. "Professional gut reaction or personal?"

"I don't know," Sawyer admitted. "Probably personal. But I'm going to keep my eye on Khalid just the same."

"So you were right," Nikos said. "Seeing the videotape actually helped Dia and Theo."

"It gave them hope." Ellen punched the remote and started the tape.

"I won't question you again about anything dealing directly with the negotiations or with handling Theo and Dia. I concede that it's your area of expertise. But I'd like for you to agree that I'm in charge when it comes to any rescues or prison breakouts. Those would fall under my jurisdiction."

"I and my agents are well-trained and quite capable of—"

"Shea and Cordell, maybe," Nikos conceded. "They

have special military backgrounds. But neither a rescue attempt nor a prison breakout is a job for a former policewoman or a couple of former FBI agents.''

"I'll agree that if—and that's a big if—we attempt a rescue, then Lucie and Sawyer stay here. Or if God forbid we're force to go through with a prison breakout, they will remain behind. But I will be a part of any team that leaves Golnar.'' When Nikos started to respond, she held up a restraining hand. "That is not up for negotiation.''

"You and Lucie stay,'' Nikos suggested. "Send McNamara with us.''

"Don't look now, Mr. Khalid, but your male chauvinism is showing.''

Before Nikos could defend himself, Worth Cordell interrupted. "There's a phone call for you, Khalid. He said it was very important that he speak to you immediately.''

"Headquarters,'' Nikos said. "Maybe it's some good news.''

"We sure could use some about now.'' Ellen exchanged a pensive look with Nikos, then they followed Worth out of the media room and down the hall to Theo's office.

Chapter 10

While Nikos spoke to Gerald Townsend, Ellen assembled her agents at the conference table. She'd made photo copies of the documents that had been inside the briefcase along with the videotape. Each agent had a copy to look over during their discussion.

"We have one week to gain the release of these three men from the Nawar Prison in Menkura," Ellen explained. "Nawar is located on the coast. Security is tight. No one has ever successfully broken out of Nawar."

"What about diplomatic attempts to secure their release?" Lucie asked.

"Of course, we'll continue trying to find a way to persuade the Menkuraian prime minister to release these men, but the odds are against us." Ellen glanced from Worth to Dom. "If we are left with no other choice than to break these men out of—"

"You're actually willing to do that?" Sawyer asked. "You'll free three known terrorists?"

"As I said, if we're left with no other choice, we will formulate a plan to free these men. Nikos has a team of his own. Highly trained professionals who will work with us."

"Mercenaries, you mean," Sawyer said.

"They're trained to do this kind of job, the way Dom and Worth were trained." Ellen pointed to the file. "The identities of two of the prisoners the Al'alim want released weren't a surprise to us. Shakir Abu Lufti and Jamsheed Abd Hamid, both top-ranking men in the organization, were captured in the Battle of the Night six months ago. But the third prisoner is someone I've never heard of, nor has Nikos."

"What's his name?" Dom asked.

"Musa Ben Arif," Ellen replied. "Despite the fact that Abu Lufti and Abd Hamid are valuable to the Al'alim, they were replaceable. We all know how these terrorist cells work—often independently of one another. One leader is killed or taken captive, another man moves up the ranks and takes his place. So if Abu Lufti and Abd Hamid aren't worth more to the Al'alim than forty million dollars, then that leaves us with one conclusion—Musa Ben Arif is worth more than his weight in gold."

"If he were that important to the Al'alim, we would have heard of him," Worth said. "Unless..." His brown eyes widened as realization dawned.

"Unless Musa Ben Arif is an alias," Ellen said.

Nikos finished his conversation, then turned to the Dundee agents assembled in Theo's office. "Good news and bad news," he told them. "We now have a few more pieces to add to the puzzle about who kidnapped Phila and why the three Al'alim prisoners are worth more than any amount of money."

All eyes fixed on Nikos.

"If we're going to be here for a while, I suggest we get

Mrs. Panopoulas to fix sandwiches and coffee so that we can have dinner in here,'' Ellen said.

''Yes, that's an excellent idea,'' Nikos agreed. ''We have a great deal to discuss and some decisions to make. And afterward, we'll have to inform Theo about what's going on and allow him to make the final decision, since it is his daughter's life that's at stake.''

''This doesn't sound good,'' Dom said. ''Exactly what did you find out?

''I'll ring the kitchen and speak to Mrs. Panopoulas.'' Lucie rose to her feet. ''It'll take only a minute.''

Joining the others, Nikos sat in the chair at the opposite end from where Ellen presided at the head of the table. ''First I request that you make no inquiries about my source of information.'' He glanced at Ellen. ''Ellen has vouched for my trustworthiness, so you can be certain that I am not the enemy. And I believe she can assure you that my information is reliable and accurate.''

Ellen nodded.

''Look, we've pretty much figured out that you're in the cloak-and-dagger business,'' Lucie said as she returned to the table, after phoning in their dinner order to the kitchen. ''You've gone so deep undercover that you probably don't even remember your real name. What we don't know for sure is whether you're working for our government or for the Brits.''

The corners of Nikos's mouth lifted in the first stage of a quirky smile, but he ignored Lucie's statement. ''The man in the photos I took—our Shabouh from the Odyssea Café—has been identified as Wasim Ibn Fadil.''

''Ibn Fadil?'' Several agents spoke in unison.

''He is the son of Omar Ibn Fadil and the nephew of Hakeem Ibn Fadil. Wasim is only twenty, but he's no servant, no common soldier. If his father sent him to handle the exchange, that alone is a sign of how important this deal is to them.''

''That really isn't news,'' Sawyer said. ''We already know that something big is going down here, that whoever the hell this third prisoner is, he's worth a great deal to them.''

''All the more reason we don't want to free those men,'' Nikos said. ''I should have more information on Musa Ben Arif in the next twenty-four to thirty-six hours, but in the meantime there's something far more important for us to discuss.''

''More important than deciding whether to free three dangerous terrorists and let them loose on the world again?'' Lucie asked.

''There's a good chance we won't have to take that route.'' Nikos focused on Ellen. Her heart skipped a beat; she suspected she already knew what he was going to say. ''We've discovered where the Al'alim are holding Phila and her nanny.''

A rumble of surprise rose from the agents, and they quickly began talking among themselves.

''Quiet down.'' Ellen spoke only a bit louder, but the intensity of her enunciation garnered the desired effect.

Everyone snapped to attention and quieted. Complete silence. Total concentration.

''Where are they being held?'' Ellen asked Nikos.

''In Subria, as we suspected. In a small village called Taraneh. Phila and Faith are being kept in the basement of a building that was once a school, but was bombed several years ago. The interior isn't much more than rubble now.''

''Are your informants one hundred percent sure?'' Sawyer asked.

''As sure as they can be,'' Nikos replied.

''Damn!'' Dom scooted back his chair and stood.

"What are our odds, if we decide to go in after them?" Worth asked.

"With the right team, our odds are good." Nikos glanced from person to person. "Dom, Worth, Ellen, I and several of my men will form a rescue team. We go in quickly, free Phila and Faith and get the hell out even quicker than we went in. If we don't run into any trouble, it should be fairly simple. They keep only one guard outside the building and one inside, twenty-four seven."

"Sounds too easy," Dom said.

"Why will several of your men make up part of the rescue team?" Sawyer asked.

"They've had military training," Nikos replied.

"Nikos and I have already agreed on the team we'll use for any rescue attempts," Ellen explained to her group. "It's a compromise and has nothing to do with my doubting either Sawyer's or Lucie's skills."

Sawyer nodded. The others remained silent.

"All right, what do we do? Do we go in after them and attempt a rescue, on the information Nikos has?" Ellen asked.

"Yes," Dom said. "If we can save the child and her nanny without having to free those damn Al'alim prisoners, then I'm all for it."

Worth nodded. "Count me in."

"Yes, I agree it's the lesser of two evils," Lucie said.

"Let's make it unanimous." Sawyer looked point-blank at Nikos. "Either way—trying to rescue them or exchanging them for the prisoners—we run a risk of not getting them out alive. But I'd say our chances are better with a surprise rescue attempt."

"Then we're agreed." Nikos stood. "Before we proceed, we need to get Theo's permission. I'll speak with him, then we can make our plans. We'll be receiving maps and directions via fax later this evening. And once we have

Theo's okay, I'll need to recruit one more member for our team. The surest, safest way to get in and out of Taraneh is by helicopter. I have one chopper pilot, but we need another topnotch man.''

''Matt O'Brien,'' Ellen said. ''He was a pave low pilot with the Air Force. There's not a helicopter in existence that he can't fly under any conditions.''

''Do you suppose we could persuade Sir Matthew to go on one last Dundee mission?'' Dom asked.

''To help rescue the Constantines' child? Yes, he'll do it,'' Ellen said.

''Then I'll speak to Matt after I talk to Theo,'' Nikos said.

Faith's heartbeat accelerated, but she didn't move when she heard the door open. Why had the guard returned? They still had food and water. Surely they didn't want to tape another video! Without lifting her head, she glanced up. Two men entered the room. Both with rifles. Both dirty and grizzly, with long hair and heavy beards. One stood in the doorway, his weapon trained on her and Phila, who sat in her lap, her little arms draped around Faith's neck.

One man spoke rapidly to the other in Subrian Arabic and the taller of the two men stormed across the room toward where Phila and she sat. He reached out and grabbed Phila's small arm, which made her cling even more fiercely to Faith. She noticed the odd tattooed emblem on the back of his large, leather-brown hand. The man snarled as he tried to pull Phila from Faith's arms.

''Leave her alone.'' Faith batted at the man, hammering her fists against his rock-hard chest. *''Min Fadilak.''* Please was one of the few Arabic words she knew.

When he released Phila, Faith sighed with relief. But that relief was short-lived. The man drew back his hand and slapped Faith so hard that she tumbled backward onto the cot. While she tried to right herself, despite the stinging pain radiating through her face, he snatched Phila away from her.

Phila screamed relentlessly and called Faith's name between frantic cries. By the time Faith managed to get to her feet, the man holding Phila had grabbed the child's hair and jerked back her head while the other guard gagged her. Faith rushed toward them, her strong, protective maternal instincts coming into play, despite her own fear. She hurled herself at the taller of the two, who still held Phila. As she barreled into him, he flung Phila at the other man and turned on Faith.

When she saw the other guard taking Phila away, Faith cried out and tried to move around the man blocking her path.

"Where is he taking her?" Faith demanded. "Please, she's just a little girl. She—"

The man with the tattooed hand slapped Faith again. She fell to her knees from the force of the blow. Her vision blurred. An intense, throbbing pain momentarily stole her breath. Then the metallic taste of blood flooded her mouth. *Oh, God, help me,* she prayed. *And protect Phila because I can't.*

Faith felt him hovering over her, could feel his booted feet punching her hips. She looked up as he bent over her, his mouth open in a frightening grin. Several teeth were missing from the bottom row. He gripped her forearms and lifted her to her feet. She staggered on wobbly legs, but willed herself to stand and look this devil right in the eyes.

The tattooed hand reached out and circled her throat in a tight stranglehold. She gasped for air. Was he going to kill her? Choke her to death right here and now?

Her entire life did not flash before her eyes. No kaleidoscope of memories. Only an overwhelming sense of regret for what her future might have held. Love. A husband.

Children. All lost to her forever. She closed her eyes and prayed.

As she prepared herself to die, Faith suddenly felt that large, sweaty hand grab the edge of her nightgown and rip it apart from neck to navel. Her eyes flew open. Her tormentor shoved the edges of her gown apart until he exposed her breasts. The cool air hit her naked skin, chilling her, warning her of the man's intent.

She slapped at him, hit him, struggled with all her might, but he only laughed. His callused hands clutched her breasts roughly. She cried out in pain and fear. He was going to rape her and there was nothing she could do to stop him. A part of her wished that he had strangled her.

His tattooed hand slid lower, over her belly and across her navel. Just as he fondled her mound, the other guard returned and yelled something in Arabic. Her attacker stopped, glanced over his shoulder and replied to his comrade. Reluctantly, as if he were considering his options, he shoved her away from him. Losing her balance, she toppled over and landed on the hard dirt floor.

For several minutes after the two men left, closing and locking the door after them, Faith sat on the floor. Tremors racked her body. She could still feel his hands on her, still smell his sour breath, still hear his labored breathing. With shaky hands, she grasped the edges of her torn gown and lapped one side over the other, then twisted the pieces into a tight knot.

What had the other man said to him that made him leave so quickly? Would he come back? Was it only a matter of time before he attacked her again?

Faith shoved herself up onto her knees, then grabbed the edge of the cot and pulled herself up on her feet. Was there anything in this spare, damp, smelly room that she could use as a weapon? Her gaze skimmed over every inch of her underground prison. But before she could mentally reg-

ister any items she might be able to use in self-defense, her
head began swimming. She quickly sat on the cot.

No matter what happened to her, she couldn't just give
up and die. That would be too easy. She refused to succumb
to her fears, no matter how real they were. With a steely
determination, Faith swore aloud, vowing to heaven and to
hell that somehow, someway, Phila and she were going to
come out of this ordeal alive.

Long after everyone else had gone to bed, except Domingo Shea who was on guard duty tonight, Nikos sat
alone in Theo's office. After pouring himself a glass of
Three Kings brandy and placing the crystal goblet on the
sofa arm, he removed his black boots and stretched out his
long legs. Reaching behind him, he grasped the brandy,
then swirled it around before taking his first sip. Unless
word reached him that there was a good reason to abort the
mission, tomorrow morning they would take the Dundee
jet to Southern Subria, which was still free from rebel control The five of them would join Geoff Monday and his
men. Tomorrow evening they would go by helicopter as
close to Taraneh as they dared, then meet up with two more
team members, who'd have ground transportation waiting
for them. Theo had given them the go-ahead, and Matt
O'Brien had immediately volunteered to join them in case
the helicopter Monday acquired needed two pilots. And
even if it didn't, taking along a backup pilot was just good
common sense. The price to rent a chopper would be exorbitant, but money was not even a consideration. This operation alone would run into several million. The Dundee
agents didn't come cheap and they got extra for hazardous
duty—and by God, running a rescue attempt into enemy
territory was hazardous, especially when that enemy was
one of the most feared terrorist organizations in the world.
Add to the cost of equipment and the Dundee agents, the

price of Monday's men, former SAS agents, now retired, but like Shea and Cordell, highly skilled professionals.

Nikos knew their only chance of pulling off the rescue without a hitch depended on their one ace in the hole—the element of surprise. If the Al'alim had only a couple of men guarding their captives, that meant they were damned sure nobody outside that specific cell within their large organization knew Phila and Faith's whereabouts.

He'd feel a lot better if an SAS team was going in, but that wasn't an option. Gerald was giving him all the unofficial assistance possible, risking his own career by doing so. There was no way the British government could become directly involved, no way their army of elite soldiers would be allowed to attempt the rescue themselves. Nikos would be working with a small but highly trained team and without backup, which left no room for mistakes. One error could be fatal to the entire group, as well as to the two hostages. And adding to his worries, there was Ellen. She was one concern he could do without; but persuading her to stay behind would take an act of God.

You can't allow her presence to distract you from the job at hand, he reminded himself. He couldn't put Ellen's welfare above the success of the operation. But how would he be able to ignore the fact that his past actions were responsible for the person she was today—a hard-as-nails, fearless warrior woman. If his selfishness and youthful lust hadn't overruled his common sense, he wouldn't have taken even the slightest risk with Mary Ellen Denby's life. But because of him, she was here on Golnar, the CEO of Dundee's, when otherwise she'd be back in the United States, with a normal, safe existence. It was his fault that the new Ellen Denby was far more afraid of living than she was of dying.

A persistent, repetitive knock on the office door snapped Nikos from his guilt-ridden thoughts. "Who is it?"

The door eased open. Nikos watched Ellen enter, then pause several feet away from the sofa.

"Is something wrong?" he asked.

"No, I'm just restless."

"So you came looking for me?" He slid his legs off the sofa until his sock-clad feet touched the floor.

"You weren't in your bedroom, so I figured this is where you'd be. I guess you're having a difficult time relaxing, just as I am."

He patted the sofa cushion beside him and held up his glass of brandy. "Come over and join me."

She hesitated for a minute, then came toward him, her shoulders squared and her chin slightly tilted. Her stance told him that she wanted him to know she wasn't afraid to be alone with him. She glanced at the sofa, then at him.

"I think I'll fix myself a drink," she said.

"Try the brandy. I recommend the Three Kings brand. It's a favorite here in Golnar. Theo's favorite, although he could afford a far more expensive brand."

She opened the bar, removed the bottle of brandy and poured a small amount into a goblet, then turned to Nikos, saluted him with the glass and downed a large swig of liquor. He watched in utter amazement when she did little more than moan softly and release a huffing breath. He'd seen grown men cough and splutter after a good taste of the hard stuff.

With the crystal goblet in her hand, she crossed the room and sat down beside him. "I can take care of myself on this mission."

"I'm sure you can."

"None of you will have to pick up the slack for me. I've done this sort of thing before. More than once."

"Have you really?"

"No, I've never tried a rescue in the hills of Subria, if that's what you're asking." She kicked off her shoes, lifted her legs and bent her knees, curving her calves along the backs of her thighs. "But I've risked my life on more than one occasion. And this is far from the first abduction case in which I and my agents have intervened."

"What makes you think I'm concerned about you?"

She shrugged. He sipped on his brandy.

She snuggled into the lush, leather sofa and lifted her glass to her lips. He tried to stop himself from staring at her, from watching the way her mouth parted to accept the liquor, the way she licked her bottom lip as she set the glass aside, the way a slight shiver rippled through her body as the brandy settled in her belly. But Ellen Denby was not a woman a man could ignore. Even wearing a pair of black tights and an oversize pink cotton shirt, she couldn't disguise the voluptuousness of her figure. With her face bare of makeup and her short cropped hair brushed away from her forehead, she was breathtakingly beautiful. As a young woman, she'd been lovely beyond words, but now there was a ripe sensuality about her that age and experience had created.

"You're staring," she told him.

"I am concerned," he admitted. "I'd rather you didn't go along on this rescue mission."

"But I've explained that I'm no amateur when it comes to—"

"The problem is me, not you."

"I don't understand." She frowned.

"I'm not usually personally involved with a team member when we undertake a mission. If I'm worrying about you, I won't be at my best."

"We're not personally involved. We haven't been in fifteen years."

"You know better. The moment we saw each other again, we connected."

"We should have learned from our past history that we're bad for each other."

"Maybe we were back then, but not now. You'd know what you're getting this time around. So would I."

He shot across the length of the sofa, grabbed her by the nape of her neck and pressed her backward against the arm-rest. With amazement bright in her blue eyes, she gazed up at him as her lips parted on a startled sigh.

He whispered her name against her lips. "Mary Ellen."

She tensed. "I'm not Mary Ellen."

"Do you think it matters what your name is or that you're fifteen years older now, and a great deal more experienced?" He rubbed his jaw against her cheek, soft beard against even softer skin. "You're a different woman and I am a different man, and yet what was between us is still there, as potent as ever."

"Animal magnetism? Lust?"

"Call it what you will, but we both know it is more powerful than anything we had experienced before our first time together or since."

"You're wrong. It isn't—"

He silenced her with a kiss. Powerful. Demanding. For a moment she responded, but then she shoved against his chest and struggled to free herself. When he lifted himself up and off her, she gasped for air, then stood and glared at him.

"I make the rules. I have the power," she told him. "Not you. Not any man alive. All your macho swagger might have impressed the hell out of little Mary Ellen from Cartersville, Georgia, but not me. I can take or leave dangerous, exciting men like you. You don't possess some hypnotic sexual spell over me. Got that straight?"

He stared at her, studying her as he listened to her tirade.

"Answer me, dammit!" Her threatening expression dared him.

"Yes, I understand." He rose to his feet and reached out for her, but she sidestepped his grasp. "I might have made the rules when we first met, but you were the one with power, even then. You're the one who cast a hypnotic sexual spell over me. Otherwise I'd never have stayed two weeks with you, and my heart wouldn't have been ripped apart by leaving you."

Their gazes linked together, but he didn't try to touch her again. Nikos could only imagine how deep her emotional scars went, the irreversible wounds inflicted by Hakeem. Nikos had spent years trying to avoid Hakeem, staying one step ahead of him and his insane thirst for revenge. If he'd known what that monster had done to Ellen, he would have turned the tables on his most deadly enemy. He would have become the hunter and Hakeem the prey. A part of him wished that Hakeem was still alive so that he could kill him with his bare hands.

"You're feeling sorry for me, aren't you?" Ellen practically snarled the words.

"I feel guilty," he told her. "And angry."

She nodded. He felt her relax, sensed it on some emotional level where the two of them were connected. She rubbed her hands together nervously, then crossed her arms over her chest and rubbed up and down on her arms.

"I was lying. To myself and to you," Ellen said. "As much as I'd like to, I can't lump you in there with the rest of the world's male population. You affect me differently. I haven't felt anything... I haven't felt any emotions that I couldn't control since... It scares the hell out of me that I can't stop what I'm feeling now. Don't you see, Nikos, you could still hurt me. No one has had that kind of power over me in fourteen years."

"I swear to you that I'll never do anything to hurt you again." He wanted to take her in his arms, to hold and comfort her.

"Then you be strong for both of us," she said. "Don't take away my power. I've already lost everything else."

He stared at her, finding what she had said incomprehensible. Before he could ask for an explanation, she ran from the room.

Chapter 11

Geoff Monday met them when they disembarked from the Dundee jet; then drove them directly to a small private airstrip outside Cantara, Subria. A café and one-level, twenty-room hotel faced the highway. Monday took them straight through the open gates connected to an eight-foot chain-link fence and stopped his Jeep with a screeching halt in front of a closed hangar. Spread out in a row adjacent to the well-lit runway, several hangars, doors gaping open, were empty while others held a variety of small airplanes. Out there on the runway, a Pave Hawk awaited their arrival.

"I won't tell you what I had to do to get hold of her," Geoff told Nikos. "She's been well used, but she's a beauty, isn't she?"

"She should be for what she cost us," Ellen said. "A quarter of a million a day rental fee is rather high, don't you think?"

"Ah, lovie, she's worth every quid," Geoff said. "Besides, we were lucky to get her at any price on such short notice. And I found her right here in Subria."

"No one's complaining." Nikos surveyed the twin-engine helicopter used by the U.S.'s Air Force Special Operations Command. Only God knew how Monday had gotten his hands on such a prize. But then the man had a reputation for being able to get the job done, no matter how impossible the odds. Of course his methods had come under SAS scrutiny more than once, which was one of the reasons why, at age 38, he'd left the service. After retirement, he had recruited other SAS retirees and formed his own independent elite unit.

Geoff Monday was a solidly built, gruff-voiced Brit with sharp blue eyes and a deceptively ordinary face. But there was nothing ordinary about this man or any member of his highly trained group. Each man had once belonged to one of the best elite forces in the world, if not the best.

"Want to take a closer look at her?" Nikos asked Matt.

"Yeah, I'd like to make a thorough inspection," Matt replied.

Monday lifted his hand and motioned to someone inside the helicopter, then pointed to Matt. "Go on over and introduce yourself to Randy. He's our other pilot. Then you two can join us in the hangar later and we'll fill you in on anything you miss."

"All right." Matt headed off toward the Pave Hawk sitting dormant on the runway.

"I've got three men with me: Randall, Perry and Blayne," Geoff said. "Come on into the hangar with me and meet Perry and Blayne. We'll introduce ourselves all around, go over our battle plans and get suited up."

While Nikos and the Dundee agents followed Geoff, he continued talking. "I've got two more—Knox and Byrd—meeting us about ten miles outside Taraneh. They left last night in a couple of Land Rovers. They'll meet us at the rendezvous point at the scheduled time. I sure will hate leaving behind two practically new pinkies that are both mounted with a machine gun and a grenade launcher.''

"Pinkies?" Ellen asked.

"They picked up that moniker during the Gulf War," Geoff explained. "The Land Rovers got doused with a coat of pink colored paint used to camouflage them in the desert."

As they approached the hangar, a side door opened and a wiry, gray-haired man in his mid-forties peered out at them.

"That's Perry," Geoff said. "He'll have coffee and tea ready if anyone wants either."

Once inside, they congregated around a gray metal table in a small room adjacent to the hangar.

With a cup of hot tea in one hand, Geoff leaned over the maps laid out on the table and pointed to a specific spot. "The town itself is an Al'alim stronghold and a couple of miles up Mount Noga, but Omar Ibn Fadil keeps a house about fifty miles west of Taraneh in the city of Zahur, which technically is still ruled by the Subrian government. During the war, Menkura didn't run any air strikes over Zahur so the wily old fox kept himself safe."

"So Omar stayed safe while his people got bombed?" Worth asked.

"These buggers are all daft," Geoff said. "The entire lot of them would die to protect their leader."

"Do you have any updates on the hostages?" Ellen asked.

"My lads there in Taraneh radioed that the old school is right in the middle of town, but most of the nearby buildings are boarded up. Best they could tell, there are only two guards."

"I still think it sounds too easy," Dom said.

"There will be eight of us and only two of them." The

wiry, freckle-faced, redheaded Blayne grinned. "I like those odds."

"And if something goes wrong, those odds will reverse," Nikos said. "There will be eight of us and forty or fifty of them."

"Then we'd better make sure nothing goes wrong, eh, lads." Geoff slapped Nikos on the back.

Three hours later, the Pave Hawk took off with two pilots and six warriors decked out in black BDUs, jackets, gloves and boots. Their faces were blackened with nighttime camouflage grease, their heads covered by helmets and their chests protected by vests. All six had Sig Sauer P226 9 mm pistols—superbly accurate and incredibly reliable. Their snipers, Dom and Perry, were equipped with M-16s and the others carried MP5 submachine guns.

The government of Subria was unofficially aware of the rescue team's mission, giving them safe passage until they reached the western region of the northern hill country ruled by the Al'alim. After that, they would be on their own. Sharing even some information with the Subrian hierarchy was dangerous, but necessary. No way could they fly across country undetected. Better to risk a breach of security than to get shot down within a few miles of takeoff.

Taraneh rested just above the foothills of Mount Noga and was a gateway into the rugged terrain held by the rebel forces. At sunset the chopper made a bumpy landing in a secluded valley flanked on three sides by snow-topped mountains. The six-person team clambered out of the Pave Hawk. The chopper stayed on the ground less than two minutes, then lifted off. Ellen didn't take time to do more than glance at her surroundings. Suddenly, as if from out of nowhere two Land Rovers skidded to dust-stirring halts. Perry, Dom, Blayne and Monday moved forward and circled the two vehicles with a security perimeter while Worth, Nikos and Ellen hopped into the Land Rover driven by a burly, bearded guy wearing a gold earring. Within a couple of seconds, the others piled into the back of the second Land Rover. And they were off in a flash, heading along a narrow, winding, dirt road that carried them away from the valley and gradually upward toward Taraneh.

Byrd and Knox were to take them as far as they could into Taraneh and wait for them. The rescue team had exactly one hour before the drivers headed back to the rendezvous point where the chopper would land in exactly one hour and thirty minutes. Matt and Perry had been instructed not to wait. If the team wasn't there, they were to leave and not return for twelve hours, at daybreak. If anyone missed the first flight, he'd be on his own in enemy territory. And if everyone didn't show up for the second flight, they'd have one final chance to get out of Taraneh, when the chopper would land a third and final time twenty-four hours from now.

Ellen shivered as the cold mountain air seeped through her heavy jacket. The Land Rovers zipped along at top speed, hugging the curves and smashing the occupants against one another. The roar of the vehicles' engines blended with the hum of the freezing autumn wind. Overhead the sky was clear and studded with stars.

Fifteen minutes after pickup, Byrd and Knox slowed the Land Rovers as they neared their destination. They parked behind what appeared to be a deserted warehouse of some kind on the outskirts of town. It was dark as pitch, but they could see from there that the streets of Taraneh were reasonably well lit.

"It's a ten-minute walk from here," Knox said, then pulled out a roughly sketched map and handed it to Nikos. "Good luck."

"Thanks." Nikos studied the map, folded it and slipped

it into his jacket pocket. "If we're not back in an hour, head out."

The team members in Byrd's Land Rover disembarked, then the ones in Knox's vehicle followed. They humped up a back road that led to a fairly steep incline and took them straight into the alleyway between the main street and the street where the school was located. Music and muted voices came from inside the buildings, and occasionally they heard footsteps along the main street.

An unexpected crash stopped the team in their tracks. A cat jumped from the rusty metal trash barrel it had just overturned against a cinder block wall. The screeching feline dashed past Nikos and straight across in front of Ellen. The whole group exhaled a collective sigh. Within a minute, they hustled down the alley, ever vigilant, aware of their precarious position behind enemy lines.

When they reached the abandoned school building, they separated into two groups. Ellen, Nikos and Worth waited for the other four to move in and eliminate the exterior guard. Just as the foursome headed out, a vehicle came roaring by. They quickly fell back into the shadows and waited until the coast was clear. On their second try, they succeeded, disposing of the single guard with expert expediency; then they signaled for the others to move forward directly behind them. The four-man team invaded the school building first and secured the area. Then with Nikos ahead of her and Worth behind her, Ellen clutched the submachine gun as they entered through the wide-open front door.

Once inside the school, the split-team formed one cohesive unit. They searched the interior for a way into the basement, constantly on the lookout for the other guard. It took them five minutes to find the staircase leading to the area below the ground floor. Dom and Geoff Monday led the way, with Perry and Blayne remaining upstairs to keep guard. Each understood his duty. Once the hostages were located and freed, Ellen would take charge of Phila Constantine, with Nikos protecting them; and Worth was to oversee Faith Sheridan's safety, keeping her with him at all times. The others would be front and rear guards during the trek back to meet up with Byrd and Knox, who were waiting with the Land Rovers.

Apparently the basement had no electricity; possibly the entire building was no longer connected to the local power source. But an eerie, dim lighting illuminated the far end of the dirty, cobweb-infested corridor. A lantern of some kind, Ellen thought. Light for the guard keeping watch? Dom advanced slowly, his M-16 held in defense mode. Ellen's heartbeat *boom-boom-boomed* inside her head. They were getting close. So close.

Dom turned the corner rapidly. The *rat-a-tat-tat* of gunfire echoed through the semidark, dank underground passageway. Dom dropped to the dirt floor. The others hugged the wall behind them. For a split second Ellen didn't know whether or not Dom had been hit. A series of rifle shots followed in quick succession. Dom rose to his feet and waved the others forward. He'd taken out the second guard, but nobody took for granted that there wasn't another somewhere nearby.

A large kerosene lantern hung on the wall beside a heavy wooden door. The dead guard lay sprawled directly in front of the threshold. Dom reached over the body and tried the door. Locked. Dom and Nikos lifted the corpse and dropped him in a corner several feet away, then searched him for the keys to the locked door.

"Voilà!" Dom pulled a metal ring with only one key on it from the dead man's pocket.

Nikos took the key and inserted it into the keyhole. Ellen held her breath. Utter silence prevailed as they waited. The distinctive click of a lock opening echoed in the hushed stillness of the subterranean dungeon. Nikos shoved open the door. Dom and Nikos, brandishing their weapons, rushed into the room.

A loud terrifying scream reverberated through the room and out into the corridor. A woman's scream.

"It must be Faith Sheridan," Nikos said.

Ellen charged into the room. Sitting there, huddled in the middle of the cot, the Constantines' nanny stared at her rescuers with fear and uncertainty. Ellen visually scanned the room, but saw no sign of another person.

After lowering her weapon, Ellen moved toward the cot. "Ms. Sheridan? Faith Sheridan?"

"Yes." The woman's weak voice quivered.

"I'm Ellen Denby. These men and I were hired by Theo Constantine. We're here to take you and Phila home."

Tears flooded the young woman's eyes. She struggled to her feet and stood on wobbly legs. Looking directly at Ellen, she swiped the tears from her face. "Phila isn't here. They took her away either last night or this morning or...I can't keep track of time down here. Not much light, no—" Faith gulped, swallowing her tears.

Nikos cursed under his breath. A couple of Ellen's agents uttered similar expletives. A cumulative buzz of disappointment groaned throughout the small, smelly room.

Ellen grasped Faith's shoulders. "Where did they take Phila?"

Faith shook her head. "I don't know. I tried to stop them, but—" she glanced down at her thin tattered gown, the bodice halves held together with a tight knot.

Ellen patted Faith's back. "It's all right. We'll get you out of here." Poor woman, Ellen thought. Only God knew what she'd been through. Her face was battered and bruised. Dried blood stained her busted lip. And her gown looked as if someone had tried to rip it off her.

"Please, y'all have to find Phila. She was so frightened.

GET 2

HOW TO GET YOUR
2 FREE BOOKS AND FREE GIFT!

1. Peel off the MIRA sticker on the front cover. Place it in the space provided at right. This automatically entitles you to receive two free books and an exciting surprise gift.

2. Send back this card and you'll get 2 "The Best of the Best™" novels. These books have a combined cover price of $11.98 or more in the U.S. and $13.98 or more in Canada, but they are yours to keep absolutely FREE!

3. There's <u>no</u> catch. You're under <u>no</u> obligation to buy anything. We charge nothing – ZERO – for your first shipment. And you don't have to make any minimum number of purchases – not even one!

4. We call this line "The Best of the Best" because each month you'll receive the best books by some of today's most popular authors. These authors show up time and time again on all the major bestseller lists and their books sell out as soon as they hit the stores. You'll like the convenience of getting them delivered to your home at our special discount prices . . . and you'll love your *Heart to Heart* subscriber newsletter featuring author news, horoscopes, recipes, book reviews and much more!

5. We hope that after receiving your free books you'll want to remain a subscriber. But the choice is yours – to continue or cancel, anytime at all! So why not take us up on our invitation, with no risk of any kind. You'll be glad you did!

6. And remember...we'll send you a surprise gift ABSOLUTELY FREE just for giving "The Best of the Best" a try.

SPECIAL FREE GIFT!

We'll send you a fabulous surprise gift, absolutely FREE, simply for accepting our no-risk offer!

Visit us online at
www.mirabooks.com

® and TM are trademarks of Harlequin Enterprises Limited.

BOOKS FREE!

The Best of the Best™ — Here's How it Works:

Accepting your 2 free books and gift places you under no obligation to buy anything. You may keep the books and gift and return the shipping statement marked "cancel." If you do not cancel, about a month later we will send you 4 additional novels and bill you just $4.49 each in the U.S., or $4.99 each in Canada, plus 25¢ shipping & handling per book and applicable taxes if any.* That's the complete price and — compared to cover prices of $5.99 or more each in the U.S. and $6.99 or more each in Canada — it's quite a bargain! You may cancel at any time, but if you choose to continue, every month we'll send you 4 more books, which you may either purchase at the discount price or return to us and cancel your subscription.

*Terms and prices subject to change without notice. Sales tax applicable in N.Y. Canadian residents will be charged applicable provincial taxes and GST.

BUSINESS REPLY MAIL

FIRST-CLASS MAIL   PERMIT NO. 717-003   BUFFALO, NY

POSTAGE WILL BE PAID BY ADDRESSEE

THE BEST OF THE BEST
3010 WALDEN AVE
PO BOX 1867
BUFFALO NY 14240-9952

NO POSTAGE
NECESSARY
IF MAILED
IN THE
UNITED STATES

I promised her that I wouldn't let them hurt her, but I—''
Faith clenched her jaw, in an obvious effort to stem the
flow of her tears. ''We've been together since they first
took us. I did everything I could to reassure her.'' Faith's
gaze fastened on Ellen's. ''God, who would do something
like this to a child? She's so dear and sweet and... Find
her. Please.''

''We'll do everything we can,'' Ellen assured Faith, then
motioned to Worth, who came forward and stood straight
and tall at Faith's side. ''Ms. Sheridan, this is Worth Cordell. He's going to take care of you now.''

Faith gazed up at the burly six-four former Ranger.
Cringing, she gasped and stumbled backward.

Ellen clutched Faith's hand. ''It's all right. I promise you
that he's a gentle giant. He won't hurt you...and he won't
let anyone else hurt you.''

Faith Sheridan is traumatized, Ellen thought. Had they
raped her or simply brutalized her? One or both would be
enough to scar her for life. Ellen knew only too well about
the lasting effects of being tormented by your abductors.

Worth braced his rifle against the edge of the cot, then
removed his jacket and eased toward Faith. ''Ma'am, you
look cold. Don't you want to let me put this on you? It'll
help warm you up.''

Timidly, Faith squared her slumped shoulders and came
toward Worth, then allowed him to help her into his jacket.

Ellen spoke directly to Worth. ''Look, you and—'' She
stopped and glanced over her shoulder at Geoff Monday.
''Send one of your men with Worth and Ms. Sheridan. I
want her safely out of here.'' Ellen looked back at Worth.
''Y'all get out of Taraneh and back to the Land Rovers.
Wait for us there. If we don't show up on time, take her
to the chopper, then go with her back to Cantara. I'm en-
trusting her entirely to your care. The rest of us will search

the building for Phila, then meet back at the Land Rovers as soon as possible.''

"I'll take good care of her," Worth said, then held out his hand to Faith. ''Ma'am, are you ready to go?''

Faith placed her hand in Worth's and allowed him to lead her out of the room in which she'd been imprisoned.

Geoff Monday issued an order. ''Blayne, you go with them.''

As soon as the threesome disappeared up the corridor, Nikos gathered the others together—Monday, Perry, Dom and Ellen. ''If Phila isn't in this building, then you know it will be impossible for us to find her. We can't even be sure she's still in Taraneh. They could have moved her anywhere in Subria.''

"Why move her?'' Ellen asked. ''Why take her away from her nanny after leaving them together all this time?''

"Once the ransom demands were delivered, maybe they decided to play it safe and separate their two hostages,'' Dom said.

"We'll search the building,'' Nikos said, ''but my gut instincts tell me Phila isn't here. We're going to have to go back to Golnar and tell Theo and Dia that we've failed them.''

"What will the Al'alim do when they find out that we've rescued Faith Sheridan?'' Ellen asked.

When Nikos didn't reply instantly, she searched his somber expression for the answer. Her stomach knotted painfully.

"They won't kill Phila,'' Ellen said. ''If they did, they'd have nothing to exchange for those three damn Menkuraian prisoners.''

"We'll have no way of knowing for sure if Phila is alive or dead,'' Nikos said. ''Not until it's too late.''

Ellen balled her hands into tight fists and clenched her teeth. God, this couldn't happen. Not again.

The cries echoed inside her head. Soft whimpering. Then frantic wails. Stop, please, stop. I'll do anything, tell you anything. Just don't hurt him.

Nikos grabbed Ellen by the shoulders and shook her. "What's wrong with you?"

She snapped out of her momentary delusional state. "Nothing. I'm okay." The deadly tempo of her pulse contradicted the validity of her denial.

"Let's head out, and remember, if Phila is here, that means more soldiers," Nikos said. "We're running out of time and we have an entire two-story building to search without alerting anyone outside that we're in here—that is if they don't already know."

Worth marveled at how tightly the woman held on to his hand, surprised by her strength because she appeared to be very fragile. She was so slender and small-boned she looked as if a strong wind would blow her away. As they climbed up the stairs, hustled through the building and rushed out into the dark, treacherous night, she tried valiantly to keep up with his long-legged stride, but try as she might, she couldn't quite make it. Deliberately he slowed his pace. Blayne glanced back at them several times. If the freckle-faced Englishman said one damn thing about them hurrying, Worth would have a few choice words for him. The woman was doing the best she could; the last thing she needed was to feel guilty for slowing them down.

The cold night air whipped around them once they cleared the schoolhouse, and Worth missed the warmth of his coat. But she needed it far more than he did. Poor little thing didn't have on anything but a badly tattered gown. Rage boiled inside Worth at the thought of how her gown had gotten ripped—by one of those black-hearted devils who'd held her captive. If the cold bothered him a bit, he could only imagine how it affected her, with nothing to protect her bare feet and legs from the chill.

Retracing the path they'd taken into Taraneh, Blayne led the way along the back alleys. When they had made it about halfway to their destination, the woman suddenly tripped over something lying in her path. Whimpering in pain, she grabbed Worth with both hands to keep herself from falling.

"Wait up," Worth called out to Blayne in a hushed tone, then asked her, "What happened? What's wrong."

"I'm all right. Please. I can go on."

"Yeah, sure you can."

Once again she gripped Worth's hands, but after taking no more than a couple of steps, she moaned and began limping. Blayne paused, glanced over his shoulder and waited while Worth knelt, lifted the woman's left foot and then her right. He felt a bloody cut along the instep of her right foot.

"I think I tripped over a broken bottle," she told him.

"Damn," Worth mumbled under his breath.

"I'm so sorry. I know I'm slowing us down, but—"

Before she could finish her sentence, Worth hung the strap on his submachine gun over his shoulder, then swept her off her feet and up into his arms. "Get going," he told Blayne.

"You don't have to do this," she said. "I can try to walk."

"Just shut up, will you? You don't weigh anything. It's like carrying a sack of feathers."

She settled her arm around his neck, laid her head on his shoulder and accepted his decision without another word. Her small body trembled at first, but within minutes stilled and softly settled against his. He didn't want to feel anything for her—no sympathy or compassion. He hadn't felt anything for another human being in so long that the stirring of emotion for this fragile, wounded woman bothered him greatly. But at the present moment, he didn't have time to analyze his feelings or decipher their meaning.

It wouldn't be long now before they'd be clear of the main part of town. Another five minutes—maybe seven minutes since carrying the woman slowed him down a bit—and they'd be near the abandoned warehouse where Byrd and Knox waited with the Land Rovers.

The woman? He couldn't keep calling her the woman. She's got a name, Worth told himself. Faith Sheridan. So, she's got a name, that doesn't mean you need to use it. If you think of her only as a rescued female and not as an individual, those sympathy pangs you're having will go away.

Just as Blayne rounded the corner of the last building that faced the main street, he stopped dead still and hugged the wall. Worth followed suit, then set Faith on her feet, put his index finger over her lips to warn her to stay quiet, pulled his MP5 off his shoulder and waited. The sound of agitated voices, speaking in what he figured was the Subrian form of Arabic, drew closer. A shout. Another shout.

A dark cloaked figure rounded the corner. Worth shoved Faith behind him and aimed his weapon. The intruder starting shooting. In a fraction of a second, Blayne opened fire and the other man went down. Holy hell! Worth thought. Suddenly a couple of other men came flying from the street into the alley, both with rifles blazing. Blayne was hit. Damn! Worth mowed down the two gunmen, then rushed over to check on his fallen comrade. Blayne lay in a pool of his own blood. Unmoving. Lifeless.

Worth hurried back to Faith, grabbed her up and threw her over his shoulder as if she were a sack of potatoes. "Hang on," he told her and began running back down the alley in the direction from which they'd come.

"What about your friend?" Faith asked as she clung on tenaciously.

"He's dead and we're going to be, too, if I can't find us a place to hide…and soon."

When they reached the Land Rovers, Ellen's relief at reaching safety was short-lived. Worth, Blayne and Faith Sheridan hadn't made it back to this point. That meant something had gone wrong. Damn, without Phila's nanny, this entire mission was a total failure. It would be difficult enough to contact the Constantines with the bad news that they had not been able to rescue Phila, but to know they had possibly lost Faith and two team members was a severe blow.

"We can wait five more minutes," Byrd told the others.

"If they're alive, Worth will handle things," Dom said. "He'll find a way to keep them safe until they can get out of Taraneh."

Ellen looked back at the town and wished they could go back for the others. "A couple of us could return into—"

"No!" Nikos said. "If somehow they ran into trouble, that means the whole town will be on alert. If we go back now, it'll be suicide. We'll leave as planned, then come back in twelve hours and hope they've found a way to rendezvous with us."

"I don't want to leave them." Ellen's shoulders slumped as she kept staring toward Taraneh.

"Nor do I," Nikos replied, "but we won't do them much good if we try to help them. We'd be a handful against at least five or six times our number."

Ellen knew Nikos was right, but that didn't make her like having to accept the truth. All she could do now was pray that the others were still alive and they'd find a way to make it out of town by tomorrow morning.

Chapter 12

When the Pave Hawk landed at the airstrip outside Cantara, the crew and ground team poured out of the chopper. Matt and Randy stayed with the helicopter, seeing to the refueling and doing a maintenance check, more to keep busy than out of necessity. Geoff Monday and Nikos led the others into the hangar where they dumped their gear in a semistraight line, leaving it to be picked up later. Perry headed toward the office area to prepare tea and coffee.

"Anybody hungry?" Perry called from the office doorway. "I can whip up a bite of something here on the hotplate, or if you'd like I'll order something from the café. I think it might still be open."

As they congregated in the corner of the hangar, near the makeshift office, everyone agreed that something hot to drink would be enough. Then Geoff Monday took his team into the office, while Ellen and Dom remained in the hangar with Nikos.

"I want to be on the team going back to Taraneh," Dom said.

"Sure," Nikos replied, understanding why Dom would need to be in on the return flight—Worth was a fellow Dundee agent, and with Dom's background he would feel compelled to rescue a downed comrade. In Nikos's business, sometimes it was every man for himself. A cover could be blown, an entire mission that had been in the works for months or even years could be jeopardized if an agent risked it all to save another. "We'll need Matt and Randy to pilot the Pave Hawk, so you, Monday and I will form the—"

"Count me in," Ellen said.

Both men stared at her.

"I thought we agreed that you're the negotiations expert and I'm the rescue expert." Nikos could feel a fight coming on. She wasn't going to let this one go unless he could give her a convincing argument. "My guess is that the Al'alim will be calling the villa sometime in the next few hours— once they realize Faith is gone. If they aren't already aware of that fact, they will be when the guards change shifts and the new guards find the old guards dead. You need to be here, near a phone, so that when Lucie and Sawyer contact you, you can make a decision about how to deal with the new situation."

He could tell that she didn't want to accept defeat, but she was struggling with the knowledge that he was right. After silently pondering for a couple of minutes, she nodded.

"Okay. I'll stay," she said. "As a matter of fact, I should call the villa now and speak to Lucie and Sawyer. They need to tell Theo what's happened and prepare him…and Dia…for a change in plans."

Nikos grasped Ellen's shoulder and gave it a squeeze. "Have Lucie paint a hopeful picture for Dia. She must have something to hang on to."

Ellen swallowed. "If only they hadn't moved Phila, we'd have her here with us. We'd be taking her home."

Nikos wondered if Ellen had any idea how emotional she sounded. Probably not. The lady wouldn't want to be reminded that beneath that rock-solid, steel-plated armor she wore, there was a feeling, caring woman. Although he longed to pull her into his arms and comfort her, he simply massaged her shoulder. She closed her eyes and sighed.

Dom glanced from Ellen to Nikos. "I think I'll see if Perry's got that coffee ready yet."

Ellen's eyes shot open. "Would you mind taking Matt a cup? And Randy, too?"

"Yeah, sure." Dom headed toward the office.

Nikos's hand drifted from her shoulder, over her back and down to where he circled her waist with his arm. She stiffened at first, then when he tugged her closer to his side, she relaxed and leaned into him.

"It's been a hell of a night," he said.

She lifted her arm and draped it around his hips. "Yeah, I hate failure, and tonight we hit the jackpot—a major double failure. We didn't even come out with the people we took in, let alone bring Phila and Faith out with us."

"We'll get Faith and Worth and Blayne when we go back in first thing tomorrow morning."

"You can't be sure. They could all three be dead."

"No negative thinking." Nikos pressed a kiss on the top of her head. "Theo and Dia aren't the only ones who need hope right now. We do, too."

When she burrowed closer and wrapped both arms around him, he urged her into motion and led her farther back into the unlit corner of the hangar. Once they were hidden by the cover of darkness, he shoved her gently up against the wall, lowered his head and kissed her. She responded with a hunger born of desperation—the same desperation he felt. The threat of death hung over them like an invisible dark cloud, reminding them how ephemeral life could be. There were no guarantees. No promise of tomorrow. All they had, all anyone had, was the present moment. Life was for the living, and God help them, they were very much alive.

Her lips were soft and sweet, her tongue moist and bold. As she nipped and licked, thrust and retreated, desire fueling her frenzied actions, Nikos pressed his erection against her belly. Whimpering, she rubbed herself against him. He lifted her off her feet, positioning their bodies so that his sex aligned perfectly with her mound. She clung to him, shivering, her mouth locked with his.

A door slammed. Nikos and Ellen froze. He listened to the sound of her accelerated breathing, felt the rapid rise and fall of her breasts against his chest, and every masculine instinct he possessed wanted to claim her here and now.

Booted footsteps crossed the hangar and headed in the opposite direction. Nikos glanced over his shoulder and saw Dom, two mugs in his hands, walking across the airstrip toward the Pave Hawk.

When Nikos turned around, Ellen placed her forehead against his. "I need to call the villa."

He nodded, then reluctantly eased her to her feet. But he didn't release her. She tilted her head and looked up at him.

"Tell Theo…" Nikos sighed heavily.

Ellen caressed his cheek, then glided her fingertips across his beard to his chin. When her index finger brushed over his bottom lip, he sucked in a deep breath.

"I'll tell Theo that you and I are going to do whatever is necessary to save Phila." Ellen offered him a tender, hopeful smile which she had no idea proved to him that a part of Mary Ellen still lived within her.

"You make the call. I'll get us something to drink."

When they entered the office together, no one looked

their way. The fact that not one soul even glanced at them told Nikos the others suspected what Ellen and he had been doing alone together. Ignoring them as they ignored him, Nikos headed toward the makeshift kitchen in the back of the room.

"I need to call the villa," Ellen told Geoff Monday.

"Go in there—" He motioned with a nod of his head toward the glass enclosed cubbyhole on the right side of the room. "There's a digital phone on the desk."

"Secure?" she asked.

He nodded.

Nikos poured two cups of hot tea, then followed Ellen into the cubbyhole and closed the door. He didn't give a damn what the others thought and was certain Ellen could care less. She picked up the phone, punched in the numbers and waited. Nikos came up beside her, placed her mug of tea on the table, then reached out and rubbed her back. She lifted her shoulders and sighed.

"Lucie?" Ellen tensed. "Bad news." She went on to explain to Lucie what had happened in Taraneh and told her that Sawyer and she should expect a call from the Al'alim soon.

Nikos could hear only Ellen's end of the conversation, but he could sense Lucie's reaction by the expression on Ellen's face. During the entire length of the four-minute phone call, Nikos continued rubbing Ellen's back. When she laid the phone on the desk and picked up the mug of tea, she moved out of his reach.

"You should get some rest," she told him. "You and Dom and…all of you who will be heading back out in a few hours. Did Geoff say something about some rooms at the hotel next door?"

"Yeah, he paid for a block of rooms for a couple of nights, just in case we needed them. But I've learned to get by on little or no sleep when I'm on this type of mission," he said. "Besides, I'd rather find another dark corner and—"

"No more dark corners. Not until... Not tonight."

"Even if I promise to behave myself?"

"What makes you think you're the one I don't trust to behave?" The corners of her mouth lifted into a tenuous smile.

Nikos chuckled. "No dark corner? No hotel room? Then how about we stay right here?" He glanced at the two chairs flanking the battered metal desk. "It's warm and cosy and—" he nodded to the glass wall separating the cubbyhole from the rest of the office "—we're in full view of the others, pretty much like fish in a tank."

"Absolutely no privacy, except to talk."

"Then talk to me, *agkelos*. Talk to me and help us both forget...for a few hours."

"That sounds good to me. There's nothing I want more right this minute than to be able to stop thinking about Phila and about Faith and Worth and Blayne."

"So, do we have a deal? You and me and some private, idle chitchat for a couple of hours?"

Ellen sat, lifted her legs and propped her feet on the edge of the desk. "Go over to the café and get us a couple of sandwiches and you've got a deal."

Worth placed Faith in the alcove of the back door to a two-story building at the end of the alleyway. "Stay here and keep quiet until I come back for you," he whispered.

Unsteady on her feet, she swayed toward him and grasped his shoulders. "Don't leave me."

"I'll be back in a few minutes. I promise." He jerked her hands away from his shoulders, placed them against the door jamb to balance her, and left quickly before she could protest again.

He'd spent the past three hours on the run, carrying Faith

whenever they moved from one location to another. Knowing they wouldn't be safe staying in one spot, he'd lingered in various hideaways only long enough to let Faith rest and to rebuild his own strength. If he didn't get them away from Taraneh before daybreak, they wouldn't have a chance of surviving. He'd begun to give up hope of finding a way out of this treacherous situation; then he spotted the old truck. He couldn't tell what make or model because the vehicle had undergone extensive body work and was now rusty, dented and covered with a heavy coat of dirt.

Worth approached the truck, all the while keeping a lookout for anyone else on the street. He had no idea if the owner lived or worked nearby, but if Worth was lucky, he'd be able to hot-wire this baby and be long gone before the owner missed his vehicle. After inspecting the truck, he felt reasonably certain he could get her going, but there was no telling how much noise she'd make when he started her. He'd have to be ready for a fast getaway.

He ran back into the alley, hoisted Faith over his shoulder, carried her across the street, opened the truck door and dumped her on the front seat. He pointed his finger in her face and said, "Sit still. Be quiet."

As she nodded, her whole body trembled nervously.

He checked the street as far as he could see in every direction. The only activity he noted was blocks away. After opening the driver's side door, he hunkered over so he could reach his objective. He worked his magic on the old truck and within a couple of minutes the engine roared to precarious life. *Chitty-chitty-bang-bang.* It was only a matter of time before someone checked outside to see what the noise was all about.

"Hold on tight, Blue Eyes," Worth said as he slipped behind the wheel. "We're getting the hell out of Dodge."

The old truck lurched forward. Worth shifted from first

to second gear. The engine spluttered; pale gray smoke rose from the hood.

"Is it on fire?" Faith gawked at the smoke, her eyes wide with uncertainty.

"I don't think so," Worth replied, then gunned it after he shifted into third."

Faith gasped when the truck picked up speed. Just as she reached down to grab the edge of the seat, Worth rounded a sharp corner. She went flying across the seat and right up against him.

He didn't even glance her way. "You okay?"

"Yes. I—"

The shouts came from behind them. Loud, outraged bellows. And then the distinct sound of rifle fire came from down the street, where the truck had been parked. A bullet hit the outside rearview mirror that shattered into fragments and scattered in the cold north wind. Worth flung out his arm, grabbed Faith's shoulder and shoved her down until her head hit his thigh. He kept his hand on her head for a couple of seconds, then when he realized she wasn't resisting, he returned that hand to the steering wheel.

There was no point worrying about being followed. They had one chance to get away and that was to keep going straight out of town, past the abandoned warehouse where the Land Rovers had been parked, and then head for the hills. The only map with directions back to the rendezvous point was inside his head, but even if he could take them to the very spot where the Pave Hawk had landed, he couldn't risk giving away their location. Just in case they were followed, and there was a damn good chance that would happen.

The Land Rovers were out there somewhere, abandoned and probably made inoperable by Geoff Monday's crew. Worth's guess would be that those vehicles weren't far from the rendezvous point, no more than a mile or so, but they wouldn't have been left out in plain sight. If for any reason he and Faith didn't make it to the rendezvous point tomorrow morning and missed their helicopter ride to safety, then he'd have to search for those Land Rovers and hope he could get one of them running. As a backup plan, it wasn't much; but it was all he had.

But first things first. Tonight their best bet was to abandon the truck once they reached the unpopulated area of the foothills. He'd dispose of the truck as best he could and seek shelter. According to the maps he'd seen, there should be a multitude of small caves in the hills. Before dawn, they'd have to go on foot to the rendezvous position. He prayed that he could find the place in time. The chopper wouldn't stay on the ground for long. Five minutes— maybe ten or fifteen, only if safety wasn't an immediate problem.

Nikos and Ellen sat side by side, their feet propped up on the metal table, where empty mugs and half-eaten sandwiches had been shoved to the side. For the past couple of hours they'd been talking practically nonstop, swapping stories about their happy childhoods, and comparing their likes and dislikes in food, music and half a dozen other subjects. They had religiously avoided two subjects: the rescue attempt and their past history.

After their last discussion—on classical music versus jazz—ended, a brief lull in the conversation made Ellen antsy. As long as they talked, she didn't think, didn't consciously worry. Think of something else to say, she told herself.

"I plan to retire soon," Nikos said.

Startled by his comment as much as him breaking the uneasy silence between them, Ellen jumped. "What?"

"I'm nearly forty. I've put in eighteen long years. I'd been thinking about it before Phila was kidnapped, but now—'' He gazed at her, his dark eyes hypnotic. ''Do you ever think about what you've missed out on?''

''Like what?'' she asked.

''Like a husband and children. A real home. A real life.''

''I don't let myself think about things I can't have.''

Nikos slung his legs off the desk and planted his feet on the floor as he swung around toward her. ''Why can't you have it? You're still young and—''

''And already have a satisfactory life.''

''Is satisfactory enough? Don't you want more?''

''A husband and children require commitment and love and risk. I don't make personal commitments. I don't take personal risks.''

''What about love?'' Nikos ran his index finger up and down her thigh.

She glanced down at his caressing finger, then reached over and knocked it off her leg. ''Change the subject.''

''Ellen?''

She surged up and out of the chair. ''Change the subject, dammit, or get out.''

Before Nikos could respond, Geoff Monday pecked on the glass partition that separated the cubbyhole from the office, then opened the door and stuck his head in.

''It's nearly midnight,'' Monday said. ''You wanted me to remind you to call the villa again at twelve.''

''Right. Thanks,'' Ellen said. ''Lucie and Sawyer will be expecting my call.''

Monday made himself scarce. Ellen eyed the digital phone lying on the table. She hadn't dreaded something this much in a long time.

''Want me to make the call?'' Nikos asked.

''No, I'll do it. I just wish neither of us had to call the villa, that there was no reason to. I wish we had been able to rescue Phila and Faith.''

''There's nothing quite like being slapped in the face by

hard, cold reality. I'd rather not have to find out what bad shape Theo and Dia are in, and I'd sure as hell rather not learn what the Al'alim's reaction has been to our failed rescue attempt.''

''However the Al'alim reacted, I've got to believe that Omar Ibn Fadil isn't stupid and that he isn't insane the way his brother was. If they kill Phila, they lose their only bargaining tool. When I speak to them again, I'll demand proof that she's alive.''

''Don't count on getting any,'' Nikos told her. ''They've agreed once to your request for proof, but that was before...'' Nikos smashed his fist against the metal chair sending it flying across the room and straight into the solid wall behind them. ''The rescue was our only other option. You know and I know that they will kill Phila if we don't get those three frigging terrorists out of Nawar.''

''I don't like the idea any more than you do,'' she told him. ''But we really don't have another choice. If Phila were mine...''

''I know. I know.'' Nikos breathed deeply, inhaling and exhaling several times. ''Theo is holding it together better than I could. If those bastards had my child, I'd find a way to kill every one of them, every son of a bitch involved in the kidnapping.''

''You'd want to do that, but sometimes what you want and what you can do are two very different things.''

They stared at each other, their gazes locking for a brief moment.

''Only one of the three men who kidnapped you is still alive, and you don't even know his name. There have to be times when you wish you could track him down and roast him alive.''

''The one I wanted dead, the one I wanted to kill myself was Hakeem,'' Ellen said. ''He was the one who tortured me. He was the one who—'' She paused, took a deep breath, then continued. "But someone else did the job for me. He's dead and I suppose that's all that really matters."

Ellen picked up the digital phone, dialed the number and waited. Sawyer McNamara answered.

"Any news?" she asked.

"Oh, yeah," Sawyer replied. "If y'all can't get Worth and his party out of Taraneh in the morning, then I suggest you hand over the job to some of Khalid's men. You're needed back here ASAP. Our kidnappers aren't happy about losing Faith Sheridan. They say they don't trust us now."

"Did they say anything about Faith? About Worth and Blayne?"

"I got the impression that they don't have them."

"That's good."

"I sure hope so," Sawyer said. "We could use some good news because what I've got to tell you is bad."

"Okay, Sawyer, just tell me what it is and get it over with."

"It seems we don't have a week to get those prisoners released from Nawar and exchanged for Phila Constantine—we've got forty-eight hours from midnight tonight."

"Forty-eight hours!"

Nikos scowled. "Forty-eight hours for what?"

"To get the prisoners out of Nawar and have them ready to exchange for Phila," Ellen told Nikos.

"You'd better start making plans right now," Sawyer advised. "We took a chance. We failed. Now, we're probably screwed."

"Damn!"

Nikos held out his hand and motioned for the phone. "Let me talk to Sawyer."

She hesitated, then handed him the phone and said, "We've dug ourselves in pretty deep."

Nikos nodded, took the phone and spoke to Sawyer. "Forty-eight hours from when?"

"About now," Sawyer replied. "We've got until midnight day after tomorrow and we'd better have those three men out of Nawar and ready for the exchange. Otherwise..."

"Yeah, I know." Nikos hesitated, his mind kicking into overdrive. Ellen could almost see the wheels turning. "Look, let me see if Geoff Monday can set up some sort of base here in Subria. We're a lot closer to Menkura from here than in Golnar. The only way we can make this work is if we launch our mission from here tomorrow."

"I've got maps, blueprints of the prison, information about shift changes for the guards...all the good stuff you'll need. Tell me where to fax it and—"

"I'll need a few hours to talk things over with Monday and see what we can pull together, then Ellen will call you back and give you the particulars."

"I'll be right here by the phone," Sawyer said.

The minute Nikos laid Monday's digital phone on the desk, Ellen said, "Can we do it? Can we put together a plan of action and execute it by tomorrow night?"

"You bet we can," Nikos told her as he grasped her chin. "Nawar Prison is on the coast. We'll go in and come out by sea. You, Matt and Randy will stay here and take charge of getting Worth and Blayne and Faith Sheridan out of Taraneh. Monday, his team, Dom and I will go into Menkura and break those goddamn sons of bitches out of Nawar."

She opened her mouth to protest, but the pleading look in Nikos's eyes calmed her. He's right, she told herself. The only way we can accomplish both goals is to form two separate teams. Nikos, Dom, Geoff Monday and his team were the ones truly qualified for this type of operation. A former SEAL, four former SAS guys and an MI6 undercover agent. This was no time to let pride and ego get in the way of doing the right thing.

"All right," she said. "You take charge of the Nawar mission and I'll see if we can salvage three lives from the failed Taraneh rescue attempt."

"Ellen Denby, you're quite a woman."

Faith didn't know how long or how far they'd driven; and had no idea where they were when Worth stopped the truck. She'd wondered how he could see where he was going without turning on the headlights, but she hadn't dared ask him. Somehow he'd managed. She knew she owed her life to this man. He'd carried her for hours, seemingly without effort, because she could do little more than hobble on her badly injured foot. He wasn't soft-spoken or even all that gentle, but she sensed an innate kindness in him that reassured her even as he barked out orders.

As they headed up a narrow road that wound around the ridge of the foothills, it began to drizzle. A soft, light rain, but enough for Worth to start the windshield wipers. He slowed the truck to a crawl as they drove higher and higher. She held her breath, praying that they wouldn't skid off the road and over into the deep ravine. When her nerves were stretched to the limit and she thought she might scream at any minute, Worth parked the truck, the hood pointed at the edge of a long drop-off. He got out, then reached across the seat, grabbed her and dragged her from the cab.

"Stand back, away from the truck," he told her.

She did as she was told and watched him, with only the cloud-obscured moonlight to illuminate his massive frame, while he shifted the gears into neutral, then grabbed hold of the truck and pushed it over into the ravine. A thunderous crash resounded loudly in the nighttime stillness.

While she stood there, her mouth agape, the cold rain

drenching her already shivering body, he came over to her and grasped her arm.

"Come on. Let's get going," he said as he lifted her and flung her over his shoulder.

"Where are we going?" she asked, her teeth chattering.

"According to the maps we studied before we came, the hills around here are pocked with small caves. All we have to do is find one before we drown, and then wait it out until daybreak."

"What—what happens at daybreak?"

"They'll fly back in and get us."

"They will?"

He didn't bother to reply; instead he marched up the road. She lay over his huge shoulder and savored the warmth of his body. She was wet, cold, injured, horribly uncomfortable and thankful to be alive.

By the time Worth discovered one of those many caves, they were both totally drenched. The rain had grown heavier and the wind had picked up enough so that she suddenly realized there was sleet mixed with the rain. He set her on her feet at the mouth of the cave, then removed a small flashlight from a cargo pocket in his pants and shone the beam into the cave.

"It's low and shallow, but it's big enough for two," he said. "You go in first and I'll follow."

Faith walked into the cavern. Her head brushed the rock ceiling. She moved to the back of the shelter, a good eight feet from the opening, then turned and watched as Worth bent over and practically crawled inside the cave. He sat down and motioned for her to do the same. With her knees drawn up against her chest, she sat there in a tight ball and silently observed while he propped the flashlight against the cave wall, then laid his gun aside and began removing his gear. When he took off his shirt, his protective vest and T-shirt, she couldn't take her eyes off him. He was thick

and broad and muscular, with a heavy dusting of dark reddish-brown hair on his arms and covering his chest in a
V-shape.

After spreading out his clothing, he turned and reached
toward her. She tensed when his fingers brushed over her
breasts as he spread apart his jacket she wore and tugged
it off her shoulders and down her arms.

"What—what are you doing?" she asked. "I'm cold and
wet and—"

"So am I," he said. "And the best way to get warm is
to get out of these wet clothes and use our body heat to
stay warm."

"Do you mean you want me to—to…?"

"Take off your gown? Yeah, that's exactly what I want
you to do."

Chapter 13

"It's all right, ma'am, you can trust me," Worth told her, his voice calm and soothing. He picked up his damp jacket, unzipped a large pocket and removed something. "This won't be large enough to cover us both, top to bottom, but if we stay close, it should just about do."

She stared at the object he held, which was the size of his big hand. When he unfolded and fully opened the square of material, and she realized it was some sort of thin blanket, she gasped.

"I don't know what happened to you back there in Taraneh, but I can promise you that you're safe now," he told her. "Nobody's going to hurt you. Certainly not me."

She stared at him and wished she could see him more clearly. Their only light came from the flashlight beam. This man was a soldier, perhaps a mercenary, trained for dangerous assignments. Was he a hired killer? she wondered. She'd seen him in action, doing a great Rambo impersonation.

He was a huge man, his body firm with muscles. With his upper torso bare and damp, his thick, auburn hair, cut military short, and streaks of black camouflage grease on his face he looked savage.

He held out the blanket to her. "I'll turn my head until you're out of your gown and covered up."

She stared at the lightweight wrap, then at his large, masculine hand. You can do this, she told herself. This man might seem lethal—might actually be lethal—but you are safe with him. She didn't know why she was so certain of that fact, but she was. Maybe it had something to do with the way he kept calling her ma'am. Or was it because he'd called her Blue Eyes? Not many people had ever noticed the color of her eyes, certainly not any other man.

Faith reached out and took the blanket. Worth offered her a faint, reassuring smile, then turned his back to her. With trembling fingers, she worked at unknotting her gown, but found the wet material wouldn't loosen easily. Bracing one hand against the rock wall, she managed to stand; then she grabbed the edge of her gown and pulled it up and over her head.

"What—what do I do with my gown?" she asked.

With his back still to her, he held up his hand. "Toss it to me. I'll spread out our clothes and hope they dry some before we have to put them back on."

She balled the wet, tattered gown into a wad and flung it toward him. He caught it in midair, shook it out and spread it flat on the ground, then did the same with his jacket, shirt and vest.

Shivery from the cold and damp, Faith wrapped the blanket around her naked body, then sat down on the ground. She squirmed about on the hard, cool, dirt floor, scooting backward; then she huddled against the cave wall. She tried not to look at Worth while he divested himself of his shoes, socks and pants, but found herself drawn to him in an oddly disturbing way. His arms and legs, corded with firm muscles, were brushed with curly dark, reddish-brown hair. He was the most utterly masculine man she'd ever seen. Something alien inside her longed to reach out and touch his back, that strong, broad back against which she'd lain when he'd carried her.

"Let me take a quick look at your foot," he said.

"It's all right. It isn't bleeding anymore and—"

Before she could finish her sentence, he lunged forward, reached down and grabbed her ankle. When he inspected her foot, she shivered uncontrollably. Her foot looked so dainty in his big hand. And she felt so small in comparison to him.

"The cut's pretty deep," he said. "But you're right, it has stopped bleeding. Your foot's filthy, but I don't have anything with me to clean it, except some water." He reached behind him, grabbed his canteen and dragged it in front of him.

"Won't it start bleeding again if you wash off the dried blood?"

"Probably, but if it's clean, it's less likely to get infected." He snatched up her tattered gown, ripped off a strip from the hemmed edge, then spread the gown back out to dry. "When did you get your last tetanus shot?" He ripped the cloth strip in two.

"I can't remember exactly," she told him. "A couple of years."

"Hmm-mmm." He uncapped the canteen, poured the cold water over her foot, and used half the ripped cloth to wipe away the grime and dried blood. "Doesn't seem to be infected." He used the other piece of cloth to bind the wound, then eased her foot back to the ground. But his callused fingers remained wrapped around her ankle.

"Thank you."

Their gazes met and locked and even in the dimly lit,

shadowy interior of the cave, she noted his eyes were the most incredible shade of brown. The color of rich cinnamon, only slightly darker than his auburn hair.

"You're welcome." His hand rose up the back of her calf, then dropped away abruptly. "We need to get some rest," he said gruffly, as he backed away from her.

When he maneuvered his massive body so that he could remove his briefs, Faith gasped silently and closed her eyes; but not before she caught a glimpse of his tight, firm buttocks. Oh, dear, reacting this way to a man was so unlike her. She'd never been the type to drool over guys, not even when she'd been a teenager. She liked men in general, had found some to be quite pleasant, but most of them seemed to look right through her as if she wasn't there. She knew she wasn't especially pretty, that her plain face and slim body never gained her a second glance. And it didn't help that she was, by nature, quite shy. She'd never had a boyfriend, although she supposed if she'd been willing to settle for just anyone, she could have snagged herself a man by now.

Being a romantic fool, she had kept waiting for Mr. Right to come along and sweep her off her feet. She wanted to hear bells ringing and waves crashing against the shore; she longed to feel butterflies in her belly and sexual excitement surging through her body. How stupid was that? She was nearly thirty, still a virgin, and was likely to die here in this godforsaken country without ever having been with a man.

"Wake up, Blue Eyes," Worth said.

Faith's eyes popped open and she hastily glued her gaze to his face. "I—I wasn't asleep. I was just thinking." She thanked the Lord that it was too dark in the cave for him to see her blush.

He chuckled. "Lie down and cover yourself with the blanket. The ground will feel cold at first, but once I crawl under the blanket with you, cuddle up to my back and you'll warm up in no time.''

"Mr....er...Worth, I wasn't...they didn't rape me," she said. "A couple of the guards hit me pretty hard and one of them..." She sucked in a deep breath. "One ripped my gown and touched me, but..."

"I'm glad it wasn't any worse for you," Worth told her. "And I'm sorry that it's necessary for you to have to...er...to strip off and... But we need to get warm and dry. And we both need to rest. We have only a few hours before daybreak, then we'll have to haul ass out of here and find the rendezvous point." He moved toward her. "Lie down and cover up. I promise that what we're doing isn't anything sexual. It's survival, pure and simple."

"I understand." She eased down onto the ground, dragged the blanket from beneath her and covered herself with it. He was right—the ground was terribly cold.

She lay there waiting, her gaze locked on the dark ceiling. When he lifted the other side of the blanket, the frigid air whooshed beneath; she shivered as chill bumps broke out on her arms and legs. Worth lay on his side, putting his back toward her; then he tugged the blanket toward him, removing half it from Faith.

When everything suddenly went black, she gasped.

"I turned off the flashlight" he said. "We may need it later."

"Yes, of course, you're right." Given time, her eyes would adjust to the darkness, but for now she felt all the more vulnerable because she couldn't see anything.

"Scoot up against me," he ordered in a commanding tone. "Get as close as you can and put your arm around me. Then go to sleep."

She inched her way closer and closer to his wide back. Even before her body touched his, she felt his heat. Irrevocably drawn to him, lured by his heat and undaunted by his powerful masculinity, Faith pressed herself up against him and lifted her arm up and over his waist.

"There, that wasn't so bad, was it?" His voice sounded deeper. Huskier.

"No, not so bad," she squeaked.

"Try to get some rest," he told her.

Of its own volition, her body cuddled to his, conforming itself to the hard musculature of his massive frame. As her breasts pressed against his back, her nipples peaked. And a fluttering sensation tingled between her legs.

Oh, Lord, no! This couldn't be happening. Not now. Not with this man.

But why not with this man? He was her rescuer, her hero, who had risked his life to keep her safe. Besides, who knew—this could very well be the last day of her life, the last day of his. If they weren't able to escape from Taraneh in the morning, there was a very good chance they'd be killed.

Nikos walked over from the airplane hangar to the hotel. He'd spent the past couple of hours going over every bit of vital information they had about the Nawar Prison. Geoff Monday and he had mapped out a plan they thought would work. *It had to work!* They didn't have any other options. They would have to free the three Al'alim prisoners and exchange them for Phila Constantine.

After getting a key from the hotel manager, he headed down the long corridor toward Room 7, which he and Monday would share. He planned to get a quick shower, change into some clean clothes and grab a short nap. But he'd be out on the airstrip later to see Ellen and the others off when they headed back to Taraneh. While Ellen's team was gone, Nikos would meet with his crew and finalize their plans for the raid into Menkura.

Before he reached his room, the door to Room 10 opened

and Ellen emerged. She wore clean BDU's; her face was scrubbed clean; and her hair was still damp from her recent shower.

"Hi, there," she said as she came toward him.

"Did you get any rest?" he asked.

"I dozed off for about an hour, then took a shower." She nodded to the door behind him. "You fixing to catch a few zees?"

"If I can," he told her. "Mostly I want a shower."

"See you later."

When she started to walk away, he grabbed her wrist.

"Don't go. Come in and talk to me for a while."

"That's not a good idea."

"What if I promise to behave myself?"

She eyed him skeptically. "We've already done an awful lot of talking. What else is there to say?"

"I spoke to Theo," Nikos said. "And I've made some arrangements I think you should know about."

While what he'd told her sunk in, she thought about it for a good sixty seconds, then said, "I'll come in and stay a few minutes. Just to talk."

He unlocked the door, swung it open, stood back and waited for her to enter. When she flipped on the wall switch, a single-bulb, overhead light came on and covered the room with a hazy, yellow glow.

The contents were meager: a double bed, without a headboard, draped with a clean but dingy cotton spread; a scarred wooden table and two equally battered wooden chairs resided beneath a high, curtained window. On the left side of the table, there was an old radio. And a well-worn, rusty red indoor/outdoor carpet spread out over the ten foot square floor.

Ellen pulled out one of the chairs and sat. Nikos eased down onto the edge of the bed, rubbed the back of his neck and groaned softly; then he bent over and removed his shoes. She watched as he wiggled his sock-covered toes.

"How's Theo?" Ellen asked.

"He's in pretty bad shape. When we spoke, he hadn't told Dia about what happened. He's waiting until morning. He wants Dr. Capaneus to be there when he tells her."

"Mmm-hmm." Ellen nodded. "I guess you and Geoff Monday have figured out a way to get inside Nawar."

"We've got a plan. Theoretically, it works."

Ellen rubbed her forehead.

"Headache?" he asked.

"Not bad," she replied.

"You're concerned about our freeing those men, aren't you?" Nikos removed his socks and massaged his tired feet, then got up and walked over to where she sat at the table. He plopped down in the opposite chair, then reached out and turned on the radio, adjusting it to a station playing music and upping the volume a little.

She glanced at the radio, then at him. She nodded understanding and said, "I realize we have no choice. Our only hope of saving Phila is to secure the release of those three terrorists." Ellen combed her fingers through her damp hair. "But how can we let them go free when we know what they're capable of doing?"

"We'll free them. But only long enough to make the exchange."

Her eyebrows lifted as her eyes widened. "Tell me about those arrangements you've made."

"Strictly between the two of us," he told her. "I'm trusting you with information that, if it fell into the wrong hands, could cost numerous lives."

"Do you trust me that much?"

"I trust you with my life, as I hope you trust me with yours."

Ellen leaned forward, her gaze scanning his face. "Once

we make the exchange and know Phila is safe, what happens then?''

"Certain segments of the British government know about the exchange. They can't take part in breaking the prisoners out of Nawar, but they can arrange for a group of elite forces to be on hand to recapture three escaped international criminals.''

"My God! Do you realize how many things could go wrong?''

"Like you said, making the exchange is our only hope of saving Phila, but there's no way in hell we can let three dangerous Al'alim terrorists go free.''

"I hope you didn't share that information with Theo.''

"No. He doesn't need to know. He has enough to worry about as it is.''

Ellen braced her elbows on the table and covered her face with her hands. He sensed her weariness because he understood it so well. Nikos rose, rounded the table and gripped her shoulders. As he massaged her neck, shoulders and back, she leaned into his caressing hands.

"And we, also, have enough to concern us right now,'' he told her. "We can postpone worrying about the exchange until we actually have something to exchange.''

She tilted her head backward and looked up at him. "Is there a problem with your plan to break the prisoners out of Nawar?''

He ran the back of his hand across her cheek. "We're going to have to trust a couple of inside guys to make our plan work. I've had to rely on traitors, criminals and greedy bastards numerous times during my career, and whenever I did, it was a crapshoot. If the money is right and they're not playing you for a fool, then you get what you pay for.''

"You're telling me that there are Menkuraian people who work inside Nawar that are willing to help you for the right price? How did you find out about them so quickly?''

"The people I work for have contacts worldwide and operatives in every hot spot. Menkura and Subria are both definitely hot spots. So getting information or setting up deals starts with a message being sent and passed on, then a request being made and an offer either accepted or declined. We have two guards at Nawar who are willing to get us inside the prison."

"And if they aren't reliable?" Ellen grabbed Nikos's arm and stared into his eyes. "You could be walking into a trap. You could get caught or worse—they could kill you. All of you."

He pulled her out of the chair, dragged her into his arms, pressed his cheek against hers and whispered, "Would you care, *agkelos*, if I were killed?"

She jerked out of his arms and glowered at him. "Would I care?"

He sensed the fury boiling inside her, but wasn't prepared for her anger to take action. She drew back her hand and brought it forward in a quick, harsh slap across his face.

"What the hell was that for?" He scowled at her, puzzled by her demonstration of pure rage.

"You want me to care, don't you? You want me to tell you that if you got yourself killed on this mission, I'd fall apart, that I'd mourn you forever." Gritting her teeth and snarling, she turned and headed for the door.

He caught her just as her hand grasped the knob. "Don't go."

She halted, then released the doorknob; but she kept her back to him. "I'm not going to fall in love with you again. Do you hear me, Nikos? I can't do it. I won't!"

What was she so afraid of? he wondered. Did she think he'd leave her again? That she'd wake up one morning and he'd be gone?

He eased into her, his chest to her back, and slowly

wrapped his arms around her. A slight tremor shimmied through her body. Leaning down, he nuzzled her ear.

"Maybe neither of us is quite ready for love," he said. "But we care about each other, whether we want to or not. And we want each other. That's not going to go away just because—"

"Yes, I'd care if you got killed." She wriggled, trying to free herself. "Now, please let me go."

"In all these years, there has never been anyone who truly cared," he told her. "Only you."

She relaxed against him, as if all the fight had suddenly drained from her body.

He nuzzled her neck, then turned her in his arms. "Stay, *agkelos*. Stay with me for a while."

The door opened, almost knocking into Ellen and Nikos, who both jumped back to avoid colliding with Geoff Monday. He stopped dead still just as he stepped over the threshold.

"So sorry." A pink stain dotted Geoff's cheeks. "I should have knocked before I barged in the way I did." He turned around. "I'll go right back out. Pretend I was never here."

"No, Geoff, wait," Ellen called. "Don't go. I was just leaving. Nikos needs to rest, and I need to talk to Matt and Randy. We'll be taking off for Taraneh at dawn."

"I'll be there to see you off," Nikos told her.

She smiled at him. And he felt as if he'd been sucker punched. *It's just a smile,* he told himself. *But it was Mary Ellen's smile.* He had a feeling that she hadn't smiled with such genuine emotion in a long time. God, how he wanted to be the one to make her happy, to put a permanent smile on her face for the rest of her life.

Worth had the hard-on from hell. How big a fool was he that he'd thought he could have a naked woman wrapped around him without getting sexually aroused? Her slender body nestled against his, her small breasts pressed flat against his back, her nipples tight. Her warm breath fanned his neck. And her small hand lay flat on his chest. He was hurting in the worst way, aching with a need that under normal circumstances he could easily control. He hadn't been with a woman in a long time and the last time he'd been with someone, she'd been a one-night stand. He wouldn't let himself care about anybody. He couldn't ask a woman to accept him as he was, emotional battle scars and all. What woman would want to be involved with a man who often woke up in the middle of the night, soaked to the skin and half out of his mind from the nightmares he couldn't escape?

She wiggled against him; her fingers glided over his chest. "Worth?"

"I thought you were asleep," he said.

"It's difficult to sleep under these circumstances."

"Yeah. And I'm sorry, but I swear you can trust me not to do—"

"I wasn't talking about our lying here naked together," she said. "I meant that knowing we might not live another day makes me want to stay awake during what could be my last hours on earth."

Hell! He thought he'd soothed her fears. Apparently he hadn't. He could lie to her and tell her there wasn't anything to worry about, that they weren't at risk of dying come morning. But she wasn't stupid. She understood that once the Al'alim found out she'd been freed from her basement prison, they would probably connect the stolen truck to her liberation.

"I won't lie to you," Worth said. "We could face a band of twenty or thirty soldiers in the morning when we try to make our way to the rendezvous point."

"And we could be killed before your friends can rescue us."

"Worse case scenario? Yeah, it could happen."

"I'm afraid," she admitted. "I'm afraid of dying before I've really lived."

"How old are you? Twenty-four? Twenty-five?"

"Twenty-nine."

"If you're nearly thirty, then you've lived, Blue Eyes." He felt her stiffen, but her small hand lying on his chest quivered nervously. He reached up and covered her hand with his. "And you're going to do a lot more living. I'm not the type of guy who gives up without a fight, so count on me to protect you."

When she snuggled closer, he willed himself not to respond physically, but his sex came to full alert. He couldn't let her even suspect the effect she was having on him. The poor little thing had been through hell these past few days. Taking care of her was the only thing he should have on his mind.

Yeah, well, his body had other ideas.

"Worth?"

"Huh?"

"How old are you?"

"Thirty-five."

"Have you...known a lot of...women?"

What the hell kind of question was that? "Known in the biblical sense?" he asked.

"Uh-huh."

"Why do you want... Yeah, I've known a few."

"Do you enjoy...well, the...er...having sex?"

Without even thinking, he flopped over from one side to the other and faced her. Only he couldn't really see her in the dark. But he could feel her. Apparently startled, she cried and jerked away from him when he grasped her naked shoulder. Her skin was so silky soft that he couldn't resist caressing her from shoulder to neck.

"Why the questions?" he asked.

She slid up against him, her breasts to his chest, her mound pressing his jutting sex. One of her small hands inched up his shoulder and around to the nape of his neck, while the other slipped between their bodies and boldly rubbed his belly.

"I've never had sex," she said, her voice a breathless whisper there in the darkness.

"What?" His arousal throbbed, the bulb tapping her belly. "How's that possible? You're nearly thirty?"

"In case you didn't notice, I'm rather plain and skinny…and when I was younger, I was very shy. As a teenager, the opportunity never presented itself. Then later on, I made a conscious choice to wait until I was in love."

"Then you should keep on waiting," he told her. "Your ideal man will come along one of these days."

Do not get yourself involved with a virgin looking for love, Worth warned himself. He hadn't been with a virgin since he was one himself.

"I may not have any tomorrows," she told her. "You might not either."

"Yeah, but if we make it out of here, you'll regret it if we do any—" Worth scooted away from her. "Hell, what am I saying? We're not going to do anything. I'm not initiating a virgin in some dark cave with no condoms and… Look, let's just pretend this subject never came up."

He waited for her to respond, but she didn't say a word. The silence between them lingered. Only the steady, rhythmic sound of their breathing penetrated the solitude. Then suddenly he heard something. *Sniff. Sniff. Sniff.* Oh, hell, was she crying?

"Hey, you aren't crying, are you?"

No response.

"Heck, Blue Eyes, there's no reason to be crying. Tomorrow at this time we'll be in Cantara and you'll be sleeping in a nice comfortable bed. And you'll be glad I didn't take you up on your offer."

Sniff. Sniff. Sniff.

He reached for her in the darkness. Big mistake. His hand brushed across her breasts. "Damn! Look, I'm sorry." Careful to move his hand higher, he reached out and grabbed her shoulder again. "You're shivering. Are you cold?" Dumb question. She'd moved so far away from him that she was out from underneath the cover. Without giving any thought to the consequences, he pulled her up against him and wrapped his arms around her. She burrowed into him and pressed her cheek against his chest.

"You're cold as ice." His big body surrounded her with its warmth, and she responded as if he were everything she needed. Sustenance, shelter, protection and comfort.

"Don't cry, Faith. It's not that I don't want you. It's just that—"

"It's dark, so you can't see me, so you could just pretend I'm beautiful," she said. "And you've got a…I mean you're already aroused. So how much trouble would it be for you to just do it? It wouldn't take long, and I'd be very appreciative, and if I die in the morning, then you'd know you fulfilled my last request and—"

"Dammit, Blue Eyes, shut the hell up!"

His mouth covered hers in a kiss that shook him down to his boots. Well, not his boots, since he wasn't wearing any. Down to his toes. Clinging to him, she responded fervently to his kiss and opened her mouth for his invasion. He cupped her hip and drew her up against his sex. She trembled and whimpered. And he knew in that very instant that he was a goner.

Chapter 14

"Faith, are you sure about this?" Worth asked when he stopped kissing her long enough to come up for air.

Was she sure? Dear Lord, she had never been more sure of anything in her life. The kiss alone rocked her off center and created a hunger inside her unlike any she'd ever known. She felt as if she'd been waiting all her life for this moment—for this man.

Sighing, she nestled against him and whispered her response on a shuddering, excited breath. "Yes, I'm sure. I'm very sure."

"You know that usually the first time isn't all that great for a woman." His lips brushed lightly along her neck and across her shoulder. "I'll be as gentle as I can. I'll try not to hurt you."

"It's all right." She stroked his chest, loving the feel of his hard muscles and curly chest hair. She'd never been this up close and personal with a man before and she loved it. She loved the feel of this particular man. "I trust you, Worth."

"Ah, Blue Eyes…" His voice trailed off as his big hands skimmed over her body, tender, caressing touches that sent shivers along her nerve endings.

"Do you mind if I touch you the way you're touching me?" she asked.

"Touch me all you want," he told her. "But when I tell you to stop, you'd better stop or I might lose it. Understand?"

"Yes, I—I understand."

Was it possible she would be able to arouse him to the point of climaxing without him being inside her? The very thought of possessing that much power over a man—over Worth—exhilarated her. She longed to explore his body and wished they weren't cocooned in total darkness. Without light, she could only imagine how magnificent his body was. When she began her exploration, running her hands over his shoulders, down his arms, across his chest and down to his belly, Worth eased onto his back and lifted her so that she had full access to the front of his torso. She slid her legs up and down against his, silky smoothness to hair and muscles. A pulsating throb between her thighs clenched and unclenched as sensation spread through her like a monsoon tidal wave.

While she made her way south, her lips brushed over his skin and her tongue sampled his unique masculine taste. When her hands reached his sex, the shaft thumped forward; she circled him and set a massaging rhythm. He was large and hard and pulsing with life. She'd never touched a man intimately, so she was surprised to find that by fondling him she was arousing herself. When he moaned deeply, she stilled her movements.

"Am I hurting you?" she asked.

"Yeah, you're hurting me in the best way possible." He manacled her wrist and lifted her hand. "It's my turn, now."

She wasn't quite sure what he meant, but when he grabbed her waist, lifted her and set her down on top of his erection, she squirmed, seeking to ease the ache strumming through her femininity. His big hand spread wide open across her lower back and urged her upper torso to lean into his. When her breasts hovered over his mouth, he reached up and danced his tongue back and forth from one nipple to the other. She whimpered with pleasure. His tongue was hot and wet and slightly abrasive against her tender nipples. When he took one tight point into his mouth and sucked, Faith's hips bucked up, her thighs parted and slid along either side of his. Aching with desperate need, she tried to find a closer union, seeking release.

Suddenly Worth slid his hand between their bodies, slipped over her mound and inserted a couple of fingers inside her. When he rocked his fingers back and forth, she cried out his name.

"Worth…oh, Worth."

"You're so ready," he murmured as his lips sought hers. He kissed her, delving his tongue into her mouth.

Just when she thought she couldn't bear another minute of this exquisite torture, he clutched her hips and maneuvered her so that she was positioned to take him into her body. But he hesitated. She waited, breathless with anticipation.

"You do it," he told her. "If you want me, take me."

If she wanted him! She'd never wanted anything more. But why didn't he just do it? "You want me to…to—"

He squeezed her buttocks. "Take me inside. Inch by inch or with one fast lunge. It's your call, Faith. You're the one in charge."

Now she understood. He was giving her the power, the control to decide when and how. She had been helpless for days, at the mercy of horrible men who could have done anything they wanted to do to her and she would have been unable to stop them. Perhaps on some empathic level, Worth even understood that for most of her life she'd been at the mercy of others. As an orphaned child dependent on the welfare system. As a shy, unattractive young woman choosing a safe, secure profession that rendered her subservient to her employers.

Faith lifted her hips, positioned herself, then took his stiff shaft in her hand; and as she mounted him, she eased the tip up inside her. Then with one swift thrust she took him completely into her body. The pain ripped through her like a hot poker. Whimpering, she lay very still atop him, afraid of more pain.

While caressing her hips, Worth whispered, "That's the worst of it. The more you move, the better it's going to feel." He kissed her, consuming her mouth as she had consumed his erection with her body.

"You do it. Please." She didn't think she had the courage to risk more pain.

He continued kissing her, deepening the penetration and increasing the tempo of his darting tongue; and while Faith's concentration centered on what he was doing to her mouth, he began moving inside her body. Slowly. Carefully. And the more he moved, the more the pain subsided. Before she realized what was happening, she began undulating to the rhythm he'd set, seeking friction on just the right spot. The sensation was pure magic, the tension building, promising her ecstasy. But before she could reach completion, Worth roared and tossed back his head as if straining. She could picture the muscles in his neck tighten, his face contort. He clamped his fingers onto her hips and pumped her up and down on top of him. Then suddenly, she felt the hot rush of his release as it shot out inside her. Her body fought for what it needed, demanding her to take action before it was too late. She rode him with a fury born of wild need. While he lay beneath her, the aftershocks of his own release rippling through him, a heady, mindless wave of pure sensation swept her away. Faith couldn't stop herself from crying out as she climaxed. Worth held her close, his lips on her face, her neck, in her hair, while she spiraled out of control and then came tumbling back to earth. She melted against him, exhausted, sated.

"Thank you," she whispered softly against his chest; and within minutes she fell asleep still lying on top of him.

Worth woke Faith at dawn and rushed her into action, not giving her time to feel awkward or embarrassed that they'd made love only hours ago. Already he was feeling guilty. Mentally he'd reamed himself out, calling himself an idiot. What the hell had he been thinking? Not only had he made love to an inexperienced woman, he hadn't used any protection. Hell, he didn't carry condoms around with him; certainly not on a mission.

They dressed hurriedly in their still damp clothes. Although she tried to refuse his jacket, he made her put it on. She needed something to protect her from the cold. He suited up, slung his rifle over his shoulder and grabbed Faith's hand.

"Time to head out," he told her.

She simply nodded, then followed him.

As they emerged from the cave, they saw that the rain had stopped sometime while they'd slept, but it was a cold, gray morning. Faith had managed to limp outside, but Worth knew she wouldn't make it far on her injured foot.

"I'll have to carry you," he said. "I know being hoisted over my shoulder isn't comfortable, but I need my hands free in case we run into trouble."

"I can try to walk." Instead of looking directly at him, she glanced down at the ground.

"Not on that foot. Besides, we'll make better time if I carry you."

Still avoiding eye contact, she replied, "All right, if that's what you think is best."

"Faith, what's wrong? If you're worrying about what happened between us, don't. These things happen between men and women. We're only human."

She shook her head. "That's not it. I don't regret what we did. It's just that I know how I must look to you this morning in the cold light of day. My hair's dirty and stringy, my face is bruised, my gown is tattered, and even under the best of circumstances, I'm not very pretty."

Worth stared at her, unable to believe what he was hearing. Their lives were in imminent danger and what worried her most was that he'd take a good look at her and find her unattractive. He burst into spontaneous laughter.

Faith's big blue eyes widened in shock. She lifted her bowed head and their gazes collided. "Am I that funny?"

Worth grasped her chin in the cradle between his thumb and forefinger. "You have no idea how appealing you are to me. You're not skinny—you're delicate. And you have beautiful eyes and a cute little nose and the most delicious mouth I've ever tasted." She stared at him, an incredulous look on her face. "If we didn't have a helicopter to catch out of this hellhole today, I'd take you back inside that cave and make love to you until neither of us could stand up for a week."

"Oh." The one word seemed to be all she could say.

Worth kissed her quickly. She returned his kiss. When he caressed her cheek, she smiled at him.

"We need to get going," he told her, then lifted her up and over his shoulder.

Worth began the long trek from the hillside back into the valley below, where they would rendezvous with the Pave Hawk sometime in the next hour or so—if nothing went wrong.

After they'd gone about two miles, Worth found shelter

in a grove of trees, put Faith on her feet and offered her some water from his canteen. She took a couple of sips, then handed the canteen back to him. Her gaze rested on his face. Something about the way she looked at him unnerved him. Not that he was an expert on women and certainly not on romance, but he had an odd feeling that what he saw in Faith's eyes was love. Not real love, of course, but a hero-worshiping, big-time infatuation kind of love.

Hell, he didn't have time to deal with Faith's feelings right now. Not with their lives at risk.

"Is it much farther to the rendezvous point?" she asked.

"Another mile and we'll be in the general vicinity."

A distant hum echoed in his ears, the sound of motors running at top speed. Hell! Not a chopper, that was for sure. Trucks or jeeps would be his guess.

"I think we're going to have company pretty soon," Worth told her. "Could be soldiers." He removed his Heckler & Koch P9S 9 mm from its holster "I've got to leave you here for a few minutes while I check out what's going on." After adjusting the automatic so it would be ready to fire, he grabbed Faith's hand and slapped the gun into her open palm. "If for any reason you need to use it, just aim and fire."

"But Worth, I've never used a—"

He grasped her face. "Stay here out of sight. And just do whatever you have to do. Can I count on you?"

She nodded.

"Sit down right there." He positioned her behind a tree surrounded by overgrown brush. She sat rigid as a statue, except for her trembling hand holding the gun.

"I won't be long," he promised as he headed out, hating to leave her behind, but having no real choice in the matter.

Five minutes later he climbed a rise dotted with trees and shrubs, enough for adequate concealment, then squatted and waited as the roar of vehicles grew closer. Lifting his head enough to get a good look at the road below, he caught site of a dirty, battered jeep leading a party of one…two…three small trucks, loaded with about ten soldiers each. He'd like to think they were out on maneuvers of some kind, but his gut instincts told him they were on a manhunt. If they stayed on the road and didn't veer off in their search, then he and Faith had a chance of making it to the rendezvous point without being detected. But if they deployed the soldiers, sent them out on foot, his and Faith's chances would be drastically reduced.

Worth watched the miniconvoy as they passed below him, then just as he started to crawl down the rise, he heard the vehicles stop. Damn! Not a good sign. The men in the jeep jumped out, three flanking the head honcho as he began shouting rapidly in Subrian Arabic. Worth didn't understand more than a few words of the language, but he didn't need to comprehend the guy's words to figure out what was going on. Within minutes the troops hopped out of the trucks, separated into groups of five and each of the six bands headed out in a different direction. Holy hell! One of those five-man squads was coming right at him.

Scurrying like mad, Worth slid down the rise, got to his feet and hightailed it back to Faith. At least he knew they wouldn't get to her before he returned.

When he dashed toward her, she looked up at him with relief in her eyes. She held out the gun to him.

He took it, adjusted the safety and slipped it back in its holster on his hip. "We've got to get out of here. Soldiers from Taraneh are heading this way."

Her mouth gaped open as she struggled to stand. Worth grabbed her around the waist, brought her to her feet and hoisted her over his shoulder. While he jogged off at a brisk pace, he kicked his mind into strategy mode. Think, man, think. You have only a few minutes head start and if they spot you, you can't outrun them. He was at most a mile from the rendezvous point, which was out in the open. But the whole area, probably once cultivated land which now lay untilled and useless due to years of warfare in the region, was surrounded by small hills; and a scattering of trees hid the main paved road from a small secondary dirt road, the two running almost parallel. Oddly enough, his best bet was to get on the main road. The soldiers were spreading out over the countryside and it probably wouldn't take long for one squad to find the remains of the truck he'd stolen and crashed into the ravine. Maybe when they radioed back to the head honcho in the jeep, their orders would be to search the caves. If so, it would buy them a little time.

Matt and Randy brought the Pave Hawk down over the valley while Ellen searched the terrain below for any sign of Worth, Blayne and Faith. The helicopter swooped low, then rose up over the foothills and circled back.

Ellen spotted a hustling band of soldiers, dressed in camouflage gear. She counted them. Five in all. No sign of Worth and the others. Damn! This was bad. The soldiers stopped, looked up at the helicopter and began firing. Matt and Randy immediately lifted the chopper out of firing range.

A few minutes later, Matt and Randy brought them back around and swooped over the soldiers, across the open field and off in the opposite direction. As the chopper sailed across the main road, Ellen spotted a man and a woman. The man, dressed in black was waving his arms. Worth!

They had to land the chopper or at least get in close enough to lower a rescue hoist. But they could do neither with five submachine-gun-equipped soldiers waiting to open fire. She had one choice. The soldiers had to be put out of commission. And she had to take action soon—before the soldiers found Worth and Faith or before they radioed their commander and more troops poured into the site.

Although she'd taken training in using numerous weapons, she had never used a 7.62 mm minigun. The Pave Hawk was equipped with two. Using the minigun was one sure way to eliminate the ground troops and clear the path for their landing. Doing what had to be done, Ellen issued orders to her pilots and when they dove the chopper toward the Taranehian soldiers, Ellen opened fire.

Bile rose from her churning stomach and up her esophagus, burning a trail in its ascent. Killing always made her sick. For others it might eventually become easy. Not for her. With each kill, a person lost some of their humanity. But Ellen forced herself not to throw up as she stared at the five lifeless bodies sprawled out on the ground. She'd done what she had to do. *You're one of the good guys,* she reminded herself.

Matt and Randy brought the Pave Hawk in for a landing, the force of the big blades whipping up a wild wind that leveled everything around the chopper. Ellen and Randy shot out of the door and hit the ground running. Within minutes they met up with Worth, who had Faith hung over his shoulder like a tow sack.

"We'd better get the hell out of here," Worth yelled. "There are a couple dozen more soldiers scanning the countryside looking for us."

"Where's Blayne?" Randy asked.

"He got it back in Taraneh," Worth said.

The foursome headed for the Pave Hawk. Ellen and Randy scrambled aboard. Worth hoisted Faith up into Randy's arms, then jumped on board. Before Randy could rejoin Matt, a second troop of soldiers came over the horizon, guns firing repeatedly. Just as the aft sliding door shut, a barrage of bullets pinged loudly off the landing gear. As they lifted off, leaving the danger behind, Ellen glanced at Worth. He sat beside Faith Sheridan, his arm draped over her shoulder. The woman clung to Worth as if he were her only lifeline. Understandable, Ellen thought. There was no telling what Faith and Worth had been through getting out of Taraneh and staying one step ahead of the soldiers. She'd seen it happen on numerous occasions—a woman becoming temporarily dependent on her rescuer after he'd saved her life. It didn't surprise her the way Faith was looking at Worth. The emotion in her eyes was very familiar to Ellen…

When they landed at the airstrip outside Cantara, Nikos and Geoff Monday were waiting. The minute they swung open the doors, the two men came running toward them. Ellen disembarked first and by the time her feet touched the tarmac, Nikos swung her off the ground and into his arms.

"I'm all right," she assured him. "Put me down."

Reluctantly he lowered her to her feet, but kept one arm manacled around her waist.

"I don't like this waiting around, worrying and wondering," Nikos said. "It's hell on a guy's nerves."

Worth hopped out of the chopper, then held open his arms for Faith. He lifted her off the Pave Hawk. She circled his neck with her arm and laid her head on his shoulder.

"What's the chances of our getting a doctor?" Worth asked. "Faith's got a badly cut foot. I think it may need some stitches."

"I'll put in a call when we get back to the hotel," Geoff said. "We've got a man I know who can get us a doctor."

"Thanks. Just let us know," Worth said. "I'm taking Faith to the hotel where she can get cleaned up and then rest. Call my room when the doctor arrives."

As Worth carried Faith toward the hotel, Geoff grinned at Nikos and Ellen. "I say, he's a bit protective of her, isn't he?"

"She needs him right now," Ellen said. "After what she's been through, I have a feeling Worth may be the only one she completely trusts."

When Matt and Randy emerged from the helicopter, Geoff looked beyond them. "Where's Blayne?"

"Worth said he was killed back in Taraneh," Ellen replied.

Geoff spouted off several expletives in a low, guttural growl, then turned from the others. Randy walked over, stood by Geoff and said something to him quietly. Ellen couldn't distinctly hear their conversation, but understood they were sharing their grief over the loss of a fallen comrade.

Suddenly, before she knew what was happening, Nikos tugged her into motion and all but dragged her off the airfield. She found herself struggling to keep up with him.

"Slow down, will you?" she called. "What's the hurry?"

"The hurry is that I've got only a couple of hours before we head out of here on our mission to Menkura, and I don't want to waste any more time."

A shiver of comprehension tingled up her spine. Not for one minute did she doubt his meaning. All she had to do was halt immediately and tell him no how, no way. But instead of using her common sense and putting a stop to things before they went any further, she kept pace with him, letting him lead her into the hotel, down the corridor and straight to his room.

Do something now, she told herself. Once you go inside his room with him, there will be no turning back.

Nikos undid the lock and flung open the door; then he grabbed her wrist and jerked her into his room. Still grasping her wrist, he slammed the door, then locked and bolted it. They stood facing each other, their gazes riveted together. The blood hummed through Ellen's veins, sending a thundering roar to her head. Nikos released his tenacious hold, then took a step toward her. She waited. Anticipatory tremors shuddered through her. Her lips parted on an expectant sigh.

Nikos reached out, yanked her to him, then whirled her around and shoved her against the wall. She wasn't afraid of him, only of herself. Afraid of her own rioting emotions, her own primeval hunger for appeasement.

He hovered over her. Tall and broad-shouldered. His long, black hair hanging free, his piercing dark eyes devouring her. Nikos was every inch the savage man. His mouth came down over hers, covering her lips with a hot, wet kiss. His actions lay claim to her as he pressed himself against her, pushing her flat against the wall. Acting purely on instinct, she brought her arms up and draped them around his neck. She opened her mouth, inviting him to take her.

He lifted his head for a moment, peered deeply into her eyes and said, ''Caring about you makes me vulnerable and I don't like feeling that way. While you were gone to Taraneh, I kept thinking about what the hell I'd do if something happened to you.''

''Nikos, you shouldn't...I won't—''

''Too late, *agkelos*. Much too late for both of us.''

He kissed her again. A ravaging, wild possession which she returned in equal measure. And in that moment she knew without a doubt that she still loved Nikos. Loved him as much as she had fifteen years ago.

Chapter 15

Somewhere inside her a frightened voice warned her against such recklessness—a cautionary wisdom she had disregarded once before and in the end paid a high price for self-delusion. But she wasn't the same girl, naive, weak and vulnerable. Whatever came later, she could handle. All she knew was that at this precise moment, she wanted Nikos—and by God she intended to have him. There might not be a tomorrow for them, no promises of a future together, nothing more than the here and now.

His fingers speared through her hair. His lips covered hers; his tongue delved inside her mouth. The heat of his large body surrounded her, seeping into her pores, spreading a sensual warmth. Her heartbeat accelerated. An adrenaline rush of pure excitement shot through her, from feminine core to the tips of her toes, from breasts to fingertips. Passion quickly replaced reason. Primitive need ruled supreme.

Her breasts ached, her nipples tightened. Moisture

gushed between her thighs, preparing her body for mating. Ellen realized that she was fast losing control and for the first time in years, she didn't care. To be with Nikos again, to know the pleasure she'd known only with him, was worth the risk of losing not only her heart, but the power she would have relinquished to no other man.

She ripped at his shirt, practically tearing it off him. Her hands were everywhere, all over him. His shoulders, his chest, his face. She couldn't touch him enough. The need to taste him urged her mouth to free itself from his kisses and move over his throat and down his chest.

With his lower body pressed intimately against hers, his erection hard against her mound, he undid snaps and opened zippers, exposing her flesh inch by inch. He tore away her clothing, removing garment after garment, until nothing stood in his way. Naked and panting, Ellen unbuckled his belt and unzipped his pants. He shoved aside her eager hands, then divested himself of his clothing and prepared himself. As she panted breathlessly with anticipation, Nikos hauled her upward, scraping her back along the wall, and positioned her to accept his fast, deep thrust. Gasping, shivering, she lifted her legs and wrapped them around his lean, narrow hips. He clutched her buttocks, steadying her for his withdrawal and second lunge, deeper, harder, more powerful than the first, embedding himself fully within her.

She clung to him, her breasts raking his sweat-dampened chest. His long hair swung rapidly back and forth about his face as he hammered into her. While the tension built, the need for fulfillment became excruciating. She felt everything. Every strong, powerful inch of him moving inside her. The friction of his muscular chest against her sensitive nipples. The tension building in her femininity. The hard wall at her back. Nikos's big hands clutching her butt.

She could hear his labored breath and her own pants and

gasps. His groans; her whimpers. Their mingled moans of pleasure. The wet slush of two bodies joined in an act of untamed mating. The bump of her buttocks against the wall as Nikos increased the tempo and momentum.

Her other senses combined in a frenzy of scent and taste and sight. Male and female, ripe with lust. When the pressure built to an almost unbearable ache, she bit down on her bottom lip and tasted her own blood. The entire world faded away, leaving nothing behind except Nikos. Nikos *and* Ellen. And pure sensation.

The point of no return came all too soon. He lunged up and into her repeatedly. Fast and furious. And then the tightly wound tension burst inside her. She cried out, clinging to him. Instinctively he went wild, pumping her like mad until she came apart in his arms, keening loudly as her climax raged through her body.

While the powerful aftershocks rocked her from head to toes, Nikos sought and found his own gratification. His hoarse, animalistic groans coincided with the rush of his release. He trembled; he shook. And then he leaned into her, rubbing his cheek alongside hers as he pressed his forehead against the wall.

She held on to him, wanting to remain a part of him for as long as possible. Passion and fulfillment rose to the apex and came to fruition, then left behind satiation and a longing for more. Once was not enough. Not with Nikos. It hadn't been fifteen years ago and it wasn't now. Experiencing the pure, raw pleasure of being his lover again only made her need him, want him, more than ever.

Worth thanked the doctor, shook his hand and escorted him to the door. The man hadn't spoken a word of English, but the best Worth could tell, he'd done a good job of stitching up Faith's foot. He'd left her some sort of pain pills, which Worth intended to make sure she used. What she needed now was peace and quiet and lots of undisturbed rest.

"I'll get you some water so you can take one of those pills," he said as he turned to face her.

God, she looked so small and helpless sitting there in the middle of the bed. Before the doctor arrived, Worth had helped her into the shower and then out again, all the while fighting an overwhelming urge to make love to her. But their lovemaking in the cave during the dark of night had been a one-time-only thing. They were back in civilization now and out of danger. After her shower, he'd helped her dress in a pair of pants and a shirt that belonged to Ellen, both a couple of sizes too large. But the clothes were clean and came closer to fitting her than anything he could have borrowed from any of the guys.

"I really don't need it," she told him. "I'm not hurting that much."

"Then lie down and rest," Worth said. "You must be exhausted."

"What about you? You're the one who should be worn to a frazzle. You toted me for miles last night and again this morning."

Worth walked over and sat down on the edge of the bed. "I'm fine. Don't worry about me."

"But I do." She held out her hand, beckoning him to come closer. When he leaned over, she caressed his cheek. "You've been so good to me. I owe you my life and… I don't even know what your full name is."

"Worth Cordell." He wished she'd stop looking at him like that—as if she wanted him in the worst way. Didn't she have any idea how difficult it was for him to resist the temptation to make love to her again?

"Worth Cordell," she repeated his name. "You're a very special man."

"Not so special," he told her. "I'm just an old boy from

Arkansas who made a name for himself in the Rangers. I'm good at being rough and rowdy, at getting tough jobs done.''

She slid her fingertips down his arm and grasped his hand. A shiver of pure male hunger ripped through him. Damn! This wouldn't do. No, sirree, this wouldn't do at all.

''You're also very good at being kind .and gentle and...loving.'' She squeezed his hand.

Get the hell away from her, Worth told himself. Faith Sheridan was the kind of woman who needed a husband and children and a white picket fence. And he sure as hell wasn't the man who could give her those things.

''Faith...I'm not the man you think I am. Because I rescued you and took care of you, you see me as some kind of knight in shining armor. Believe me, I'm not.''

''You left out the fact that you made love to me.'' She scooted toward him until she was close enough to wrap her arms around his neck. ''You haven't forgotten, have you? I know I'll never forget what it was like being with you. It was the most wonderful experience of my life.''

''Ah, Blue Eyes, don't you realize what saying something like that does to a man?''

She might think she wasn't pretty, but she was wrong. Faith had a china doll delicacy about her. Peaches and cream light complexion, luminous silvery-blue eyes and long, silky brown hair. She was a good foot shorter than he, and he doubted she weighed much more than a hundred pounds soaking wet. But every ounce of that hundred pounds was pure woman. Tiny waist. Softly rounded hips and small, high breasts that just barely filled his big hands.

Just looking at her made him hard.

''I don't know much about men in general,'' she admitted as she leaned into him, her lips only a hairbreadth from his. ''But I know something about you and I'd like to learn more. A lot more.'' Her warm breath fanned his mouth. And heaven help him, he had to kiss her.

His lips hovered over hers and of their own volition tasted her luscious sweetness. Damn! She was like an enticing Lorelei luring him into her snare. He jerked away from her and stood.

''Worth, what's wrong?'' she asked, her voice shaky with emotion.

''Nothing, Blue Eyes. Nothing's wrong.'' He couldn't turn around and face her. She'd see his erection. And if she did no more than look at his face, she'd be able to tell that he wanted her something awful. ''I'm going down to the café to get us some grub. I'm starving and I'll bet you are, too.''

''Yes, as a matter of fact, I am hungry.'' She sighed. ''How kind and thoughtful you are.''

Jeez! He wasn't kind or thoughtful. He was a world-weary former soldier and a mean son of a bitch, with a tormented mind and a dark soul. Yes, he'd rescued her, taken care of her and saved her life. But that was his job. Nothing personal about it. Even making love to her hadn't been anything personal. But she'd never understand. Not a woman like Faith. Hell, she'd begged him for it, hadn't she? What man alive could have resisted?

''You take a nap,'' Worth said. ''I'll be back soon.''

He all but ran from the room. Maybe, if he took long enough, she'd be asleep when he got back.

Musa Ben Arif shared the evening meal with his fellow inmates. Shakir and Jamsheed sat across from him, their eyes downcast as they soaked the hard bread in the watery gravy on their plates and ate hungrily. The three men spoke in hushed tones so as not to alert the guards. Their conversation masked the truth to protect them from the others who could not yet be told of Musa's real identity.

"Last night I dreamed of freedom," Jamsheed said. "The gates of Nawar opened for me and for you, Shakir, and you, too, Musa. We three walked past the guards and were escorted to the sea where a boat waited to take us home."

"What a sweet dream," Shakir said. "Would that it could come true."

"Tonight we must pray to Allah," Jamsheed said. "Tonight our combined prayers will be heard."

"Be quiet," one of the other prisoners said. "Talking is not permitted during our meals. If the guard hears you, you will be beaten."

"Forgive me," Jamsheed said. "I simply wanted to share my dream with my friends."

Musa nodded solemnly, understanding the hidden message in Jamsheed's words. A message had come from Subria and through the network of true believers within Menkura that tonight was the night they would be freed from captivity. His brother Omar had found a way to rescue him, as he'd known he would once he learned that Hakeem Ibn Fadil was alive in Nawar, having lived incognito for the past eight years.

Within Nawar, many revered Hakeem as a great general in the Al'alim army. Even among the Menkuraian guards, there were a few sympathetic to the cause. But he had been unable to trust anyone with the truth about who he was—not until Jamsheed and Shakir were brought to Nawar.

Once he was home again in the hills of Subria, he would not forget his years of imprisonment. He had learned much from his captivity. And the long years of confinement had fueled his anger and hatred. Outside these walls, there was much to be done. First he would destroy El-Hawah; only then could he concentrate on more important matters. He had always known it was his destiny to change the world.

* * *

Ellen lay in bed beside Nikos, her head resting on his arm. Her gaze focused on the water-stained ceiling of his hotel room. They had made love twice. Once in an animalistic frenzy. And then slower the second time, exploring each other's bodies with hands and mouths. No words of love had been exchanged, only earthy, erotic demands and promises.

Nikos ran his hand gently down her arm, then leaned over and kissed her shoulder. "I have to dress and meet Geoff and the others."

She sighed. "I'll get dressed, too. I want to see you off."

He rose up and over her, then gazed down into her eyes. "When this is all over—"

She placed her index finger across his lips. "Shh. When Phila is safely home, we'll go away somewhere for those two weeks of wild, unbridled passion I offered you a few days ago."

"What if I want more than two weeks?"

She stared into his black eyes, seeking the truth that lay beyond his words. "I'm not prepared to offer anything more. Not now. Maybe not ever."

"Then what was this all about today? Just a sample to whet my appetite for those two weeks?" Nikos said angrily, then bounded out of bed, went into the adjoining bathroom and slammed the door.

Ellen lay alone on the rumpled sheets and considered the situation. If she allowed their relationship to progress beyond the physical, then she would have to tell Nikos the truth—the whole truth. And she wasn't sure she could ever be that honest with him. All these years, it had been her secret, her burden to bear alone. For fourteen years, she had kept the pain buried deep inside her, but if she shared it with Nikos, she would have to unearth the agony, lift it from the depths of her soul and experience the torture all over again.

Her father had used his wealth and political power in Georgia fourteen years ago to have the files on her case sealed. Only those directly involved would ever know even half the truth. The body of the terrorist she had killed in order to save her own life had been retrieved and buried according to Georgia law. No charges had been filed against her.

Her father had taken charge and made all the arrangements for her life while she was in the clinic. On her family estate, there was a small grave, marked only by a three-foot marble angel. And after a six-month stay in the Paget Clinic, where she'd received intensive psychological therapy for six months, she had emerged a new and stronger woman. Leaving the weak and vulnerable Mary Ellen behind, the new Ellen Denby had visited that tiny grave in Cartersville one time, then she'd left and never looked back. Not once had she ever returned.

Nikos emerged from the bathroom dressed in his clean, black BDU, with his hair pulled back in a ponytail and a frown etched on his features. He surveyed her from head to toe, his gaze lingering over her naked breasts. She bounced out of bed and breezed past him on her way to the bathroom.

"I'm going on out to the airstrip," he told her.

"Go ahead. I'll catch up with you in a few minutes."

She held her breath, waiting for a reply, but he said nothing. The slamming door reverberated through the room. Ellen socked her fist into the bathroom door. Dammit, he didn't understand. He wanted her to be Mary Ellen, and she could never be that sad, pitiful, helpless girl ever again. Mary Ellen had given him her body, her heart, her very soul and had expected him to fulfill all her dreams of a happily-ever-after life. But Ellen had no dreams, no false hopes. She could give him her body, abandoning herself to passion. And he had always possessed a part of her heart. That would never change. But she had no soul; it was bur-

ied in a small grave on her family estate outside Cartersville, Georgia.

By the time Ellen reached the airstrip fifteen minutes
later, the men were loading their gear onto the Pave Hawk.
Matt and Randy were already on board, preparing to pilot
the chopper from Cantara to Olabisi, a seacoast town that
lay within forty miles of the Menkuraian coast, near the
Nawar Prison.

She knew that even with help from the inside, success
was not guaranteed. On a mission such as this there were
too many uncertainties, too many things that could go
wrong. First, the waters off the coast of Olabisi could be
treacherous for boaters and swimmers unaccustomed to the
region. Then once the six-man team made it ashore, they
had to get past the border patrol before facing twenty nighttime guards at Nawar Prison. And after that, the hardest
part would come in getting the three Al'alim prisoners out
of the country and aboard the boat waiting off the coast of
Menkura. A part of her wished she could go with Nikos,
while the sane, sensible side of her knew she wasn't really
qualified for this mission.

"Where's Nikos?" Ellen asked Geoff Monday when he
came out of the hangar and headed toward the helicopter.

"Taking care of a last-minute phone call," Geoff replied.
"He wanted to find out how Mr. and Mrs. Constantine were
doing and give them an update."

"Nikos promised Theo that he'd bring Phila home. He's
willing to take any risk to save her."

"A man shouldn't go off to battle the forces of evil without the right send-off," Geoff told her. "I don't know
what's going on between you and Nikos. But he'll be off
his game if he's distracted by anything."

Ellen understood what Geoff was trying to tell her. She

had to make things right with Nikos before he left; otherwise he might take their problems with him on this mission.

"I'll talk to him," Ellen said.

"Good girl." Geoff patted her on the back, then walked on across the tarmac.

Ellen hurried into the hangar and found Nikos in the office. He glanced at the door just as she walked in.

"How are Theo and Dia?" she asked.

"They're doing a lot of praying."

"Sounds like a good idea." She took a hesitant step toward him. "I'm going to be doing my share of praying while you're gone."

"Thanks. This mission needs all the prayers we can get."

"Please, be careful. Don't get shot or anything."

"I'll do my best."

"In case you don't already know..." she took a deep breath. "I care. If anything happened to you..." She moved slowly, hesitantly, getting closer and closer to her objective. "Dammit, Nikos, you'd better come back to me!"

He reached out, grabbed her and hauled her up against him. "I have every intention of returning to you in one piece." He grinned. "You've promised me two whole weeks of unbridled passion. That alone is worth living for."

"What if I want more than two weeks?" Her words echoed the question he'd asked her back at the hotel.

He studied her expression as if seeking proof of her sincerity. "I'll be willing to negotiate for more."

Emotion lodged in her throat. She seldom cried. Tears were such a silly, feminine weakness.

Nikos leaned over and brushed his lips across hers. Wanting more, she stood on tiptoe and wrapped her arms around his neck, pulled him down to her and kissed him with a passion born of fear and love.

He deepened the kiss, then broke off and eased her arms from around his neck. "I have to go."

She nodded.

He turned, left the office, walked through the hangar and out onto the airstrip. Ellen stood alone, her heart thumping rapidly, the sound a deafening cadence inside her head. She closed her eyes to stave off the threatening tears.

The turbulent roar of the Pave Hawk taking off shook the office windows. Ellen ran out of the hangar and onto the airfield just in time to see the twin engine helicopter rise into the air. She stayed there, looking up at the afternoon sky, until she could neither see nor hear the chopper.

Nikos was gone. If she lost him again... Dammit, she would survive. She'd done it once; she could do it again. She was stronger now, better able to cope.

A lone tear slipped from the corner of her eye and trickled down her cheek. She didn't bother to brush it way.

At that very moment, she made herself a promise—if Nikos came back to her, she would tell him about his son.

Chapter 16

The two speedboats bounded from one forceful wave to the next, occasionally leaping four or five feet into the air in the choppy waters off the Menkuraian coast. Perry and Knox piloted the high-powered vehicles at approximately forty knots. When they were less than two miles from the shoreline, they shut off the running lights and Nikos sent a secure radio transmission to Olabisi, alerting his SIS contact there that they were preparing to land. Pulling off this mission was only half the job. If they made it through Part One, Nikos had to make sure Part Two ended in the recapture of the freed terrorists. The SIS had to be involved in every step, and several SAS teams would remain on standby.

The chopper pilots waited back in Olabisi, ready to whisk the six-man unit and the three Al'alim prisoners to Cantara and then to wherever the exchange would take place tomorrow. Nikos knew that his MI6 contact would inform Matt and Randy what was going on, and Matt in turn would get in touch with Ellen. *Ellen.* His Ellen. This morning he'd seen a glimpse of Mary Ellen in her, although she would deny the possibility that any part of her old self still existed. Leaving her fifteen years ago had been difficult, but leaving her earlier today had been one of the hardest things he'd ever done. He'd dodged the bullet time and again, so he realized that he'd about run out of luck. In the past, making it through a mission alive hadn't been constantly in the forefront of his mind. But that had been when he'd had no one waiting for him. Now he had Ellen. Not for the rest of his life, but for two weeks—and maybe more. God knew he wanted more. He wanted that cottage in England, the dull life of a country gentleman, spaniels frolicking on the lawn with a couple of children and a loving wife to warm his bed and his heart.

Perry and Knox parked the boats off an isolated beach seldom checked by the border patrol because few people knew about the passageway through the towering limestone cliffs. They killed the motors. The roar of the crashing waves obliterated every other sound. An eerily cloudy night sky canopied the rough sea and narrow beach, giving the men a feeling of being trapped in a wet cave. Less than twenty feet of sandy beach lay between the sea and the grassy slope that quickly melted into the jagged rock wall in front of them.

The six-man team emerged from the boats, arranged their gear and prepared to head out. Geoff Monday led the way. He was the only one familiar with the territory. He'd been part of another mission into Menkura less than a year ago. This entire operation depended upon Monday's ability to find the passage that would take them from the shore to the cliffs above.

Four of them were armed with Heckler and Koch MP-5 machine guns and two carried M-16 rifles fitted with grenade launchers. As backup weapons, they all had pistols secured to their waist belts and knives strapped to their legs. With their hands and faces darkened by camouflage grease, the six men adjusted their haversacks and headed up the beach.

Nikos breathed a sigh of relief when Monday, equipped with night vision, found the entrance to the passageway within minutes. The climb upward was steep and sometimes the opening between the craggy rock walls narrowed so much that they were forced to remove their haversacks and shove them through in front of them. After what felt like an endless climb, they reached the top, then took a couple of minutes to readjust their gear and check out their surroundings. From their SIS information, they knew a patrol passed along the winding gravel road that skirted the cliffs every two hours. They had timed their arrival halfway in between that one hundred and twenty minute span and would have to time their departure in the same way. The army patrol didn't concern Nikos; getting into Nawar did. He sure as hell hoped nothing went wrong. If it did— He couldn't allow himself to even think about it.

Monday led the pack as they tramped through the rugged mountainous terrain. Ten miles to Nawar. A brisk hike in the cool night air for well-trained soldiers in prime physical condition. As they trekked inland, keeping off the road but following its snakelike path, they stayed alert to the possibility of trouble. If the Al'alim-sympathetic guards did their part, getting into Nawar would be a hell of a lot easier than getting back to the boats.

Ellen spoke to Matt for only a couple of minutes, just long enough for him to relay the message that all systems were go and the crew was within striking distance of its destination. When she laid the phone down on the table, Worth Cordell handed her a cup of fresh coffee.

"Are you all right?" he asked.

"I'm fine. Why do you ask?"

"You're concerned about this fellow Nikos."

"Am I that obvious?"

"Just to someone who's very observant," he replied.

Ellen offered him a weak smile. "I've come to realize that men who don't talk much tend to be observant and often pick up on things they shouldn't."

"I figure the guy's got nine lives. So, unless he's already used up all of them, he'll be coming back in one piece."

Ellen crossed her arms over her waist and rubbed her elbows. She drew in a deep breath, then exhaled slowly. "Quiet men also tend to be good listeners." She looked directly at Worth. "Are you a good listener?"

"I can be. You got something you want to get off your chest?"

"I never thought I'd say this, but what I need is another woman to talk to."

"Mmm-hmm."

"Have you ever been in love?" she asked, then when she noted the stricken look on Worth's face, she laughed. "Thanks."

He shrugged. "For what?"

"For making me laugh at a time like this."

He grinned sheepishly. "I figure everybody's been in love at least once. Right? For me, it was so long ago and I was so young that I barely remember her. Teenage stuff. Nothing serious since then."

"If you barely remember her, it wasn't love. Just hormones."

"You're probably right."

Holding her coffee mug tightly in her hands, Ellen strolled out of the office and into the open hangar. As she gazed up at the dark, cloudy night sky, Worth followed her.

"Were you and Nikos in love?" Worth asked.

"I was." She took a sip of black coffee. "I suppose he was. You'd have to ask him."

Ellen and Worth stood side by side for several minutes, neither of them speaking. She liked Worth and felt that on some level she understood him. He was a wounded soul, just like she was. According to his records, he'd mustered out of the army after a Ranger mission turned into a blood-bath for both the U.S. troops and the enemy soldiers. She had no idea what had happened to him on that assignment, but she suspected he had returned stateside with at least one major demon chasing him. If anyone knew about demons, she did.

"I need to get back to the hotel and check on Faith," Worth said. "She was asleep when I left. If she wakes up and I'm not there, she'll—"

"You've got a problem with Faith," Ellen told him. He eyed her quizzically. "You are aware that she probably thinks she's in love with you."

"She doesn't. She's just dependent on me right now. That's all. The poor little thing has been through hell. I'm not about to walk away from her when she needs me."

Ellen's brows lifted as she widened her eyes in a perceptive expression. "If I didn't know better, I'd say you cared about this woman, that she meant something to you personally."

"Don't be stupid. She doesn't mean a damn thing to me, other than the fact she's a human being who's had it pretty rough."

"Do you want me to go check on her?" Ellen asked. "I can take over baby-sitting duties if you'd like."

He shook his head. "You stay close to the phone in case Matt calls again anytime soon. I can handle things with Faith...with Ms. Sheridan."

Ellen nodded. "I think I'll get myself another cup of coffee."

"If you need me, call over to the hotel."

"Sure thing."

As she watched Worth walk away, a sudden, inexplicable sadness overwhelmed her. What was wrong with her? She understood that all the worrying in the world wasn't going to help bring Nikos and the others safely back to Cantara.

But maybe saying another prayer would.

The six-man squad entered Nawar through an unlocked back door in the basement area that was above ground. The door had been left open for them. One checkpoint passed without incident. The stone structure was over a hundred years old and consisted of three above ground levels and a basement that had once housed a dungeon. As they stalked through the dark corridors, they discovered the dank, rat-infested underbelly of Nawar was vacant of all life, except the rodent and insect variety.

Their informant had told them the three Al'alim prisoners were in three separate cells, but all on the second level of the prison, all in the south wing. There was no way a guard could arrange to have them all together in a single cell, so the team would have to secure their release, one by one.

Dom would get Shakir Abu Lufti. Monday would get Jamsheed Abd Hamid. And Nikos would be in charge of the mysterious Musa Ben Arif.

Byrd, Perry and Knox would keep watch. The guard, who by his actions betrayed his country, waited for them on the first floor at the south stairs where he had night watch. He passed them through the security check and radioed to his accomplice, who was set to meet them when they arrived on the second level. Nikos didn't know these men's names; didn't need to know. A simple password phrase was all that either he or they required for identity. *Sorirart Biro'aitak.* Nice to meet you. Oh, yes, it was nice to meet them all right. Nikos knew what had to be done once these guards had served their purpose. He and Monday had been in agreement concerning the fate of their Menkuraian helpers. Perry and Knox would take care of that little chore on their way out.

They had now passed the second checkpoint.

The stairs were dimly lit, but even that much was more than Nikos would have liked. Darkness had its advantages. They split into two units, one advancing up the right side of the stairs while the others came up the left side precisely two minutes behind them. When they reached the second level, they hugged the wall. The long corridor that ran the length of the south wing in front of the row of cells lay before them empty and quiet. As they listened, they could hear an occasional snore or cough or heavy breathing. Some prisoners slept peacefully while others struggled even in their sleep.

Nikos spotted the guard at the same moment Geoff Monday did. Monday motioned them back. They waited, breaths held until the guard called out softly, *"Sorirart Biro'aitak."*

Monday repeated the phrase, then came out of the shadows and motioned the guard to come to him. The tall, skinny young man rushed forward and came to a halt when he saw the squad of mercenaries.

The third checkpoint cleared.

"Shakir is in cell six, Jamsheed in cell ten and Musa in cell thirteen. I will open those three cells from my command post," the guard whispered in remarkably good English. "Say the man's first name only, then repeat the code phrase and he will do the same."

"Are you alone up here?" Nikos asked. "Do we need to be concerned about other guards?"

"I've already taken care of the other two guards in this

section,'' the young man said. ''When you leave you will knock me out. Understand?''

Monday grinned wickedly. ''Oh, I understand. You can count on us.''

A shiver raced up Nikos's spine. How easy killing had become for Monday and for others like him. Hell, it was easier for Nikos than he liked to admit. Another reason he needed to retire. If he stayed in the game too long, there would come a time when he'd be hard pressed to see the difference between himself and the enemy.

''The other prisoners may awaken,'' the guard said. ''If they do, it is only a matter of time before guards from another section will check to see what is happening.''

''Don't worry,'' Monday replied, ''we don't intend to hang around that long.''

As soon as the guard returned to his command post, the team went into action. Nikos had farther to go, so he headed out first. Silent and deadly he made his way down the long balcony-style corridor until he reached cell 13. The prisoner inside stood by the metal bars, his dark eyes trained on Nikos. Suddenly the door slid open.

''Musa?'' Nikos asked. *''Sorirart Biro'aitak.''*

''Sorirart Biro'aitak,'' the man replied, his voice gravely and hoarse, as if his vocal cords had sustained some type of permanent injury.

''Hal Tatakalm Alingli'zia?'' Nikos asked the man if he spoke English.

''Yes,'' came his succinct reply.

''Come with me. Now.''

Nikos stood back to allow his prisoner room to walk out of his cell, then Nikos nudged him forward and they soon met up with Monday and Dom, both escorting their charges. Byrd remained behind for a couple of minutes—to take care of the guard. Then the team reunited as they headed down the stairs to the first level. Upstairs in the south wing a rumble of voices rose higher and higher. The other prisoners were awake and aware that three of their comrades had been rescued.

While the team retraced their steps, heading down to the basement, Knox lingered long enough to administer retribution to the second traitor, then brought up the rear just as the team and their prisoners emerged from the dungeon. Lights began coming on inside Nawar and spotlights scanned the perimeter as a siren wailed like an earsplitting scream.

Chapter 17

The chase was on! The six-man squad hustled their rescued prisoners into high gear. Cloaked in darkness, they made their escape; however, the black obscurity worked as much against them as for them. But Monday seemed to possess a sixth sense about direction, much like a nocturnal animal. Nikos knew the only way they were going to get out of this alive—all of them—was to get a good head start. The *rat-a-tat-tat* of machine gun fire peppered the ground around them. When they were less than a hundred yards from the prison, Shakir grasped his chest, doubled over in pain and dropped to his knees. Dom squatted, checked the man's wounds, then looked up at Nikos and shook his head.

"Leave him," Musa Ben Arif said. "If he is dying, we cannot help him and he will only slow us down."

Cold-hearted bastard, Nikos thought, but then he figured anybody who joined up with the Al'alim was a brother to the devil. Besides, these crazed fanatics seemed to be more than willing to die for the glory of their cause. And Ben

Arif seemed perfectly at ease giving orders. Hell, he acted as if he knew no one would buck his command.

Nikos wished he could get a really good look at Ben Arif. This guy had to be "somebody." A very important somebody. But who? Headquarters had better figure out this guy's identity before they took him in for the hostage exchange. Knowing who he was would alert them to whether or not the man was on the international list of those who were wanted dead or alive.

"Leave me," Shakir said, his voice weak as he gazed up at Musa. "I am not important. You must go. Go now."

Shakir believed his own life wasn't important; he was willing to sacrifice himself to help save Musa. All the more reason for Nikos to believe that Musa was the central figure in this kidnapping/rescue scheme. He wished he could say it would bother him to leave the dying man behind—but it wouldn't. After working undercover for so many years in various countries, infiltrating numerous terrorists organizations, he had come to think of men like Shakir as less than human. They were demons, capable of unimaginable brutality.

Hurriedly Nikos and Monday consulted in a terse strategy meeting, then Monday issued orders. Dom and Knox positioned themselves at precise angles to the lookout tower, while the others scampered away from the prison and toward the nearby rocky hillside, sparsely dotted with vegetation. Each using his M-16 fitted with the M203 40 mm grenade launcher attached under the rifle barrel and possessing its own trigger and sighting system, Dom and Knox launched the first attack. As the grenades exploded with deadly force two hundred yards away, Dom and Knox made a hasty retreat. Then from three hundred yards away, they repeated the attack, wreaking more destruction and buying the team what they needed most—time to get away.

Nikos didn't look back. During their succinct planning

session, Monday and he had checked their watches. Timing was an all important factor in the success of this mission. The border patrol should have passed the cliff roadway fifteen or twenty minutes ago, leaving the beach area clear for the squad's return. If they were lucky, no one at Nawar would figure out that the intruders had come in by sea—at least not soon enough to contact the patrol in time for the Menkuraian soldiers to prevent their escape. But there was nothing to stop some of the guards from coming after them once they regrouped following the grenade attack. If the guards picked up their trail, they could track them all the way back to the beach.

Hustle, hustle, hustle, his mind screamed the command.

The next ten mile trek seemed more like fifty, but they made good time and managed to stay well ahead of any guards who might or might not be following them. When they reached the cliff road, they saw no sign of the patrol. If their luck would just hold out for a while longer, Nikos thought, they'd all make it back to Olabisi alive. With Monday taking the lead, they bounded down the passageway in the cliff wall, single file, then came out on the beach and headed straight for the speedboats. Just as they reached their destination and split into two units, a well-equipped Menkuraian patrol vehicle skidded to a screeching halt high above on the cliff's edge.

Damn! The patrol was supposed to be miles away right now. Undoubtedly the prison had contacted them about the breakout and they'd made an educated guess that the rescuers had come in by sea.

Monday started yelling orders. Knox and Perry revved the boats' engines, while the others boarded posthaste. Dom stayed on shore long enough to launch a grenade that blasted a huge chunk from the cliff wall and sent the Land Rover airborne in a blaze of flames that licked across the black sky. Immediately Dom waded toward the nearest boat and climbed aboard. A second later the two highspeed crafts jetted away from the Menkuraian shore. Nikos released a deep sigh. They would soon be in Olabisi; then it was a brief helicopter ride back to Cantara. Back to Ellen.

Nikos wondered how the death of one of the prisoners would affect the exchange for Phila Constantine. His gut instincts told him that Shakir Abu Lufti's demise wouldn't cause the Al'alim to blink an eye. No, Shakir and Jamsheed were dispensable. They'd been used as little more than a smoke screen to divert attention from the main attraction. The real prize, the man whose release was of monumental importance to the Subrian rebel cult, was sitting right beside Nikos. Musa Ben Arif.

But who the hell was he really?

Worth and Ellen waited outside the hangar as the Pave Hawk descended and made a smooth landing on the tarmac. As soon as the rotary blades slowed and the aft sliding doors opened, Worth and Ellen ran to meet their returning comrades. Nikos jumped out first, then a tall, thin, barefoot man in ragged pants and shirt came out directly behind him. Dom hopped out next, and he and Nikos flanked the Al'alim prisoner. Ellen noted the others as they emerged from the chopper: Monday, Byrd, Perry, Knox and another prisoner. Ellen studied the two Subrian rebels. The one guarded by Monday was younger than the other and several inches shorter. His hair and beard were black, his shoulders broad, his posture straight. She recognized him from the photos Nikos had shown them. General Jamsheed Abd Hamid. The older man guarded by Nikos and Dom kept his head bowed so that Ellen couldn't see his face clearly, but she noticed the patch covering his right eye. His shoulder length hair and long, scraggly beard were steel-gray and his leathery skin sallow, as if he hadn't spent much time in the sunlight.

Suddenly she realized the team was one prisoner short. "Where's the other—"

"The Nawar guards opened fire with a machine gun and Shakir was killed," Nikos said. "But we've got what we went after."

In her peripheral vision she caught a glimpse of the man who, by process of elimination, had to be Musa Ben Arif. Was it her imagination or had the man actually tensed slightly when he'd heard Nikos's comment? That meant he understood English. But did it possibly mean more than that?

"We've got a nice room waiting for these two guys," Worth said. "No windows. Only one door in or out. And I'm taking the first watch."

Nikos handed Musa over to Dom, then grabbed Ellen's arm and pulled her aside. He waited until the others were out of earshot, then said, "Any updates from Sawyer and Lucie?"

"Not yet."

"News about the rescue should be spreading like wild-fire," Nikos told her. "The minute word reaches Omar Ibn Fadil, he'll get in touch to give us our instructions about the exchange."

"How will losing one of the exchange prisoners affect things?"

"If our guess is right and Musa Ben Arif is what Phila's kidnapping and the hostage exchange is all about, then it won't affect a damn thing."

"Did you take a good look at him?" Ellen asked. "He's not a young man by any means. Probably close to sixty, wouldn't you say?"

"If he's somebody important, I should recognize him, but I don't. But years in Nawar could age a man and change him so drastically that he'd be unrecognizable." Nikos shook his head reflectively. "I kept getting odd vibes from him, and several times I felt as if he were watching me, maybe studying me.''

''Just because you didn't recognize him doesn't mean he didn't recognize you.''

''A sobering thought.'' Nikos's gaze connected with Ellen's. She laid her hand on his shoulder. ''What if he is someone from my past? Maybe I've been somehow involved in this whole affair from the very beginning, from the planning stages. That would mean I'm responsible for Phila's abduction.''

''If that's the case, then we need to find out before we make the exchange, not afterward. We don't need to discover, too late, that there's a wild card in the deck and Musa plans on playing it.''

Jamsheed stood aside and waited for Musa to enter the motel room. As the door closed behind them, the two made eye contact and Musa held a finger to his lips in a warning signal. Jamsheed nodded.

''We should rest,'' Musa said. ''But first we should pray and thank Allah for our deliverance.''

They knelt on the floor and prostrated themselves, then began their chanting supplication. As the memorized words rolled off Musa's tongue, his mind filled with other thoughts. Thoughts about the irony of life. What he wanted most in this world was his freedom, but there had been a time when destroying Yusuf Ben Amir had been his main objective. Ben Amir, sometimes referred to as El-Hawah, had murdered his only son. He had known that when he became a free man, his search for El-Hawah would begin all over again. But not once had he thought finding the man would be so easy.

How very wise of his brother Omar to not only unearth El-Hawah's true identity, but to actually find a way to maneuver him into being the one to rescue Musa from Nawar

Prison. Curiosity frustrated him. There were many unanswered questions. But soon enough he would learn the particulars of Omar's brilliant plan. From what he'd surmised by listening to the infidels' brief conversations, he and Jamsheed would be exchanged for another hostage.

But there would be no exchange. At least not the one agreed upon by his rescuers and his brother. The person Omar held captive must be of great importance. But was this person's life worth more than the life of El-Hawah, his son's killer? If so, then that would be the new terms of the exchange. Even if he had to die to accomplish El-Hawah's destruction, so be it. But before he took the man's life, he would reveal himself. Odd how Yusuf had changed so little in all these years, how easily Hakeem had recognized the man; whereas he himself was greatly changed—stooped with age, gray, wrinkled and missing an eye. Before he'd been captured, Hakeem had shaved his beard and mustache and cut his hair so that he would more readily resemble his servant Musa Ben Arif. Then during the time he'd spent in Nawar, he'd lost an eye in a vicious knife fight and had lost at least fifty pounds due to the starvation diet he'd endured those first years of imprisonment. He doubted his own brother would recognize him today. Hakeem smiled. He wanted the last thing Yusuf Ben Amir, the legendary El-Hawah, saw before he died to be Hakeem Ibn Fadil's laughing face. The pain Yusuf suffered would be exquisite. Just the thought of inflicting such torture aroused Hakeem's senses.

Of course, there was the woman. An added delight to Hakeem's revenge. He had been surprised to see that she and El-Hawah were together. Memories of her pathetic cries, her moaning pleas were like sweet music inside his head. He had thought the woman would hate Yusuf after what had happened, that she would blame him for her pain and suffering. But women were such weak, spineless creatures. All of them. Yusuf's woman had undoubtedly run back to him. Like others of her sex, she needed a master. And any man who remained loyal to one woman was a fool. Apparently the great El-Hawah was just such a fool.

Geoff Monday took over Worth's guard duty shortly before dawn. ''Any problems?''

''Except for their prayers, I haven't heard a peep out of them,'' Worth told him.

''They're probably sleeping like babies,'' Geoff said. ''They know they're going home soon. Sorry bastards. I'd like nothing better than to execute them myself.''

''Take 'em out and shoot 'em down like dogs,'' Worth mimicked the words from one of his favorite classic Western movies.

Geoff chuckled. ''I like the sound of that.''

Worth headed off down the corridor. He was tired, sleepy and horny. While keeping vigil over their rescued prisoners he'd allowed his mind to wander down the hall, to the woman asleep in his bed right now. Becoming her lover had been a huge mistake, but he knew, given the same set of circumstances, he'd do it all over again. There was something about Faith Sheridan that got to him. It was more than sex—and that's what scared the hell out of him.

When he reached his room, he undid the lock, eased opened the door and walked in as quietly as possible. She'd left the bathroom light on and the door cracked halfway so a beam stretched across the carpeted floor and cast shadows on the walls. He eased toward the bed. Faith lay cuddled against one of the pillows, hugging it close to her body. He stood over her and watched while she slept. What would it hurt if he lay down alongside her? He was bone weary. All he wanted was sleep. *Liar*, an inner voice taunted. If all he wanted was sleep, he could bunk in with Dom.

Worth sat on the edge of the bed, removed his shoes and

socks, then eased down atop the covers and lay perfectly still. After a few minutes he rolled over on his side. Faith didn't stir. Worth cursed himself for his stupidity. He was aching with a powerful need to hold her. Several minutes later, after fighting an inner battle, he knew he'd lost the war. His willpower gave out on him. He reached over, draped his arm across her and pulled her up against him.

She mumbled in her sleep. He brushed aside several tendrils of dark hair from her cheek and kissed her. Her eyelids fluttered.

"Worth?"

"Yeah, Blue Eyes, it's me."

She turned over, shoved back the covers and moved right into his open arms. Nothing in his entire life had ever felt so right.

Shortly after daybreak, Nikos woke Ellen. He'd gone to sleep holding her in his arms after a fast, frenzied mating. Now he wanted her again, but he intended to take her slow and easy this time. She opened her eyes and stared up at him, then smiled. Arousal combined with tenderness as he studied her features. She was the most beautiful creature he'd ever seen, her face and form absolute perfection.

He kissed her forehead, her cheeks, her chin and then her mouth. A telltale ripple shimmied through her, and he knew she was already as aroused as he was. Just the touch of his lips excited her, as the sight of her body stimulated him.

"I don't think two weeks will be nearly long enough to satisfy me," he whispered in her ear.

She rubbed against him like a kitten curling about its master's ankle. "How long do you think you'll need to become thoroughly satisfied?"

When he skimmed his open palm across her back and down over her behind, she emitted a throaty purr. He clutched her hips and lifted her just enough so that she could feel his erection. Her purr deepened to a feral growl.

"I believe forty or fifty years should be enough."

She stilled against him, her muscles tensing. "Nikos?"

He understood what she was asking. He had intended to wait until after they had freed Phila and taken the child home to her parents before he told Ellen how he felt about her.

Had he loved her all these years? Or had the seeds of love been planted fifteen years ago and only now come to fruition? He didn't know; didn't care. If he could change the past, take away the torment she had endured, he would. But he couldn't. All he could do was offer her a future—the two of them together for the rest of their lives. Once he freed himself from the Firm, he could offer Ellen what the young Mary Ellen had wanted—marriage and children and a happily-ever-after life.

"I want to spend the rest of my life with you," he told her. "I'll retire and we'll buy a country estate in the English countryside, or if you prefer, I'll move to America with you and—"

She laid her index finger over his lips. "Aren't you getting ahead of yourself?"

He grinned. "Yes, I suppose I am. I'm taking for granted that you want what I want. Marriage. Children. A real family."

"It's what I wanted…once. Years ago. But we can't go back and simply pick up where we left off. Too much has happened. There are things about me that you don't know. Things you have a right to know."

Nikos grabbed her wrist and jerked her finger away from his lips. He tossed her onto her back, straddled her hips and hovered over her. "We both have things in our pasts that are probably better left there. I don't care about other men, just as other women in my life shouldn't matter to you. All that's important is that we love each other." He rubbed his body against hers and elicited a hungry gasp from her parted lips. "We want and need each other, *agkelos*. Now, even more than fifteen years ago."

"Nikos, are you sure?"

He flicked his tongue across one pebble-hard nipple and then the other. "I'm very sure."

"Sex isn't love," she told him.

He swooped his hands beneath her and lifted her hips higher, then positioned himself between her thighs and surged his rock-hard sex up and into her. She cried out as he embedded himself fully, going deep, stretching her to the limit.

"I know the difference," he said. "And so do you."

Her hips undulated, rising and falling to meet his powerful thrusts. "You told me once before that you loved me, but you left me. You weren't there for me when I needed you."

He stilled instantly. "That was then. This is now. I swear to you that I will never leave you again. Forgive me, Ellen. Forgive me and give me a second chance. Give us a second chance."

Clutching his shoulders, she bucked up against him and brought her lips to his. "I love you."

Nikos had wanted this mating to be slower, gentler, to last a long time, but those plans disappeared like smoke in the wind. Their hunger for each other was too urgent for them to linger over the finer points of lovemaking.

Their coupling took on a primitive edge as they kissed and touched, as Ellen possessed him as surely as he possessed her. He delved deeply, then retreated, only to plunge harder and faster. They rolled and tumbled, reversing dominant positions more than once in their raging hunger for appeasement. Need rode him hard, a demented taskmaster with only one goal—fulfillment.

His hot, lurid words and phrases excited him as much as her. He told her explicitly what he wanted to do to her, what he *was* doing to her. She responded with her own earthy, erotic replies as she tossed him onto his back and straddled him. He grabbed her hips and pumped her up and down until she took charge and set the frantic rhythm as she rode him. She the demanding mistress; he the powerful stallion beneath her.

The moment he felt completion nearing, he flipped her over onto her back and hammered into her. Madly. Savagely. And then he came. A mind-blowing, body-exploding climax that made his ears ring and his nerves tremble. Her gratification came seconds after his. Her whimpers and shudders intensified his own pleasure. As fulfillment claimed her, she raked her nails across his back and bit down on his shoulder to stifle a scream.

He collapsed in sated pleasure on top of her, his breathing ragged, aftershocks still pummeling through his body. She clung to him, her lips all over his shoulder, his neck, then searching and finding his mouth. He lifted her hands up and over her head and held them there as he kissed her.

A loud pounding on the door brought them both to instant alert. Nikos cursed under his breath, then slid off her and got out of bed. He jerked on his pants, then tossed her his shirt. Before he opened the door, he glanced over his shoulder to make sure Ellen was properly covered, then he cracked the door a couple of inches and peered outside at Domingo Shea.

"Sorry to bother you," Dom said. "But I thought you'd want to know that we just got a call from Sawyer. The Al'alim contacted him at the villa. He's on his way here with the details of the hostage exchange."

Chapter 18

Sawyer McNamara arrived at the airstrip shortly after nine. He'd taken the Constantine jet into Cantara and rented a car at the airport. Ellen and Nikos met him in the hotel lobby. Ellen knew she didn't have to tell Sawyer that she was with Nikos, in the most basic way a woman can be with a man. There was something very proprietorial about Nikos's attitude, subtle hints in his manner that was nothing more than the primitive male warning off another. Sawyer would have to be blind not to pick up on the signals.

"We have things set up over at the hangar," Ellen said. "The troops are gathered and waiting."

Sawyer nodded, glanced from Ellen to Nikos, then looked down at the suitcase he carried. "Once I deliver the instructions and this—" he handed the case to Ellen "—I'll wait around here in Cantara until the mission is over, unless Ms. Sheridan is eager to return to Golnar. The Constantines would like for her to call them. They want any news she has about Phila."

"After our meeting, you can speak with her and find out what she wants to do," Ellen said.

The three of them left the hotel and made their way expeditiously to the hangar. The entire team, except Knox, who had relieved Geoff Monday on watch an hour ago, were assembled in the office.

Ellen placed the suitcase in the middle of the table, then sat beside Worth. Nikos stood behind Ellen, one hand resting possessively on her shoulder. All eyes were on Sawyer as he sat in the empty chair at the head of the long, metal table.

"The exchange is to take place today," Sawyer said. "I was given some very specific instructions and told that if they aren't followed to the letter, Phila Constantine will be killed."

"Today?" Geoff Monday scowled. "Not giving us much warning, are they?"

"The less time, the less likely we are to double-cross them," Dom said.

That comment gained Dom everyone's attention.

He shrugged. "Hey, I'm not stupid. At least not as a general rule." He looked directly at Nikos, then glanced from Worth to Sawyer. "There's a backup plan, isn't there? Tell me there is, because none of us are going to accept the reality of freeing those two Al'alim scum. Not permanently."

"Why keep the plan a secret from us?" Worth asked.

"We can discuss contingency plans once we hear what Sawyer has to tell us." Nikos squeezed Ellen's shoulder.

"They want the two prisoners brought by helicopter to Taraneh. I have the coordinates." He nodded to the suitcase on the table. "They're in there, on top of the four million."

Ellen reached out, unzipped the case and lifted the cover. A couple of the men let out low whistles when the cold hard cash came into view. Ellen removed the manila file folder atop the money, laid it aside and closed the suitcase. She flipped open the folder, studied the information, then passed it around.

"They want us to set the chopper down right outside of town," Ellen said. "Not a stone's throw from the abandoned warehouse we passed on our way into town."

Ellen noticed the way Geoff Monday glared at Nikos. She understood their silent exchange. Monday was no doubt privy to the plan for the SAS to recapture the freed terrorists.

"The helicopter is to set down at precisely three o'clock, Subrian time. Jamsheed Abd Hamid and Musa Ben Arif are to be escorted off the helicopter by me and Nikos." Sawyer's gaze connected with Ellen's. "No one else is to accompany the prisoners. We are to give the four million dollars to Musa before disembarking, then turn over Musa to the Al'alim first, after which they will give us Phila Constantine, releasing her as we release Jamsheed."

"I don't like it," Geoff said.

"Neither do I," Dom agreed.

"It doesn't matter whether or not any of like the terms. It's their way or else," Sawyer reminded them. "But no doubt about it, y'all will be like a bunch of sitting ducks when you go into Taraneh."

"Sawyer's right," Ellen said. "We'll be going into a bad scenario, but it's the only hope we have of saving Phila. And we have to remember that the most important thing in this entire situation is making sure we're able to take Phila Constantine out of harm's way. I'm willing to do whatever is necessary to accomplish that goal."

"There's something else about this arrangement that stinks," Worth said. "Why were they so specific about which agents they want to escort Musa and Jamsheed?"

"Who knows?" Dom skewered Nikos with a sharp gaze. "You got any ideas, Khalid?"

"I might," Nikos responded.

"How about sharing with the rest of us?" Sawyer asked.

Tension radiated around the room like a deadly invisible gas. Suddenly Geoff Monday's digital phone lying atop the maps spread out on the table rang. A collective pause stilled everyone in the office.

Geoff Monday picked up the phone, punched the receive button and said, "Monday here." The person on the other end of the line spoke, then Geoff replied, "Yes, sir, he's with me now." Geoff handed the phone to Nikos.

Nikos took the phone, then left them and went inside the glass cubbyhole connected to the office space, obviously wanting privacy for the conversation. While the others talked among themselves, Ellen watched Nikos. She knew the exact moment he heard some sort of horribly frightening news. He looked through the glass partition directly at her and their gazes locked instantly. A tremor of pure fear shuddered through her. Dear God, what was it? What had he just been told?

Two minutes. The entire conversation lasted only two minutes. But in that short length of time, Ellen knew that her life had changed dramatically.

Nikos returned to the rescue team, laid the digital phone down in front of Geoff and returned to his former position behind Ellen. When he reached down and grasped her shoulders, she felt a slight quiver in his touch. She sensed his fear, absorbed his rage, and understood how devastating the news must be to have affected a man such as Nikos in such a powerful way. He was a brave, fearless secret agent who had lived with danger most of his life.

No one said a word. Everyone waited. Ellen lifted her right hand and laid it atop Nikos's left hand that gripped her shoulder.

"Musa Ben Arif was the personal servant of Hakeem Ibn Fadil," Nikos said, the fury in his voice undisguised.

"Musa was with Hakeem when Hakeem was killed in battle. It was Musa who identified Hakeem's body. Now it is not so certain that it was Hakeem's body."

Murmurs rose from those gathered at the table. Questions. Speculations. Ellen's mind whirled with the news. She fought the realization of the truth exploding inside her mind. No, no it wasn't possible. Hakeem was dead. Worldwide newscasters had broadcast the story of Hakeem's death in battle over eight years ago. His body had been ripped limb from limb by the Menkuraian soldiers. She remembered every vicious detail of Hakeem's death as recounted by the soldiers who were there. She had taped news reports and listened to them over and over again until she had them memorized.

He was dead. Dead! Killed in battle. His monster's soul was rotting in hell.

"He's dead!" Ellen screamed. "Hakeem is dead!"

In her haste to stand, she knocked over her chair as she got up, shoving Nikos's hands from her shoulders in the process. She ran from the room, out into the hangar, disregarding Nikos's shouts for her to wait.

Rushing onto the tarmac, the sun warm on her face as she looked up at the bright blue sky, Ellen stopped abruptly and went dead still.

The baby's cries echoed inside her head. Soft whimpering at first. The fussy little sobs of an infant. *I'm coming, sweetheart. Mommy's coming to you.* But she couldn't find her child. The cries grew louder, more insistent. A baby weeping for a mother who couldn't save him. *Don't cry, baby. Please, don't cry. Mommy's coming. I'll make it all right. I'll take care of you. I promise.*

Agitation, anger and then fear overwhelmed Ellen. She doubled over in agony, then dropped to her knees.

When Nikos caught up with Ellen, he found her on her knees in the middle of the runway. Tears streamed down her face. God, forgive him. He'd had no idea she would react this way. She gave every indication of being in control of her emotions. Hadn't she told him that she'd put the past behind her, that she was invincible? But that was when she'd believed Hakeem was dead.

"Ellen?" He went down on his haunches in front of her. "*Agkelos,* let me help you." He reached out to her. She lifted her head and stared right at him. The torment he saw in her eyes was more than he could bear. "Come with me. Talk to me. I'll find a way to make things right."

She didn't respond, but kept looking directly at him. When he grasped either side of her waist and lifted her to her feet, she allowed him to maneuver her as if she were a puppet. Just as he got her on her feet, the others came barreling out of the hangar. When he turned Ellen around and lifted her up into his arms, Geoff Monday, his mercenaries and the Dundee agents hovered nearby, but stood back and waited.

"Is she all right?" Geoff asked.

"Is she sick?" Sawyer broke rank and started moving toward Nikos.

Dom clamped Sawyer's arm, preventing him from interfering. "Do you know what's wrong with her?" Dom asked.

"She'll be all right," Nikos told them. "I can't explain what's wrong with her. Just take my word that I'll look after her."

"Is there anything we can do?" Worth asked.

Nikos shook his head as he walked past them. "No, nothing."

By the time he shoved open the door to his hotel room and carried Ellen inside, she had stopped crying and lay limply in his arms. He set her down on the bed, knelt before her and clutched her shoulders, then shook her gently.

"Ellen, talk to me."

She closed her eyes, took a deep breath and then hurled herself into his arms, almost toppling him to the floor. He caught her, righted himself and cocooned her in a tight embrace.

"Musa Ben Arif is Hakeem, isn't he?" she asked, her voice deceptively calm.

"Yes, I believe he is."

"Then he isn't dead. He's been hiding away all these years in Nawar Prison, pretending to be his own servant. But he's free now. He's free! My God, Nikos, *you* freed that monster!"

Nikos shook her again, more soundly the second time. "Listen to me. He is not going free. Once Phila is safe, we'll recapture Hakeem. He won't get away."

"But the exchange is set for three this afternoon. It's too soon...too soon."

"Trust me, Ellen. Trust me. I swear to you that Hakeem will not go free."

Their gazes collided, locked and held for endless moments, then she said, "I want him dead, not recaptured."

"That can be arranged."

"No, you don't understand." She gripped the front of Nikos's shirt. "I want to kill him."

"Let me do it for you." He grabbed her hands and held them between his. "For what he did to you, I could kill him with my bare hands."

Ellen tugged her hands free, lifted one to caress Nikos's cheek and choked back fresh tears. "Hakeem intends to kill you before you can kill him. He is obsessed with revenge against you."

"No matter what happens—"

She kissed him to silence his reply.

"I need to tell you something, but before I tell you, you must promise me something."

He stared at her, puzzled by her statement. "Name it."

"Promise me that you won't kill Hakeem until we make the hostage swap—Hakeem and Jamsheed for Phila. The past is the past and can't be changed. But Phila is alive and she must come first."

"I don't understand." What was she trying to tell him? Why did she think he'd even consider risking Phila's life simply to kill Hakeem?

Ellen took Nikos's hand and urged him to sit beside her on the bed. They sat side by side, his arm around her. He could feel her slow, steady breathing.

"When Hakeem kidnapped me, I wasn't alone," Ellen said.

"You weren't—who was with you?"

"My baby."

"Your— You had a child?" Frigid cold encased his body. He knew. Oh, God, he knew, but he could not bring himself to say more.

"After you left me—" When he groaned, she took his hand into hers and held tightly. "I went home. Back to Georgia. A few weeks later, I discovered I was pregnant."

"With my child." A precognitive fear wound tightly in his gut.

"My parents were wonderful," Ellen told him. "I wish you could have known them. They were so good to me. They stood by me, helped me. They adored Nicky."

"Nicky." The name reverberated inside his head. Nicky, Nicky.

"He was beautiful." Ellen smiled. That tender mother's smile ripped Nikos's heart in two. "He looked so much like you. Your black hair. Your dark eyes."

Nikos swallowed hard. "When Hakeem abducted you, Nicky was with you?"

"He was three weeks old and I'd put him in the carryall and strapped him in front of me so we could take a walk together. It was the most beautiful spring day. He lay against my breasts, sound asleep. I heard the car, but thought it was one of our neighbors taking the old road. It happened so fast. One minute I was walking with Nicky, singing to him...and the next minute, they grabbed me.''

Nikos marveled at how suddenly calm Ellen had become. Unnaturally calm. ''You don't have to relive every moment. I don't have to know every detail, if it's too painful for you.''

''There is no pain,'' she told him. ''I have it under control again. I've pushed it deep down inside me.''

''Ellen, where is Nicky?''

She stared at him, an incredulous expression on her face. ''Nicky is dead. He's buried on our family estate outside Cartersville with only a marble angel marking his grave.''

''How did Nicky die?'' He knew. God help them both, he knew! But he had to hear her say it, no matter how much it hurt her.

''Hakeem killed him. An eye for an eye. A son for a son.''

Rage tore at Nikos's insides like the sharp talons of a hawk. The word *no* screamed repeatedly inside his head.

''Hakeem took Nicky away from me,'' Ellen said in that eerily calm voice. ''He threatened me and beat me and... He tortured me, but I couldn't tell him what he wanted to know. I didn't know what your real name was. I didn't know where you were. But Hakeem didn't believe me. He felt certain that since I had borne you a son, you would keep in touch with me because of the child. When he threatened Nicky, I started making up lies and telling him anything I thought he'd believe.

''Then he told me that if I didn't tell him the truth, didn't hand you over to him, he would kill Nicky. I begged him. I pleaded with him. I bargained with the devil. But he never intended to allow Nicky to live. You had killed his son. He told me that he had every right to kill your son. I even lied and told him that Nicky wasn't yours, but he didn't believe me.''

Nikos could no longer see Ellen's face. Tears glazed his eyes as unbearable pain gripped him in its clutches.

Ellen continued, ''Hakeem left me alone with his two henchmen and went into the other room where he had put my baby. Nicky was carrying on. He wanted me, but they wouldn't let me go to him. Then suddenly the crying stopped.''

Nikos didn't think he could bear to hear any more. The pain was so intense that he felt as if he were dying.

''Hakeem came back into the room where I was and told me that he'd killed my baby—our baby.''

Guilt ate away inside Nikos like a strong, deadly acid. Ellen had given him a son. A son he'd never known existed. And Hakeem had killed that precious innocent baby because of who and what Nikos was. His child had died because of him!

''I didn't believe him,'' Ellen said. ''I couldn't believe anyone would kill a tiny, helpless baby. After Hakeem received that phone call—remember, I told you about that—and they left me with... After I killed the man Hakeem had left to interrogate me and made my escape, I went to find Nicky. He was lying on the floor in the other room. I thought he was asleep.''

God no! Nikos's mind screamed. Don't let it be true, his heart pleaded silently.

''I went down on my knees and lifted Nicky into my arms. He was still warm. But—but he wasn't breathing. That's when I remembered Hakeem saying that he'd been merciful, that he'd killed Nicky quickly. He had smothered our little boy.''

Fury born of guilt and hatred and a pain beyond anything Nikos had ever imagined possible guided his actions. He shot up off the bed, ran across the room and out the door. Ellen ran after him, calling his name.

"I'm going to kill the goddamn son of a bitch," Nikos said as he stormed down the hallway.

Ellen chased after him. When she caught up with him, she grabbed hold of his arm, but he simply dragged her along with him.

"Nikos, you can't. You promised me. You can't kill him. Not yet. Think about Phila."

He heard her talking to him, but her plea didn't really register in his mind. He was going to kill Hakeem. Slowly. Painfully. And then he was going to carry the bastard's body out into the forest and let the wild animals pick his bones clean.

When they reached the room where the two prisoners were being guarded, Knox came to attention.

"Is something wrong?" Knox asked.

"I'm taking Musa Ben Arif with me," Nikos said.

"No!" Ellen cried. "You can't."

Nikos grabbed and turned the doorknob, but the door didn't budge. "Unlock the door."

"Don't," Ellen told Knox.

"Open that damn door or I'll rip it off its hinges." Nikos glared at Knox.

"What the hell's going on?" Knox grasped Nikos's arm.

Before Ellen could intervene, Nikos landed a hard blow to Knox's jaw and the man went reeling backward onto the floor.

Ellen let out an ear-piercing scream. Within seconds Worth Cordell emerged from the room he was sharing with Faith and came racing down the hall.

"What's wrong?" Worth asked.

"You have to stop Nikos from getting in there to Musa Ben Arif," Ellen said. "He's going to kill him."

"What the hell's happened to make him—" Worth

stopped midquestion when Nikos turned on him, a vicious snarl on his lips and pure violence controlling his soul.

When Nikos charged Worth, the two began struggling. While Worth tried to contain Nikos, Knox came to, shook his head, then rose to his feet. Knox joined Worth in an attempt to control Nikos's rage. But it wasn't until Geoff Monday and Dom showed up and joined forces with the other two men that they were able to physically overpower Nikos. They held him down while he fought them like a madman.

Geoff Monday looked up at Ellen. ''Want to tell us what set him off this way?''

''I told Nikos that Hakeem Ibn Fadil killed our infant son,'' she replied. ''Fourteen years ago.''

Chapter 19

An hour later, Ellen and Nikos sat alone together, on opposite sides of the small table in his hotel room. Nikos was frighteningly silent and had been for quite some time. Ellen had tried to talk to him, but he'd simply glared at her.

"Don't you think I want to kill him?" Ellen spoke softly. "I am going to kill him. But not until I know that Phila Constantine is safe. I will not put my need for revenge before a child's safety."

She saw a flicker of understanding in Nikos's black eyes. It was the first sign that she might be getting through to him.

"After what Hakeem did to Nicky and to me, I spent six months in a private sanitarium and underwent intensive therapy," Ellen reached out across the table and turned her hand palm up, but didn't try to touch Nikos. "I became a different person after that. I've had fourteen years to deal with my hatred and anger, to find ways to manage my pain. This is all very new to you, as if it just happened."

"You buried your emotions so deep inside you that you thought nothing and no one could ever hurt you again." Nikos scowled at her. "You didn't deal with anything. You just pretended not to care."

"Maybe I did," Ellen admitted. "But I managed to survive. I have a job, a productive life. I cope."

"But you've been dead inside all these years. You survived by killing Mary Ellen Denby, by destroying the very essence of what made you you."

"I left out an odd little twist to my sad tale," Ellen said. "I carried Nicky in my arms when I escaped—after I killed one of my captors. When the police found me wandering aimlessly, I was holding Nicky in my arms. They had to pry him away from me."

"Ellen...?"

"The police actually accused me of killing him." Ellen emitted a fractured, agonized chuckle. "Can you imagine? The doctors told the police that I had been brutalized—physically tortured—and the police eventually withdrew their accusations. I told my father what had really happened to me and to Nicky. He was the only one who ever knew. He hired a very good lawyer and called in favors from everybody he knew to have all the files on me and Nicky permanently sealed. Then he arranged for me to go away to Paget Sanitarium."

"And you permanently shut off your emotions. You stopped living and merely existed."

Ellen nodded. "And I was doing all right until you came back into my life. You made me remember what it was like to love, to be happy...to have hope."

Nikos extended his hand and laid it beside Ellen's there on the table, but neither of them made that final move to touch the other.

"Do you have any idea how guilty I feel?" Nikos swallowed. "My son, our child, was murdered because of me."

Tears pooled in Nikos's eyes. Ellen put her hand in his. He closed his eyes and squeezed her hand. Teardrops cascaded down his cheeks.

"I haven't cried since my parents and sister were killed," he said. His gaze linked with Ellen's. "Why don't you hate me? How can you bear to look at me?"

"Because what happened to me wasn't your fault. And you're not to blame for what happened to Nicky. Hakeem is a monster. A mad dog who needs to be destroyed." Ellen leaned forward, brought Nikos's hand to her mouth and pressed her lips tenderly against his palm. "First we rescue Phila. Then we take care of Hakeem."

Nikos nodded. "Whatever it takes to save Theo's child, I'll do. I wasn't there to protect my own son, but I swear to you that I will not let Hakeem or any of his blasted followers harm Phila. Even if it means…"

"I know. Even if means we have to forfeit our lives to save her."

Clasping Ellen's hand, Nikos rose to his feet and pulled her around the table and into his arms. He wrapped her in his embrace. She laid her head on his chest. This was where she belonged; where she had always belonged. She felt the rightness of it in every pore of her being.

He stroked her back lovingly and whispered softly in her ear, "No one knows, except Geoff, that several SAS teams are already within ten miles of Taraneh."

Ellen's heartbeat accelerated and a warm flush of relief settled over her. A fragile smile tilted the corners of her mouth.

On the helicopter ride from Cantara to Taraneh that afternoon, the two prisoners were kept bound, gagged and blindfolded in the back of the Pave Hawk. Matt and Randy piloted the craft while Ellen and Nikos sat silently together.

They planned to follow the Al'alim's orders to the letter—up to a point.

Nikos had decided that no matter how this thing played out when they reached Taraneh, he wasn't going to let anything happen to Ellen. If necessary, she was willing to sacrifice herself to save Phila. He understood where that willingness to die came from—it came from guilt. She might not see it, would probably deny it, but deep down inside, Ellen blamed herself for not being able to save Nicky. There certainly was enough guilt to go around. He didn't think he would ever be able to forgive himself, and found it amazing that Ellen could.

The flight to Taraneh seemed endless, and yet when the Pave Hawk landed, Nikos couldn't believe they had arrived. Before they opened the door, Matt and Randy stationed themselves in front of the miniguns mounted in the cabin windows. Nikos jerked Hakeem—alias Musa—to his feet while Ellen brought Jamsheed out of his seat.

Nikos removed Hakeem's blindfold and then the gag in his mouth. Ellen repeated the process with the other prisoner.

"You will remove the ropes from our wrists, also," Hakeem said as he looked Nikos squarely in the eye.

"Not on your life, *Musa*," Nikos replied, stressing the man's false name.

Randy let out a long, low whistle. "There must be fifty soldiers out there. And looks like old Omar Ibn Fadil himself has come to meet us."

"Imagine that." Nikos glanced at Jamsheed, then grinned at Hakeem. "You two must be a couple of really important men for the leader of the Al'alim to oversee the exchange himself."

Hakeem returned Nikos's smile and in that moment Nikos realized Hakeem knew that Nikos had recognized him. *So be it.*

Nikos grabbed Hakeem by his bound hands tied securely behind his back, jerked him close and whispered, "I'm going to cut out your heart and ram it down your throat."

Hakeem tensed. "But not today, old friend. Today we play the game by my rules. And you will lose."

Nikos picked up the suitcase filled with four million dollars, strapped it to Hakeem's back and shoved him toward the door. Ellen brought Jamsheed with her when she came up beside Nikos.

The aft doors swung open. The cold November wind blasted Ellen and Nikos as they jumped out of the chopper. The orange sun leaned westward in a clear afternoon sky. Nikos scanned the area, taking note of the fact that the Pave Hawk was surrounded by at least three dozen soldiers, some on foot, others sitting in vehicles. This scenario was every bit as bad as he'd anticipated.

Nikos ordered the two prisoners to disembark. The moment Jamsheed's and Hakeem's feet hit the ground, Nikos and Ellen grabbed the men. With their backs protected by the helicopter, they jerked the prisoners around in front of them, using them as shields.

A young man came forward and stood approximately twenty feet from them. Nikos recognized him as Shabouh who had met with Ellen at the Odyssea Café. Of course, Shabouh was really the Al'alim leader Omar's son, Wasim. Hakeem's nephew. This was turning into a real family affair, Nikos thought.

Fully covered from head to toe, with only her huge dark eyes visible, a woman stepped from behind the line of soldiers and dragged a child with her. A small, wide-eyed little girl in a dirty, tattered, pink nightgown, with a dog's harness strapped over her chest, stood before them trembling. Phila Constantine appeared to be alive and well, if somewhat traumatized.

Nikos glanced quickly at Ellen's stricken face. Fear and

haunted memories blanched her complexion. Sensing her pain intensified Nikos's own anguish.

The woman brought the child to Wasim, then scurried away, back behind the soldiers. Wasim positioned Phila in front of him, holding her in place by the leash attached to the harness.

"You will release Musa Ben Arif," Wasim announced loudly.

"We want the child," Nikos countered.

"Once we have Musa, then we will give you the child."

Ellen and Nikos exchanged a hurried glance. They both knew this was going to get dirty. And soon. Very soon.

Nikos shoved Hakeem forward. Hakeem balked, then turned around so that he faced Nikos, who realized the bastard was showing his nephew his bound hands.

"Untie him," Wasim ordered.

"You untie him," Nikos replied, then gave Hakeem another, much harder shove. Hakeem growled, but he kept moving forward, closer and closer to Wasim.

Nikos held his breath. Waiting. Realizing the inevitable and knowing there was absolutely nothing he could do to stop it.

When Wasim reached his nephew, he spoke quietly in a tone so low that Nikos couldn't make out what was being said. But he could guess. Wasim whipped out a large knife from a belt sheath and cut the rope that bound his uncle's hands.

Nikos's gaze subtly scanned right and left, searching for a sign of any kind, but knowing there shouldn't be even a hint. *Let them be there, God,* Nikos prayed. If the SAS teams weren't already in place right now and ready to strike, then heaven help him and Ellen and little Phila.

Once his hands were free, Hakeem unstrapped the suitcase from his back and tossed it to the ground, then he reached out, grabbed Phila and lifted her up into his arms.

Holding the child in front of him, he looked directly at Nikos.

"Let her go," Nikos said. "Unless you want us to kill Jamsheed."

"I die gladly," Jamsheed shouted as he dropped to his knees, presenting himself in a sacrificial manner. "I give my life for you, great one." With wild eyes, Jamsheed proclaimed to his fellow Al'alim rebels, "Hakeem Ibn Fadil has returned to lead his people to greatness and revenge himself upon his enemies."

A thunderous clamor of joyous shouts rang out all around them. The Al'alim welcoming a fallen leader back from the grave.

"You must realize that you have no bargaining tool," Hakeem told Nikos, a smug, self-satisfied look on his ugly face.

"Maybe not, but I have two men ready to open fire with a couple of miniguns." Nikos knew his threat was an idle one. Two miniguns against nearly fifty armed soldiers would take out at least a third of them, but probably not before they'd killed Ellen, Phila and Nikos.

"If you issue such an order, the child will be the first to die." Hakeem glanced over his shoulder at Omar. "Thank you, my brother, for such a magnificent scheme. You not only free me from captivity, but you put my worst enemy in the palm of my hand."

"Let Phila go," Nikos said. "I'll give you whatever you want in exchange."

"Of course you will." Hakeem looked at Ellen. "Did you tell him about his son?"

"She told me." Boiling hot fury raged inside Nikos.

"I held my hand over his little mouth and nose until he stopped breathing," Hakeem said. "It gave me great pleasure to see the life drain from your son, to know that I had taken from you what you had taken from me."

Every instinct within Nikos went into kill mode, demanding he charge into immediate action. *Not yet,* he told himself. *Think about Phila. You know what Hakeem is trying to do. Control yourself.*

Nikos walked forward slowly. "Here I am," he said. "Take me and let Phila go."

"So very noble of you. A man willing to give his life to save a child." Hakeem glanced at his nephew. "Who is this child to him?"

"She is Phila Constantine," Wasim replied. "She is the daughter of El-Hawah's friend, Theo Constantine."

Hakeem laughed, then looked once again at Ellen. "You told me that you and your lover had attended a party at the Constantine villa, but I thought little of it." Hakeem turned and saluted Omar. "How wise of you, my brother, to discover this vital information about El-Hawah's friend."

Nikos moved closer and closer. If he could get close enough, he had a good chance of killing Hakeem. The Al'alim soldiers would mow him down immediately after he attacked Hakeem, but what did it matter—he was going to die one way or the other.

"Put Phila down and let her go to Ellen," Nikos said. "You've got what you want."

Hakeem grinned. A wicked, fiendish grin. "Ah, but I do not want you." He pointed his long, bony index finger directly at Ellen. "I want her."

"No!" Nikos bellowed.

"I will kill you later," Hakeem said. "But before you die, I want you to know that I not only killed your son, but I killed your woman. You are very weak to allow a woman to become so important to you."

"You'll take me or there's no deal," Nikos said.

When Ellen tried to walk past him, Nikos grabbed her arm and pulled her back.

"You have to let me do this," she told him. "I couldn't

save Nicky, but I can save Phila. If we let anything happen to that little girl, we could never live with ourselves afterward. You know that as well as I do.''

''You're not going to sacrifice yourself.'' Nikos glared at her. ''Do you hear me?''

Ellen kissed Nikos's cheek, then whispered hurriedly, ''It's a good day for Hakeem to die.''

Before his mind had a chance to register and decipher her comment, Ellen turned and walked toward Hakeem. It took every ounce of Nikos's willpower not to go after her. He watched and waited, his heart trapped in his throat. When she was within ten feet of Hakeem, she paused.

''Release Phila,'' Ellen said.

Hakeem removed the dog's harness from the child's thin body and gave her a gentle forward shove. Ellen motioned for Phila to come to her. The little girl hesitated, then took several weak, tentative steps. Ellen reached out, grabbed Phila into her arms and hugged her fiercely.

''Do you see Mr. Khalid over there?'' Ellen pointed at Nikos. Phila nodded. ''Go to him as fast as you can.''

The minute Ellen released Phila, the child ran toward Nikos. He swooped her up into his arms and rushed toward the Pave Hawk. By the time he deposited Phila inside the chopper, Ellen had taken those last few steps to put herself within Hakeem's reach. A surge of blinding fury swept through Nikos. Every instinct within him urged him to save Ellen. But how?

Hakeem reached out, grabbed Ellen by the nape of her neck and yanked her toward him. She stood there, staring up at him, then grinned and boldly spit in his face.

Snarling, Hakeem wiped the spittle from his face, then slapped Ellen so hard that she reeled backward from the blow and would have fallen to the ground if Hakeem had not been holding on to her.

Nikos balled his hands into tight fists. Adrenaline surged through his body.

"I do not remember you being so brave," Hakeem said. "You were such a spineless, sniveling creature, begging me to spare your child's life. You would have done anything I asked of you. You were my slave."

"Is that what you want?" Ellen asked. "Do you want to see me on my knees begging?"

What the hell was she doing? Nikos wondered. Why was she goading Hakeem this way?

Hakeem laughed, then removed his hand from Ellen's neck. "If you wish to beg, then beg. Let your man see what a worthless, helpless female you are."

Ellen lunged forward and pressed herself up against Hakeem. A murmured roar rose from the Al'alim soldiers. Nikos held his breath.

With lightning speed, Ellen took the knife in her hand—the knife she had only seconds before slipped down from inside the sleeve of her jacket—and as she looked him square in the eyes and whispered, "Surprise," she rammed the blade directly into Hakeem's heart.

Chapter 20

Ellen held Hakeem as he slumped over, his one good eye wide-open and staring sightlessly off into space. Knowing she could balance his weight for only another minute, two at the most, she tried to prepare herself for what was to come. The instant Omar Ibn Fadil realized his brother was dead, he would issue an order for his troops to kill her. Using all her strength, Ellen maneuvered Hakeem's lifeless body just enough so that she could catch a glimpse of Nikos, who stood several feet this side of the Pave Hawk.

"Get out of here," she screamed. "Go! Now!"

Nikos froze to the spot. Ellen prayed for him to move, to jump into the helicopter and get away before all hell broke loose. Hakeem's deadweight became too much for her to support, so she had no choice but to release her hold on him. The very second his body dropped to the ground, a deafening rumble rose from the Al'alim soldiers.

Everything that happened next seemed to occur in slow motion. Nikos made a mad dash in her direction. Wasim snapped around and glared at Ellen, then slipped the strap holding his rifle from his shoulder. Just as Wasim aimed his weapon at Ellen, Nikos barreled into him and tackled him to the ground. Omar yelled orders as fast as the Pave Hawk's miniguns spit out their firepower on both sides of the helicopter. Ellen nosedived onto the ground. When she saw a soldier not five feet from her get hit and go down, she crawled over and snatched his rifle out of his death grip. Surrounded by Al'alim troops, the odds sure as hell weren't in the good guys' favor. But by God, Nikos and she would fight as long as there was a breath left in either of them.

Suddenly the Pave Hawk's rotary blades began to spin. A tumultuous roar blocked out every other sound. The turbulent wind whipped up by the chopper created a whirlwind of dust that made it difficult to see more than a couple of feet.

The helicopter whirled into the sky. Ellen sighed. Thank God, Phila was safe. Matt and Randy would take her to Cantara and then on home to Golnar, straight into the loving arms of her parents. In that one moment, Ellen realized she didn't want to die. She wanted to live. She wanted to marry Nikos, have other children with him and the two of them grow old together.

Wherever the SAS troops were, she prayed they'd show up very soon.

As the dust settled and the Pave Hawk's roar died away, Ellen heard the rumble of approaching vehicles, their occupants firing their GPMGs—General Purpose Machine Guns. Her prayer had been answered! She looked up from where she lay on the ground and saw black clad SAS troops storming the area. The Al'alim soldiers were so distracted by the SAS attack that it seemed they'd forgotten about Nikos and her. The Al'alim who had surrounded the Pave Hawk broke apart in small groups, scattering like leaves in the autumn wind. While the battle ensued, Ellen scrambled behind an overturned vehicle, positioned herself and began firing.

Just as one of the SAS Land Rovers swept past her, in hot pursuit of the enemy, she caught a glimpse of Nikos standing over a dead Wasim, directly in the midst of the battle. Suddenly she realized that he saw her. His facial features contorted with fear and he yelled something at her she couldn't hear over the rumble of warfare. Her heart stopped for a millisecond when Nikos aimed Wasim's rifle in her direction. Oh, God! Oh, God! She immediately sensed the danger behind her. Nikos fired repeatedly. She swung around just in time to see two Al'alim soldiers fall.

Nikos hurled over dead bodies and debris, fighting each inch of the way toward her. But before he could reach her, several other soldiers headed toward her from the opposite direction. She opened fire on them and took one of them out, then another. Nikos bounded up on and then over the wrecked vehicle and came between Ellen and a bullet with her name on it. He took the slug in his shoulder. He clutched the gaping wound for a second, then as he went down, he got off several more rounds, taking out another man. Ellen finished off the fourth soldier, then turned to Nikos.

"How bad is it?" She shoved aside his hand covering the wound. Blood stained his shirt and continued oozing from the bullet hole.

"Hurts like hell," he admitted. "But I don't think it'll kill me."

"It damn well won't. I've got plans for you, big boy." Ellen lifted her gaze and scanned the section around them.

"Big boy?" Nikos chuckled, then winced.

An SAS Land Rover skidded to a halt not ten feet in front of them and a couple of British soldiers jumped out, submachine guns ready to fire, their stern gazes moving slowly from left to right as they searched the area.

"We're here," Ellen yelled. "I'm Ellen Denby and I've got an injured man with me."

The two SAS team members approached Ellen and Nikos carefully, then moved in to assist.

"We'll get you out of here soon. You hold on, mate," a lanky young soldier said to Nikos. "We've got those bastards on the run, back into Taraneh. Nothing I'd like better than to go in there and clean out that vipers' nest, but that's not our assignment."

"Hakeem Ibn Fadil is dead," Ellen said.

"Yes, ma'am. And so is the other Nawar prisoner, that General Abd Hamid. And Omar Ibn Fadil has been captured. He's wounded and I doubt he'll live to make it out of here."

"You can add another Ibn Fadil to the count," Nikos told them. "Omar's son Wasim is dead."

One of the soldiers helped Ellen lift Nikos to his feet, then the four of them loaded into the Land Rover and headed south, along with the remainder of the SAS rescue team.

Worth, Sawyer and Matt flew back to Golnar with Phila Constantine and Faith Sheridan. Lucie had escorted Theo and Dia to the Dareh airport and the couple were waiting impatiently when the jet landed.

When Matt and Randy had brought Phila to Cantara, Faith had immediately gone into nanny mode, taking charge of Phila with gentle maternal concern. The first thing Faith had done was put in a phone call to Theo and Dia so that Phila could speak to her parents; then once the child had been cleaned up, dressed and fed, they'd boarded the jet and headed straight for Golnar.

While en route to Dareh, Sawyer had received word that

Nikos and Ellen were alive. Worth had said a hasty prayer of thanks. He wasn't a guy who did much praying, but he figured nothing short of a miracle—and a damn good group of elite soldiers—had saved two people who sure as hell had had the odds stacked against them.

Once they emerged from the airplane, Phila ran across the tarmac and straight into her mother's waiting arms; Theo encompassed his wife and daughter in his embrace. Tears streamed down Dia's face as she kissed Phila repeatedly. The reunion between parents and child was enough to make a grown man cry.

Lucie socked Worth on the arm. "Glad to have you back. Any word on Ellen and Nikos?" She glanced at Sawyer, deep concern in her gaze.

"They're alive," Sawyer replied.

"Thank God!" Lucie's face brightened as she smiled broadly.

"Khalid got hit," Sawyer said. "But he'll make it. They'll patch him up as soon as the SAS guys bring them back to Cantara."

"The SAS guys?" Lucie's eyes rounded.

"It seems our friend Khalid had a damn good plan to make sure the terrorists he broke out of Nawar didn't go free," Worth said.

"It also would appear that he's got quite a lot of clout with the British government," Sawyer added.

Lucie draped her arm across Sawyer's shoulders. "Chin up, old chap. The better man won. Can't fight true love."

Sawyer knocked Lucie's arm from around his shoulder, growled at her and headed straight for the airport terminal.

"The man has no sense of humor," Lucie said, then hurried off right behind Sawyer.

Worth shook his head and chuckled; then he noticed Matt's wife, Princess Adele, her eyes filled with tears, rushing toward her husband. Matt lifted her off her feet and hauled her up against him, as he kissed the breath out of her.

"You can't ever do something like this again," the princess said. "No more dangerous assignments. I can't have anything happening to the father of my child."

Matt set his wife on her feet, then clamped his hands on either side of her face and stared into her dark eyes. "Did you say the father of your child?"

The princess smiled through her tears of joy and nodded her head. Matt swung her around and around, then let her glide slowly down his body until her feet touched the ground.

While Worth was watching the happy couple, Faith came up beside him. Her small hand reached out hesitantly and grasped his big hand. He glanced down at her; she gazed up at him. Hell, this wasn't going to be easy. No doubt about it, she expected something from him he wasn't sure he could give her. She saw him as her hero and thought she was in love with him. But he didn't know how he felt about her. Did he care? Yes. Too much. Was it love? He didn't know. *Love* wasn't a word in his vocabulary.

"We need to talk," he said.

"Yes, we do." She smiled at him, all the love she felt showing plainly in her adoring gaze.

"We'll be heading back to Cantara right away," Worth told her. "Lucie, Sawyer and me. We'll pick up Dom and go from there back to the states."

"Are you coming with us, Faith?" Theo Constantine called to her as he lifted Phila onto his hip and curled his other arm around Dia's shoulders. Matt and his wife joined the Constantines as they prepared to leave the airport.

"I—I—" She looked at Worth.

"She'll be with y'all in a minute," Worth said.

Theo nodded, then he and his family headed for their

waiting limousine. After he assisted his wife and child into the limo, Theo turned back to Worth and Faith.

"Have you heard any news about Nikos and Ellen?" Theo asked.

"They're alive and on their way into Cantara," Worth replied.

Theo smiled. "We owe them—and all of you—so very much."

"We were just doing our job," Worth replied.

"Yes, I understand. But I am in your debt. Forever." Theo glanced at Faith. "Take as much time as you need to say goodbye."

When Theo got into the limousine, Matt and Adele followed, then his chauffeur Peneus closed the door. The loyal servant crossed his arms over his chest and stood guard.

"I'm going home, too," Faith told Worth.

"Home?"

"Back to South Carolina. I grew up there and I suddenly feel a great need to go back to the United States for a while. Besides, with you home based in Atlanta, I thought—"

Worth grasped Faith's shoulders. "Look, Blue Eyes, you shouldn't plan your future around me." When he saw the look of disappointment in her eyes, he amended his statement. "What I mean is we shouldn't rush into anything. Our entire acquaintance has been only a few days and we can't plan our lives based on…" Hell, he wasn't doing a very good job of this. Maybe if he were a little more certain about his own feelings, he'd be able to explain things better to Faith. "Right now, we're still pretty much in the moment, if you know what I mean. You're still seeing me as your knight in shining armor and I'm still caught up in the whole hero scenario and—" Worth lowered his voice "—the great sex probably has both of us confused."

Faith smiled timidly and whispered, "The sex is great, isn't it?"

"Yeah, it is. And that's one of the reasons we need to slow down and not rush into anything."

"You need time to think about us, to make sure what you feel for me is the real thing. Is that it?" she asked.

He nodded. "Yeah, that's it."

"I think waiting is a good idea."

"You do?"

"It'll take me a couple of weeks to work out a notice with the Constantines," Faith said. "And then it'll take me another few weeks to find an apartment and look for a new job and settle in back in the states." She mused thoughtfully for a couple of seconds, then gasped. "I know. I know."

"You know what?"

"The perfect time and place for us to meet after you've had a chance to decide if you truly love me."

Worth swallowed hard. He hadn't said anything about love. "The perfect time and place?"

"Whitewood, South Carolina, my hometown." She stood directly in front of Worth and grasped both of his hands. "If you decide that you really love me and want us to be together, come to Whitewood on Christmas Eve—that's only about six weeks from now—and meet me at eight o'clock that night, under the lighted Christmas tree in the town square."

What a hokey, purely feminine plan, Worth thought. Romantic for sure. And sentimental. He shouldn't give her any false hopes. He should just tell her right now that he didn't love her and there was no point in her hoping he would.

"Don't you think it's a marvelous plan?" she asked.

"Yeah, honey, it's just…it's marvelous."

She stood on tiptoe and kissed him. Instinct kicked in immediately. He lifted her off her feet and hugged her to him possessively, then kissed her. When they were both breathless, he eased her back to the ground.

"I'll see you in six weeks." She began walking away from him. "Christmas Eve. Under the tree in the town square." When she reached the limousine, Peneus opened the door for her. She looked back over her shoulder at Worth, smiled and said, "Whitewood, South Carolina." Then she disappeared inside the limo.

Worth stood there and watched the Constantine's big, black stretch limo until it was out of sight. Why the hell hadn't he just told her outright that he wasn't going to show up on Christmas Eve? *Because, you big dope, you aren't a hundred percent sure what you'll do come Christmas Eve, are you?*

The doctors at the Cantara Hospital patched Nikos up enough so that he could be transported by Dundee jet back to Golnar, where he spent five days in the hospital there. Ellen stayed with him. She knew that if she had her way, she would never leave his side ever again. Theo, Dia and Phila came to the hospital every day to visit with Nikos and check on his progress. Faith Sheridan dropped by to thank Ellen and Nikos and to tell them she had given her notice to the Constantines and planned to return to her hometown in South Carolina before Thanksgiving. Curious about Faith and Worth's relationship, Ellen had been tempted to ask Faith how they'd ended things, but she managed to keep her nose out of their business.

Matt and Princess Adele stopped by for a visit on their way to the airport for their flight back to Orlantha. The happy couple had shared their news of impending parenthood. Despite her happiness for the newlyweds, thoughts of a newborn baby had resurrected bittersweet memories in Ellen's heart.

Sitting in a chair by the window, Nikos held up his hand

to Ellen, who stood behind him as she gazed outside. She caught sight of his offered hand in her peripheral vision, then reached down and grasped his hand in hers.

"Someday, you will tell me more about our little Nicky," Nikos said. "I need to know everything."

She squeezed Nikos's hand. "His name was Nicholas, but I called him Nicky. Nicholas was such a big name for such a little—" Her voice cracked.

"I can't do anything to change the past," Nikos told her. "Neither of us will ever forget our first child or the way he died, but...but we can have other children." He tugged on her hand until she came around in front of him so that he could see her face. "Marry me, *agkelos.* I love you and want to make you happy."

"I love you, too," she told him. "But I'm afraid. I've spent fourteen years protecting my heart, constantly being on guard against caring too much about anyone."

"I know that I let you down once, that because of me, you suffered unbearably, but I promise—"

She placed the tips of her fingers over his lips. "The only way we can have a future together is if we put the past behind us. No guilt. No regrets about what might have been. No looking back, only forward."

"Agreed," Nikos said. "Mary Ellen Denby, will you marry me?"

A fragile smile formed on her lips, then broadened to a full, vibrant smile. "Yes, Nikos Pandarus, I'll marry you."

He yanked her down and into his lap. She gasped, then flung her arm around his neck, careful to avoid putting any pressure on his healing shoulder.

"Let's get married here, on Golnar," he said. "I'm sure Theo and Dia would be happy to host a wedding at the villa."

She caressed his cheek with the back of her hand, then shook her head. "Let's get married in the church on Stoffel

Avenue. Remember that day when we took shelter from the unexpected rainstorm when we were on our way to—''

He kissed her. Tenderly, yet passionately. Then when he ended the kiss, he said, ''I remember that day and that little church.'' He closed his eyes and pressed his cheek against hers. ''I remember every moment I spent with you those two weeks.''

''Those are beautiful memories,'' she told him. ''But now we're going to make new, even better memories.''

Ellen stayed there in Nikos's lap, held securely within his strong embrace as she let his love wash over her, a soothing balm to heal the wounds of the past. Her heart and soul filled with the promise of a thousand-and-one happy tomorrows.

Epilogue

Nikos placed three red roses from their garden in a crystal vase and set it on the tray beside the plate of chocolate chip pancakes, the freshly brewed coffee in a nonspill mug and the handmade Mother's Day cards.

"You carry the tray, Daddy," six-year-old Melina said, her huge brown eyes sparkling with excitement. "And I'll carry Mommy's present." She lifted the gaily wrapped rectangular box from the kitchen table.

Nikos returned his daughter's dazzling smile. From the moment he had cut the umbilical cord and placed this child in her mother's arms, he had worshiped Mary Melina Pandarus, named for her two grandmothers. Her beautiful facial features were identical to Ellen's, but her coloring was his—black hair, black eyes and olive complexion.

"Me carry something, too," three-year-old Zale whined.

Nikos picked up the cards the children had made for Ellen and handed them to his son. "Here, you carry these."

Zale smiled broadly. Every time he looked at Zale Denby

Pandarus, named in honor of his two grandfathers, Nikos's heart swelled with pride. The boy was his spitting image, except for the brilliant blue eyes, so like Ellen's.

"Are we ready?" Nikos asked.

"We're ready," Melina replied.

"Me ready. Let's go." Zale ran ahead of them as fast as his chubby toddler's legs would carry him.

"Tell him to wait," Melina complained. "We should all wake Mommy together."

Nikos grinned. Melina, his little drill sergeant, with her mother's take-charge, aggressive personality. "Don't worry. Zale probably can't open the bedroom door. He hasn't learned how to maneuver the plastic restraints covering the knobs on all the doors."

"Oh, Daddy, where have you been? Of course, he can open the doors with those plastic covers on the knobs. He learned how to do that last week."

"I see. I must have been busy that day."

"You were," Melina told Nikos as he followed her up the stairs, directly behind a tottering Zale who had managed to make it halfway up the steps. "It was the day you were helping Dr. Murray deliver Bonniebelle's baby. Zale opened the front door and was nearly at the end of the driveway before we knew he was gone. You should have heard Mommy screaming."

"Mommy was scared," Nikos explained. "She worries about you and Zale because she loves you so much."

"I know. It's because she doesn't want anything bad to happen to us."

When Nikos and Melina reached the bedroom, Zale had indeed opened the door. They walked in behind him, just as he bounded up the footstool and into the four-poster bed with Ellen, who turned over, tossed back the covers and grabbed Zale into her arms. She spread kisses all over his face, then flopped him down on the bed and nuzzled his belly with her nose. Zale squealed with delight.

"Happy Mother's Day," Melina said as she rushed to join the romp in her mother's bed. Melina tossed the gift box on the pillows, then Ellen held out her hands, grasped Melina around the waist and dragged her into bed. As she draped her arms around her children, they cuddled in her lap.

"Make room for breakfast." Nikos came forward and held out the tray.

"We made pancakes," Melina said. "Chocolate chip. Your favorite."

"Me, too," Zale added as he shoved the homemade greeting cards directly into Ellen's face.

She giggled happily and took the cards from Zale. The one from Melina was made out of pink construction paper and decorated with hearts and flowers—and she'd printed the word *Mother* in block letters quite well across the top of the card and her own name across the bottom.

"It's beautiful." Ellen kissed her daughter, then turned to the second card, which was made of green construction paper and covered with multi-colored hen scratch—Zale's unique brand of writing. "Yours is beautiful, too." She rubbed noses with Zale, then had to repeat the snookie-nose process several times before he was willing to allow his father room on the bed. Nikos placed the tray across Ellen's lap, then lifted Zale. When Nikos sat, he positioned his son on his thigh.

Melina rose to her knees, wrapped her arms around Nikos's neck and said, "Open your present, Mommy. It's from all of us. Zale and I helped Daddy pick it out and Daddy paid for it. He said you'd like a shawl just like this."

Ellen reached behind her for the two foot square box lying on the pillows. With the breakfast tray teetering on her lap, she held the present over the plate of pancakes,

eased the ribbon from the gift and removed the box lid.
Three sets of eyes focused on Ellen's face. Nikos held his
breath. The gift was certain to bring back memories. During
their seven year marriage, he had avoided evoking old
memories, choosing instead to rely on making new memories to make Ellen happy.

Carefully Ellen spread apart the white tissue paper covering the gift. She stared at the item lying inside the box.

"Take it out," Melina said.

"Me see, too," Zale added.

Ellen lifted the bright red shawl and tossed aside the
empty box. Her gaze met Nikos's for one brief moment,
then she glanced away. His heart caught in his throat.

"Do you like it?" Melina asked. "Isn't it the prettiest
thing you've ever seen. And it's your favorite color, too."

"Pretty, pretty." Zale's small, plump hand patted the
soft, silky material.

Ellen draped the red shawl around her shoulders, then
stroked her hand over Zale's where he clutched the front.
"Yes, it's beautiful." Ellen smiled at Zale. "Pretty,
pretty."

"She likes it." Melina winked at her father.

"Yes, I believe she does." Nikos scooped up both of his
children, one under each arm. They giggled happily. "Eat
your breakfast, Mommy," Nikos said. "I'll get these two
dressed and you can find us down at the stables taking a
look at Bonniebelle's new foal, when you get ready to join
us.

Fifteen minutes later, with the coffee mug drained and
half the stack of chocolate chip pancakes eaten, Ellen laid
the breakfast tray aside and got out of bed. She hugged the
red shawl around her shoulders and closed her eyes. Memories of a summer day long ago in a faraway land envel-
oped her in a warm, comforting fog. A carefree time of first

love and sexual awakening. A red shawl purchased at an open air market and worn about her naked body that night in bed. Then the sweet memories evaporated in the flames that had burned the first red shawl Nikos had given her. Ellen shuddered, then opened her eyes and sighed.

Pushing the unhappy thoughts out of her mind, she showered quickly, then dressed hurriedly in jeans, plaid shirt and red leather boots. Before leaving the bedroom, she picked up the red shawl her family had given her as a Mother's Day gift, wrapped it around her hips and tied the ends in a knot high on the left side of her waist. Just as she headed out the door, she stopped, glanced at the vase of red roses and smiled. She and Nikos had planted a garden of rose bushes when they'd first moved into her family home seven years ago.

When she reached the stables, Ellen found Nikos and the children petting Prince Charming, the four-day-old colt sired by Caesar, the prize stallion on their Arabian horse farm, located here on Ellen's family estate outside Cartersville. Robby and Bobby, the families Irish Setters sat beside the children. Melina stroked Robby's shiny coat, while Zale had a stranglehold around Bobby's neck.

"Oh, Mommy, you look so pretty." Melina eyed the red shawl draped around Ellen's hips.

"Pretty, pretty," Zale repeated.

"We need to teach him some new words," Melina said.

Nikos lifted Zale up and placed him on his shoulders. "Don't worry about it, son. The ladies love the word *pretty,* especially when you're using it to describe them." He ruffled Melina's long, dark curls. "Isn't that right, Mary Melina?"

His daughter wrinkled her nose when she frowned. "Ah, Daddy."

"Ready for our walk?" Ellen asked.

"Are we going to see if the roses have bloomed for Nicky?" Melina asked.

Nikos and Ellen came up on either side of Melina and clasped her hands. "Yes, let's go see. Then we can come back to the house and fix a picnic lunch to take down by the pond this afternoon."

The foursome, along with their two frolicking dogs, followed a gravel path alongside the fenced pastures, through a wooded area and then out into a small open field. Standing there alone, with green grass for its bed and the blue sky for its canopy, a three-foot-high marble angel kept watch over an unmarked grave.

"Oh, Mommy, look, look," Melina broke free from her parents' hold and raced across the field toward the angel. "The roses are blooming."

Tears misted Ellen's eyes as she gazed up at Nikos. She smiled at him. A lone tear trickled down her cheek. Nikos returned her smile, his own eyes damp.

As they approached Melina, who stooped to smell the white buds covering two small rosebushes planted on either side of the statue, Zale squirmed to get down, so Nikos put the toddler on his feet.

"Angel," Zale said as he patted the marble statue's face.

"That's our big brother Nicky's angel," Melina said. "Nicky's in heaven, but this angel is here to let us know that Nicky is always looking out for you and me, Zale. Nicky's our guardian angel." Melina looked to her mother for confirmation. "Isn't that right, Mommy?"

"Yes, darling, that's right."

Melina took Zale's hand and led him toward the path back to the stables. "We're very lucky to have Nicky up in heaven watching out for us. Not everybody has their own big brother as a guardian angel."

"Angel, angel, angel," Zale said in his customary sing-song.

While they watched their son and daughter, Nikos pulled Ellen into his arms.

"Are you happy, *agkelos?*" Nikos asked.

Ellen glanced at Nicky's angel, then at her laughing children. Her life was almost perfect. Except for that little piece of her heart that had been ripped out of her when Nicky died. But it was not a sorrow she bore alone. She had been able to share it with Nikos for the past seven years.

"Yes. Yes, I'm very happy."

She threw her arms around Nikos and kissed him.

"That's what mommies and daddies do," Melina explained to her baby brother. "When they're in love."

* * * * *

Don't miss Worth and Faith's story,

FAITH, HOPE AND LOVE,

in the anthology,

SO THIS IS CHRISTMAS,

available now from Silhouette Books!

EXPLORE THE POSSIBILITIES OF LIFE—AND LOVE—
IN THIS GROUNDBREAKING ANTHOLOGY!

Turning Point

*This is going to be our year.
Love, Your Secret Admirer*

It was just a simple note, but for the three women
who received it, it has very different consequences....

For Kristie Samuels, a bouquet of roses on her desk can mean
only that her deadly admirer has gotten too close—and that
she needs to get even closer to protector Scott Wade,
in this provocative tale by **SHARON SALA.**

For Tia Kostas Hunter, her secret admirer seems a lot like the man
she once married—the man she *thought* she was getting a divorce
from!—in this emotional story by **PAULA DETMER RIGGS.**

For secretary Jamie Tyson, the mysterious gift means her romantic
dreams just might come true—and with the man she least
suspects—in this fun, sensuous story by **PEGGY MORELAND.**

Available this December at your favorite retail outlets!

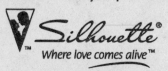

Where love comes alive™